CHRISTMAS EVE FROLIC—*Page 17.*

MAUM GUINEA,

AND

HER PLANTATION "CHILDREN;"

OR,

HOLIDAY-WEEK ON A LOUISIANA ESTATE.

A SLAVE ROMANCE.

BY MRS. METTA V. VICTOR,
AUTHOR OF "ALICE WILDE," "UNCLE EZEKIEL," ETC.

BEDFORD, MASSACHUSETTS
APPLEWOOD BOOKS
128 The Great Road

Maum Guinea was originally published in 1861 by Irwin P. Beadle & Co., New York.

ISBN 1-55709-550-7

Thank you for purchasing an Applewood Book. Applewood reprints America's lively classics—books from the past that are of interest to modern readers. For a free copy of our current catalog, write to: Applewood Books, P.O. Box 365, Bedford, MA 01730.

10 9 8 7 6 5 4 3 2 1

Library of Congress Catalog Card Number: 99:64870

PUBLISHERS' NOTE.

In presenting "Maum Guinea" to their readers, the publishers feel that no word of theirs is necessary to create an interest in its behalf. The peculiar and novel nature of the subject is treated with such power, pathos, humor and keen apprehension of character that it must stand out in relief as one of the most original and thoroughly delightful romances in our literature.

In the illustrations, both artist and engraver have added to their enviable repute. As pictures of Southern and Plantation Life the designs are all that could be desired.

"Maum Guinea" is the publishers' Holiday Offering to an appreciative and critical public, for whom it is their pleasure to cater.

BEADLE AND COMPANY

NEW YORK, 1861.

INTRODUCTION.

Negro life, as developed on the American Plantations, has many remarkable as well as novel features. The native character of the black race under the Slave system is toned down rather than changed. We find among the slaves all those idiosyncrasies which distinguish the negro type in its native land. Superstitious, excitable, imaginative, given to exaggeration, easily frightened, improvident and dependent, he forms a most singular study; and, so differently do the negro character and the relation of slave and master impress different observers, that the philanthropic world is greatly at a loss for some settled opinion regarding the normal condition of the African in the drama of civilization.

In writing of the race, I have sought to depict it to the life. Seizing upon the Christmas Holidays as the moment when his exuberant, elastic nature has its fullest play, I have been enabled, in the guise of a romance, to reproduce the slave, in all his varied relations, with historical truthfulness. His joys and sorrows; his loves and hates; his night-thoughts and day-dreams; his habits, tastes and individual peculiarities, I have drawn with a free, but I feel that it is a perfectly just, hand. There will, indeed, be found so much that is real in the narrative, that it will scarcely be deemed a romance by those who read to be informed as well as to be pleased.

The several slave-stories given are veritable historical transcripts. That of Nat Turner's insurrection is drawn from the most reliable authorities. That of the leading character, with slight embellishment, is drawn from a life history, stirring and novel though it be. The various descriptions of barbecues, negro-weddings, night-dances, hunts, alligator-adventures, slave-sales, are simple reproductions of what is familiar to every Southerner.

"Maum Guinea" has not been written to subserve any special social or political purpose. Finding, in the subject, material of a very novel and original nature, I have simply used what was presented to produce a pleasing book. If the moralist or economist should find in it any thing to challenge his or her attention, it will be for the reason that the book is a picture of slave-life as it is in its natural as well as in some of its exceptional phases.

M. V V.

MAUM GUINEA,

AND

HER PLANTATION "CHILDREN."

CHAPTER I.

FLIRTATION.

"Gay as the indolent poppy-flowers,
Sleepy and sweet as they,
With love, like a golden butterfly,
Deep down in her heart at play."

Daughter of Egypt, vail thine eyes!
I can not bear their fire.—BAYARD TAYLOR.

By dark bayou and cypress-swamp,
By rice-field and lagoon,
Her soul went wandering to the land
That scorches in the moon.—ALDRICH.

"You go 'long, 'Perion!"

"I wan' to, druffully, but I *can't*."

"W'y?"

"'Cause my feet is fastened to de yearth, Miss Rose."

"I don' see nuffin keepin' 'em—'less it's cause dey so big, you can't luf 'em."

"Dem's massa's own shoes I's a wearin', anyhow, t'ank you; I 'mired de buckles in 'em, dis mornin', and he says: 'Go 'long, take 'em;' and den he gibs me dis note to bring ober, safe and soun', and tell no tales. I wears massa's shoes, and eberybody knows *he* got han'some feet. No, no, Miss Rose, 'tain't dat; it's suthin else is a fastenin' ob 'em. Can't you guess?"

"Laws, no—course I can't."

"It's 'traction—'traction of grabity tow'd de lubly bein' in whose presence I now revolbe."

"Laws, Mister 'Perion, you uses such obbrobrious language!"

"We's had opportunities, Miss Rose; we ain't common folks. 'Sides, I's 'spired by de occasion."

"'Spec's if you was conwersin' wid Miss July, de likes ob me couldn't understand it at all,"—and the crimson turban of the young mulatto girl gave a coquettish toss, and the black eyes flashed at him a quick, sidelong look.

"Now *don't* go to saying dat," answered her companion, with a gesture of distress. "You knows I neber speaks to July 'less I can't help it. Course, bein' fellow-serbants, and eatin' to de same table, I has to be perlite to her. But I guess I knows who I wishes was missus' maid, 'stead of dat pert niggah."

"*I* wouldn' belong to nobody but my own young missus. She's de bestus young lady in de hull Lousiany State. Don't you t'ink she's *berry* han'some?"

"She's mighty han'some for a white lady—mighty han'some, and I don' wonder young massa t'ink so; but I know who suits my taste better!"

"Who, now?"—with the most innocent interest

"W'y, de lubly bein' who waits on her, in course,"—with a flourishing bow.

Again the crimson turban was tossed.

"Laws, Mister 'Perion, you is such a flatterer!"

The young colored man leaned against the gate-post, surveying her admiringly; her lithe, slender form, clear, yellow complexion, and flashing eyes, were doubtless his ideal of female beauty.

"Truf isn't flattery, Rose."

"Hadn' bettah let July know w'at you been sayin'."

"You knows you's better lookin' dan July. Wish you wouldn' refer to dat indiwidial ag'in, Miss Rose; it hurts my feelins."

"Oh, it does!"—with provoking incredulity. "But you see, Jim was ober here, Sunnay night, and he tol' me you and July was gone to meetin' togedder."

"Oh, gorry, Jim'll get thrashed for tellin' dat story. I had a sprained ankle, and couldn' go nowhar. I was as oneasy as a fish out of water all de ebenin', for I 'spec' he come and tell you some lie. Hope you wouldn' have nuffin to say to *him*, Rose—he's nuffin but coachman. Massa don' set no great store by *him*."

"He plays de banjo bestus eber I heard—Jim does."

It was very cruel of the girl to make this assertion so coolly; Hyperion kicked the gate-post, and looked sullen.

Although it was the middle of December, the rich sunshine of the South melted over the landscape, of which the figures of the speakers made at this moment a vivid and picturesque part; the girl, graceful in form and motion, with her red head-dress, and gold ear-rings glittering with every movement; the boy, dressed in the extremest elegance of a *valet*, in his master's left-off clothing, lounging indolently; both of them belonging to the finest specimens of mulattoes, young and handsome. They preferred the full warmth and light of the noonday sun, to the shadows on either side of the tree-bordered avenue, at the foot of which they stood; and as they basked in the bright day, they seemed a natural part of the bloom and gorgeousness of the climate.

The road which ran past led through a rich and level country, divided into such extensive plantations, that only two or three other dwellings were anywhere visible, besides the low, large cottage which stood at the head of the avenue, a veranda extending around the first story, and trees embow ering the broad roof, making, with its French windows, and vine-wreathed pillars, an attractive residence. Glimpses could be had of the out-buildings, and negro-houses further back, but the profusion of shade was such that these objects were almost hidden, showing just enough of themselves to give life to a scene which might otherwise have seemed lonely, from the absence of neighbors.

While the servants stood at the gate, happy in their broad flirtation, the curtains were parted from one of the upper windows, and a young lady looked forth, her pink lawn dress and dark hair fluttering in the light breeze.

"Rose!" she called, after leaning out a moment, to be sure that there was no one at the front of the house whom she did not wish there.

"Laws, dar's missus, callin'. 'Spec' dat answer's writ a'ready,"—and the young girl ran at the summons, leaving her companion thinking how "mighty quick that young lady mus' be at writin',"—when the truth was, she had been longer composing the brief note than its limits seemed to warrant.

The missive came wavering down into a rose-bush as Rose reached the spot. The writer watched till she saw it deposited in Hyperion's vest-pocket, and himself mounted upon the horse that had borne him from a neighboring plantation, when she disappeared from the window.

"Don' belieb any more dat Jim's lies. You kin see for yourself my ancle's lame, else massa wouldn' 'lowed me to ride dis hoss. Will you be to home next Sunnay night?—'cause I got suthin *berry* pertikler to say, Rose."

"Ef I don' make no promise, I shan' break none. Jim said he'd hab his banjo ober to mammy's cabin, Sunnay night."

"Berry well, Miss Rose. You can dance to banjo all yer life, if you want to. Shall I gib Jim your complimens?"

He straightened himself so finely on the spirited horse, and looked at her so fiercely, that the saucy laugh went all out of her brilliant face, and with downcast eyes she murmured:

"Laws, no. I don't care a straw for Jim, nor his banjo neder. I 'spises him, he's so set up about hisself. He may come to mammy's ef he wants to—*I* shan' be dar. I shall be down beside de spring, under the hill, 'less it's too cold. Dar's a nice bench dar, and nobody spyin' roun',"—and with a flash of her eyes at him, to see how he received this information, she darted off toward the house.

Hyperion's face shone like gold in the sunshine all the way home. He was so full of anticipations of the "berry pertikler" communication he had to make, that the reins fell on the neck of the horse, who walked home at his leisure, mindful not to overheat himself. When the *valet* came in sight of his young master impatiently pacing the portico, awaiting his return, he suddenly gathered up the reins and dashed up the carriage-path, with a speed which intimated he had ridden post-haste.

"You've been absent twice as long as you ought, you rascal."

"Gorry, massa, I didn' wan' to kill your favor*ite* hoss. 'Sides, the young lady took time to do her writin',"—and Hyperion handed the dainty note, confident of its mollifying influence.

In this he did not miscalculate, being motioned away by the eager hand which took the missive, the seal of which was instantly broken, and the young gentleman engaged with the contents. The smile which broke over his face proved these to be of an agreeable character; he read the few words over and over, and finally kissed them, before he deposited them in his vest-pocket. Yet this important note was a simple acceptance from Miss Virginia Bell, of Mr. Philip Fairfax's invitation to a Christmas festival which was to be celebrated in the neighborhood. All that charming secrecy which had invested the manner of its delivery and reception, was only that consciousness which attends every little act of two persons who have just begun to dream of that which they have not yet put into words. There was no more reason why Hyperion should have conveyed his message as subtly as if it had been a challenge to a duel, and its answer have been dropped as cautiously as if it had been the key to a conspiracy, than there is why two young people should blush when they chance to meet each other's glances, or tremble when their hands touch accidentally. These are the indescribable "airy nothings" which make the first stage of courtship so charming—delicious in experience, and hallowed in recollection.

Philip walked up and down the portico, thinking nothing, but dreaming every thing sweet and vague, the blood coursing through his heart to a music which thrilled every nerve—the music of his own hopes; though his step kept time unconsciously to the melody which floated from the direction of the stables, whither Hyperion had taken the horse. His *valet* was singing; though remarkable, even among the rich-voiced colored people, for the purity and power of his voice, it seemed to the young master as if it had never poured forth before so deep, unrestrained and joyful a strain. And perhaps it never had; for the colored man was dreaming, too; and his memory was welling and full of the gold of somebody's smile—the toss of a crimson turban, the glitter of a pair of ear-rings, darting through all his visions.

"'Pears to me yer mighty happy to-day."

"Well I is—'spects because it's comin' Cris'mas," answered Hyperion to the colored woman who addressed him; and so surprised was he to think she should speak to him at all, that he stopped and looked at her. "It's comin' Cris'mas, Maum Ginny."

He was on his way back to the house, and paused before the cook's cabin, in the door of which sat the woman who addressed him. She was a tall, good-looking person, also a mulatto, although two or three shades darker than the boy, almost entirely without the laugh and sparkle which sets off the dark features of her race so pleasantly; stern, even commanding in appearance, with a strange look in her eyes which might be sadness or might be hate, or both—nobody could read it. She was usually so silent that Hyperion felt especially honored by her addressing him, waiting for her to say more.

Maum Guinea was a new-comer, compared with himself. *He* had been born on the plantation, and brought up with his young master, changing gradually from his plaything, to be teased and worried like a good-natured dog, to his servant and *valet*, with all the ease and privileges of a favored house-slave.

Maum Guinea had been with them but five or six years, Colonel Fairfax having purchased her during one of his visits to New Orleans, his former cook having become too old to move with the desired alacrity. She had the confidence and respect of the family in a high degree, and was liked by all the slaves; though to the latter she was an object of mystery and conjecture. Her moody silence in the midst of their thoughtless gayety, her ability to keep her own counsel, the gloomy fire of her eyes, awakened their awe, while her gentleness to the sick, her skill in nursing, her accomplishments in cooking, and the many favors she contrived to do them all, inspired their affection.

Maum Guinea's advice was law with house-servants and field-hands. They came to her in their joys and troubles, and she gave them a kind of wise sympathy, asking none in return for her own cares, if she had any.

"Plenty ob good times, Cris'mas," continued Hyperion.

"*I* don' like it; it's black to me—blacker 'n my own blood."

She spoke this with such sudden fierceness, and a look of such terrible passion leaped out of her eyes for an instant, that the laugh was frightened out of her companion's face. He scraped the ground with his shoe, not knowing what reply to make, though his curiosity was keenly alive.

"Mos' folks likes it, specially collud pussons," he continued, at length; "nuffin to do, den, but play an' dance and hab good times. Gorry, I guess dem poor field niggers glad ob it."

Maum Guinea did not appear to hear him. Her sudden fit of communicativeness was over, and her eyes were fixed on the distant sky with a far-away look; after waiting a short time, he moved on, not thinking it safe to interrupt her mood.

"'Spec's you found Rosa well?"

He wheeled around suddenly and met her half-smiling look—a look which never grew into a real smile—with a puzzled, embarrassed air.

"'Clare for it, Maum Guinea, I b'lieves you know *eberyting* going on—eben what one's t'inking."

"Birds sing sweet afore Valentine—ask Massa Philip," she replied, rising and going in-doors, muttering to herself, when there, "blackbirds better not try to sing—no use—no use!"

"I's got a more importan' questing to ask massa," whispered Hyperion to himself—"old massa, too; ef it was only young massa, shouldn' car'. Gorry, but I hates it! I orter to do it dis berry day, while Massa Philip so tickled wid his letter; p'raps *he'll* ask ole massa for me,"—and he turned the corner of the house, whistling softly, and stealing a subtle glance out of the corner of his eye to see if Mr. Philip was still in the favorable mood. That young gentleman was leaning against a pillar of the veranda, looking off in the direction of Judge Bell's plantation, and smiling as if he saw a certain beautiful face through all the intervening space; he looked handsome, with that expression in his features, though he was not a particularly handsome man. His complexion was sallow and his features irregular; but his hair was glossy and abundant his form good, and his air frank and pleasing.

Hyperion—he had given this fanciful name to his *valet*, on account of his flowing curls, purple and shining, and with scarcely a trace of the original wiry kink — subdued his whistle, approaching his master with the air of one who has a favor to ask.

"How now?" asked the latter, pleasantly, when he finally perceived him, after he had stood several moments near him. "Speak out, what is it?"

"Oh, Massa Philip—" here the *valet* stopped, shuffling his foot on the ground; a vision of the coquettish turban again inspired his courage, and he proceeded: "Oh, massa, nex' week comes Cris'mas, you know, and I 'spec's—'spec's—"

"What, you rascal! you haven't come to me to beg spending-money, have you? It's only last week I gave you five dollars, and you ought to have a hundred dollars of your own by this time. Can't afford to have you so extravagant—I really can't,"—and the young gentleman shook his head gravely.

"Oh, Massa Philip, 'tain't de Cris'mas money—I's g t plenty; it's—it's—"

"Been playing off any your old tricks, ha?"

"No, massa; but you see it's comin' Cris'mas. and I was a t'inking as how Massa Fairfax he don' like to let any his people go 'way from home to get married."

"Why, no, certainly not; it's a bad practice," answered the young man, growing serious, while a shadow fell over the brilliant face of the "boy;" "but I hope *you* don't think of getting married, at home or abroad, Hyperion?"

"I *was* a t'inking, do I hadn' spoken to her 'bout it, nor wouldn' till I'd asked *you*. 'Twon't be no trouble to you, massa; I'll jes' step ober and see her once-and-a-w'ile, and she's a berry, berry nice pusson, and t'inks a heap of me."

"How do you know, if you haven't asked her?"

"Oh, massa! I *guesses* it,"—with a sly chuckle.

"Who is it? If you want to be so foolish as to get married, why don't you take July, here at home? that would be sensible."

"July!"—with a queer contortion—"she's such a bad temper, massa,"—peering up at the window to see if that person was within hearing—"'sides, she's 'gaged to Jim."

"I don't think the Colonel will consent to your marrying off the plantation; and I don't know as I shall let you marry at all—bad practice. But you haven't told me who it is."

"It's Miss Bell's Rose, massa."

The young gentleman flushed up in the guiltiest manner, he couldn't help it, for the shrewd eyes of the poor fellow were reading his face.

"Oh, it is, is it?"

"Yes, massa; and maybe 'twill be all in de family, arter all—hi! hi!"

"Clear out, you rascal! Go and dust my clothes, they need it."

"But, massa—"

"Well! well! clear out, I say. Maybe I'll speak to the Colonel, though I guess you're capable of managing your own business. It isn't best to be in too much of a hurry about it, though."

"I know, massa; but Cris'mas is comin', and it's a good time to get married."

"What, so soon? Short courtship, hey, boy? And all the better for that," he added to himself, thinking of somebody else, and of the ceremonies and delays attending "marriages in high life."

CHAPTER II.

CHRISTMAS EVE.

Joy for the present moment! joy to-day!
  Why look we to the morrow?—SARGENT.

Hi, pretty Kitty! hi, jolly Polly!
Up with the heels, girls, fling, lassies, fling!
Hi, there! stay, there! that's not the way, there!
Oh, Johnny, Johnny,
Oh, Johnny, Johnny,
Ho, ho, everybody, all around the ring!—SYDNEY DOBELL.

Christmas comes but once a year,
And when it comes, it brings good cheer.—OLD SONG.

These eight days doth none require
  His debts of any man;
Their tables do they furnish out
  With all the meat they can.—OLD SONG.

"Wildly and gorgeously flashes the fire,—
  The squeak of the fiddle flies high and higher."

IT was Christmas Eve. The sound of the fiddle floated through the darkness over Colonel Fairfax's plantation. Guided by this, as also by the fitful flash from distant bonfires, we might come upon a curious scene. The field-negroes were having a grand frolic. As none of their cabins would allow of much dancing within their limits, and there were twenty or thirty ready for a regular "break-down," they had chosen an open shed belonging to the sugar-house, which they had brilliantly illuminated by fires in the open air. About these were gathered all the aged and rheumatic, whose dancing days were over, toasting their unshapely feet at the glowing embers, and looking on at the more active revelers. The air was almost balmy, soft as spring, but damp enough to make the warmth of the blaze welcome to those who were not exercising. Fantastic as the flames whose light played and quivered around them, were the groups which they revealed — uncouth creatures, the most of them, even the younger ones; while the old seemed more like caricatures of humanity than realities. Yet all of them—the young and stout, and the old, distorted by hard labor beyond their natural ugliness, branded by servitude, withered by years—were as gay and free from care as a meeting of chattering apes in a Bornean forest. They had none of them lost that rich capacity for enjoyment which is the boon and blessing of their race. They were happy in their new clothes, in their week's holiday, the warmth of the fire and the exhilaration of the music. Each one had received a new suit that very day; the homely cotton gowns and trowsers were new, as were the shoes; and some were bedecked with turbans, gorgeous as the poppies of the Orient. And some of the dandies—for even among field-hands on a sugar-plantation, there are dandies—flowered out in vests of superfluous brilliancy, which they had purchased for themselves from their allowance of spending-money.

Perched on a box at one end of the shed was the musician an old negro with white wool and wrinkled face, who evidently felt the importance of his position, for he rosined his bow, and screeched it across the strings, until the anticipation of the dancers was wrought to a pitch with his highest note. The red hue of the fire gave a weird glow to the rolling eyes, and shining faces; the soft, oily chuckle of the girls and the easy laugh of their partners sounded pleasantly on the air.

Everybody was laughing at the least provocation, or none at all. Some ancient crone, with her knees drawn up to her chin, before the fire, has said something, at which all her companions "hi! hi!" "hi! hi!" and some stalwart dancer has hurried up the fiddler, whose answer is followed by a chorus of "yah! yah! yah!" "yah! yah! yah!"

In the mean time, somebody sings:

"De ladies in de parlor,
Hey come a rollin' down—
A drinkin' tea and coffee;
Good morning ladies all.

De gemmen in de kitchen,
Hey come a rollin' down—
A drinkin' brandy toddy;
Good morning ladies all."

At which everybody laughs, and the fiddle squeaks violently.

"Say, dah! hain't ye got dat fiddle ground?"

"Min' yer bisness, and don' be in a hurry. 'Fraid I shall break a 'tring if ye hurry me,"—and Uncle Zip grins to himself, at the thought of the discomfiture he has threatened.

"Berry well. Me and Chloe is a going to get along widout yer help,"—and the speaker catches a girl around the waist, sets up a clever, lively whistle, and they begin to hop and jump in a grotesque jig, the steps of which could never have been set down in any "art of dancing." The fiddle gives a triumphant squeal, which extinguishes the whistle, Uncle Zip's head drops on his breast, his monstrous foot beats time, his arm moves methodically, and out jumps an invigorating reel, which sets the beaming, giggling, uncouth couples into wild and indescribable feats of motion.

There seems, in all the features of this fantastic picture, a harmony; the dark sky, the flashing, leaping flames, the crimson glow, the grey head-dresses, the black faces, the bright eyes, the shrill, merry music, the untutored gestures.

Fast and faster flew Uncle Zip's bow, and wilder grew the frolic, until musician and dancers paused from sheer exhaustion. The performer refreshed himself from a jug which stood on a box beside him, the gift of the company in part reward for his arduous labors. Some of the old women began to rake out sweet potatoes from the embers, which those disposed took in their hands and munched; there were also corn-cakes, baked on hot stones; and eggs which had been stolen or purchased, and saved for this occasion. It was rumored by some that there was a pig to be roasted; but this, it seems, had been reserved for Christmas-day proper, when there was to be a barbecue, and good times generally.

In the midst of the first "recess," while these refreshments were being handed round, a group of house-servants approached, led by the tall figure of Maum Guinea.

"Oh, dar's Maum Ginny. Oh, I's glad," cried the children, some of whom had been permitted to keep up and see the fun

"How is yer, Maum Ginny?"

"W'at yer got? w'at yer got?"

The whole crowd pressed around, knowing by instinct that she came for their benefit, as she never went to merry-makings for her own. July, the chambermaid, was with her; and Hyperion, looking much less bright than on the day we made his acquaintance, though he was dressed with an elegance that made the "niggahs" stare; likewise Rose and another girl from Massa Bell's plantation, and one or two others. Maum Guinea carried a large basket, covered with a cloth, and Hyperion, with another man, two large buckets full of steaming coffee, seasoned with sugar. The girls brought tin-cups to drink from.

"Here, chil'un," said the cook, "is my treat."

As she spoke, she uncovered the basket, which was heaped with cold ham, buttered biscuits, and any quantity of small sweet-cakes. To the cries of delight she made no response, not even smiling at the thanks and flatteries which overwhelmed her, but went quietly to work distributing the dainties in such a way as to secure to each a fair portion.

"Oh, Maum Ginny, how could you 'teal so much nice 'ings?" asked one eager urchin, as he grasped the cakes she gave him.

"Didn' 'teal 'em," she replied, indignantly; "bought ebery t'ing wid my own money—eben de eggs an' sugar—an' bake 'em myself."

"Oh, Maumy, you is awful good."

"Woll, woll, neber mind dat. I's got no pickaninnies spend money fur, and ole women don' need finery."

The eager creatures grunted and chuckled their admiration and satisfaction. In their eyes, Maum Guinea, although colored and a cook, was almost as superior a being as any of the white race they had ever seen. They regarded her with almost the same awe and adoration which they would have bestowed upon a *fetish*—they believed that something of a supernatural character attached to her.

While the others were eating and resting, Hyperion bribed Uncle Zip, with a piece of silver, to continue his playing; and he and Rose, Jim and July, danced French-four, half-cotillion, and some of those regular dances which they had copied from the lessons set them by the ladies and gentlemen at whose balls and parties they served as attendants. Very well they danced, too; especially Rose, who had something of the mixture of fire and languor which distinguishes the Creole women. Hyperion was distressingly graceful and impressive; while Jim bowed lower, and threw out his heels more freely than was admired by the critical eye of the *valet*. But, of course, a coachman could not be expected to rival a *valet* in refinement and elegance. Alas, for Hyperion! alas, for Rose! though they gradually warmed to the music, and entered into the spirit of the dance, there was evidently something wrong with them. The glow which had lighted up their golden faces, as they flirted in the sunshine, but a few days previous, was softened down by a decided shadow. Sometimes, when she looked at her lover, a slight quiver would weigh down the lashes over her dark, liquid eyes, and compress her lips; while his gaze followed her every moment with a sad, unsatisfied longing.

They had met by the spring, on the previous Sabbath night, as they had agreed; and there, very much after the fashion of whiter and freer lovers, had, all coquetry aside, solemnly promised to marry each other—provided, they were allowed. They knew very well that it was against the rules to marry off their own plantations; but they were both especial favorites and pets, and relied upon carrying the matter with the young white lady and gentleman, whom they suspected of a tender interest in each other; and when they parted at the spring, it was with the hope of being married this very Christmas Eve

Rose's imagination had already selected the very dress, out of her young mistress' wardrobe, which she was to beg for her own wedding-dress—a corn-colored tissue, with crimson trimmings, which was now in its second season, and which she had always admired exceedingly. She felt certain, too, "that Miss Virginny would give her a real gold ring," to be married with, and a wreath of flowers for her hair, and plenty of cake to make merry with. They would be married Christmas Eve, and then they would have a whole week to spend together—a whole week of regular honeymoon; and after that—why, they could see each other pretty often, and perhaps, before many months, they would belong to the same family, with a bride and groom to wait upon, and every thing so nice and happy.

This was the pretty dream they had cherished when they parted; but when they met again, a few days later, their prospects were changed. Miss Virginia had no idea of allowing her favorite maid to marry, and be having interests of her own, which might interfere with dressing her hair and humoring her caprices at all times—at least, not at present—not for a year anyhow. She was going to Saratoga next year, and should need Rose as much as her trunks or purse, and Rose might be ill or something—no, no, decidedly—not until she returned from the Springs. By that time, matters might be arranged, if they were still so foolish as to wish it, so that they could marry; a contingency might arise—here Miss Virginia blushed, and looked out the window, confused by the pleasant thought which had swept across her mind, sweet as a breeze from a garden of roses. It was but a thought—nay, but a fancy—for no lightest whisper had yet been breathed; but it awoke a bashful, tumultuous stir in her pulses, and set her to dreaming, so that she leaned against the window-sill, forgetful entirely of the downcast girl, who, with tearful eye and heavy heart, was striving to keep on with her embroidery, and not injure it by the rain which dripped over her cheeks.

Poor Rose! her brilliant hopes had been blotted out, corn-colored tissue dress, gold ring, and all. During that half-hour, almost for the first time in her life, she wished she were not a slave—which was very unreasonable in her, for there are many free white people who can not marry whom they please nor when they please, nor have a silk tissue dress to be married in. Turbulent thoughts swelled her bosom, and once or twice a defiant glance flashed through her tears at the young mistress whom she loved, and who was usually indulgent to a fault. Virginia made a pretty picture as she leaned against the window-frame, the dark braids of her hair, heavy and shining, framing a face of delicate oval, tinged with the warmth of a southern climate; lips like rubies; cheeks just a shade brighter than the clear brunette color of neck and brow; the fancies of eighteen summers floating in her eyes, the anticipations of maidenhood heaving her breast with a breath quick and tremulous. She was young, wealthy, beloved; ease and happiness were her birthright, and it would have been cruel for her to have been robbed of them thus early. She looked kind, too, and gentle; indolent, as a southern temperament is apt to be, but not ill-tempered. Her air was that of a person of refinement and intelligence above that of ordinary young ladies.

"Oh, dear! I hope the dress-maker won't dissappoint me about my ball-dress," she said, at the close of her reverie. It was natural she should think of the festival, since Philip Fairfax was to be her escort, and that her thoughts should finally settle upon her attire, which was to be so charming. "You must go and see her to-night, and find out how she is getting along with it, Rose;" and, singing to herself, she glided out of the room, forgetful of her momentary vexation at her maid for wanting to marry.

Hyperion had had no better success with his suit; indeed, rather worse. The old Colonel chanced to be in a bad humor when the matter was proposed, and had not only utterly refused to hear of his marrying off the plantation, but had insisted on his taking July if he wanted a wife.

"July's sixteen now, and not much to do. It's high time she was doing her share toward keeping up the population," said the matter-of-fact master. "She's a good-looking wench, too; I don't know what better you could ask, boy."

Mr. Fairfax had not the same reason for favoring the match which Philip had, as he did not suspect the state of affairs between the young people. He was a good master—a model master—but a strict disciplinarian, and would not allow such irregular proceedings as having one of his slaves go to a neighbor's plantation in search of a partner.

Almost discouraged, Hyperion returned to Massa Philip to get him to intercede for him, and was told that it was not wise at present.

"Wait a while, you rascal, wait a while. I'll see that you aren't obliged to marry July, if you have such a bad opinion of her. Maybe you can get Rose yet, if you are patient; there's more Christmases coming."

This was the shadow which had fallen upon the slave lovers—a light shadow, compared to darkness which might be, but which gave a sad, cold look to the faces usually so vivacious, and drew the sharp eyes of Maum Guinea upon them with no common interest, as they threaded the mazes of Uncle Zip's not very intricate music.

"'Tain't weddin'-cake," she said, meaningly, as she offered them of the stores in her basket when the dance was finished; "But I guess yer can eat it. Pr'aps, when Maum Ginny bakes weddin'-cake for de young massa, some oder folk'll get der share too."

"Laws, how you do go on!" ejaculated Rose; but she sighed afterward.

In the mean time, if one couple was in the shade, another was in the light. Jim, the coachman, was in exuberant spirits; he flung himself around so, during the dance, that there was danger of his getting himself into a fatal tangle—in fact, once, leaping up and hitting his long heels together in the air, he came down differently from what he expected, to the "inextinguishable" merriment of the whole company, from the toothless negress mumbling over the ashes, to the pickaninny rolling on the ground near by.

"Tell yer what, Maum Ginny," spoke Jim, after Rose,

rolling his eyes mysteriously, and chuckling at July, who rolled her eyes also, and smiled like a sunflower, "yer may sweeten a hoe-cake for *us*, and we'll be eberlastingly obleeged to you, t'ank you, and do as much for you on suitablum occasion."

"Ho! ho! dat so, July?"

"Yis, Maum—we jis' made it up."

"To-morrer ebening I 'spec's we'll need de preacher. My complimens to yer, Mister Hyperion, and hopes you and Rose won't refuse us der perliteness of yer countenance, to stand up with us,"—and he flourished a bow, to which the *valet* replied with one still more impressive.

"T'ank you, Mister Jim, I don' know as I's any engagements as will pervent my doing yer the honor of bein' yer groomsman—dat is, ef yer goin' to do it up brown, as der coachman of a fust family oughter."

"Oh, I's got a w'ite dress," spoke up July.

"And I calkerlates to spend t'ree dollars in refreshments, and I 'spec's missus will give us a bottle of wine, like as not—July missus' maid, and missus said she might chuse a partner, ef she liked."

"You'll come, Rose?" asked the bride-expectant.

"W'y, yis, I s'pose so."

It was hard for Rose to stand up at somebody else's wedding, instead of her own; but she choked down the lump in her throat, and began to question July about her dress and "fixins," as the visitors gathered up the now empty buckets and basket, and left the "niggers" to finish the ball.

Maum Guinea promised Jim she'd bake them a splendid cake, with frosting on it; for the family was going to take dinner out on the morrow, and she should have less than usual to do.

When they came to the cook's cabin, a cheerful light shone

through the little square window: none of the party were sleepy, and she asked them to come in and sit awhile; so they went in, squatting themselves upon the floor in a semicircle about the fire. There was a good deal of screeching and laughing, pretended anger and rude flirtation among the young people; but the mistress of the cabin had grown silent, gazing into the deep, red heart of the fire with a steady, stern look, which almost made the superstitious creatures about her tremble, when they chanced to observe her in the midst of their merriment.

There was something in Rose's soul that night—we suppose she had a kind of half-in-half gold-colored soul, seeing there was so much white blood in her veins—which brought her into sympathy with the quiet woman near her; she gradually sidled up to her, though she still held her lover's hand, and finally dropped her head against the stately bosom of the cook.

"Oh, Maum Ginny," she cried, looking up, half-frightened at her own boldness, "tell us a story. I do like stories so; and you tell such queer ones. Tell us suthin 'bout *yerself*, Maumy, when you was a girl 'bout my age."

Maum Guinea started as if a hissing snake had suddenly sprung out of the glowing coals; but she was soon calm again, shaking her head in refusal.

"Chile, chile, hush!"

"Jim, you tell us 'bout dat big snake you cotched last summer," interposed July, who was proud of the exploit of her lover, as well as a little frightened by Maum Guinea's voice.

"Well, you see," he began, nothing loth, "massa sent me out in de swamp to—"

"We's all heard dat, forty times ober," murmured the *valet*, who always held himself superior to Jim, and did not hesitate to criticise.

Den I was out in de swamp, wid an ax, to cut some bark to make wash for Bill's foreleg, which was swelled; and I found de right kind of tree, only der was a big black wine twisted around der trunk, w'ich I t'ought I'd cut down; but w'en I teched it wid de ax, golly, didn't it untwist itself mighty quick time, and stan' right up on its tail, and look me in de face, sassy! Yer see it was a snake, de biggest eber *I* see—w'en it stood up it was just my height, and as ugly as it was big. He look at me so wicked, golly, I t'ought my time was come. I couldn' lif' han' nor foot, but jes' look him in de eye; yes, sir"—mysteriously—"dat snake was de debbil hisself, sure 'nuff, and he put a spell upon me, so I couldn' help myself. His eyes were as green as grass, and he winked at me so sassy—he *did;* you needn' stick your tongue in yer cheek, 'Perion; if you'd been dar you'd *see*—and den he jes' drew back a little, and I don' know now how it happen, but de ax it flew up itself, for I couldn' lif' it, and hit him on de neck and cut his head cl'ar off. It was de debbil, sure 'nuff, for he hollered 'ouch!' when his head fell off; but I didn' stay to bury him, nor to get de bark nudder. Golly, I wouldn' go in dat swamp ag'in for a silber dollah."

"We's mighty glad you's killed de debbil, Jim," said a shining, good-humored-looking fellow, the darkest of the group of mulattoes; "'kase we all feel easy in our mind now."

They all giggled at this sally; nevertheless, three or four of them, with dilated eyes, stole furtive glances under the bed and into the corners of the room, as if they expected his majesty might still be alive and near at hand.

"Somebody tell anodder story—suthin *new*, that nobody else eber heard," suggested another.

"Don' tell any thing skeery," said July, creeping closer to Jim.

"'Kase might make July's hair stand on end," suggested

the wit of the company again; "an' eberybody knows it's so kinky, hain't no end to stand on."

"It's 'traiter yourn, anyhow," retorted the young lady.

"Look-a-heah, chil'ren, 'tain't more'n 'leben o'clock, and nobody can't go to bed till de blessed Cris'mas comes in. S'posin' somebody tells each oder de *trute*—suthin as has happened to hisself, some time anodder. We's all slaves, and we's all been sold once or more, 'ceptin' 'Perion here. Les' tell suthin 'bout w'ere we cum from, w'en we's little, or w'en we had anodder massa," said Jim.

They all looked at Maum Guinea.

"Go on, chil'ren," said she; "ole woman'll listen."

"But you ain't ole, Maumy," said Rose, "and you know more'n any de rest."

"Woll, woll! let oders tell dere's first. Dar's seben ebenings comin', and we can tell lots ob stories. Who'll begin?"

"Draw cuts," suggested Hyperion.

Jim brought the broom out of a corner, and pulled as many splints as there were persons present; Maum Guinea, who declined to take part in the lottery, arranged them in her hand so that but one end should be visible—the one who drew the shortest splint to tell the first story. The lot fell upon Johnson, a house-servant from the Bell plantation, a slender, thin, rather sullen-looking man of about thirty, with glittering, Italian eyes, and a good deal of the nervous white element in his temperament.

"Mister Jonsing, please purceed."

"Don' be bashful, Mister Jonsing."

"Let him alone honey; he's a-getting ready."

Johnson looked over at Rose; her hand was in Hyperion's, but her eyes were fixed upon him coaxingly; although his fellow-servant, she knew nothing of his history previous to his arrival at Massa Bell's, two years ago.

"Oh, yes, tell us," she pleaded, with lively curiosity.

"'Twon't be nothin' to make you laugh," was the answer.

"We don' want to laugh, jes' now," said Maum Guinea, gravely; "it's going on to Cris'mas now, and we oughter be singing hymns of glory. If you've any thing heavy on yer mind, maybe you'll feel easier for sharing it, dough—w'en it lays *too* long, it grows so heaby, can't be lifted nohow."

"If I must, I must," said Johnson, and his auditors crowded a little closer about him, opening both ears and eyes, excepting July, who was dropping asleep on Jim's shoulder, dreaming of her wedding-dress.

CHAPTER III.

JOHNSON'S STORY.

> And the slave, where'er he cowers, feels the soul within him climb
> To the awful verge of manhood, as the energy sublime
> Of a century, bursts, full-blossomed, on the thorny stem of time.
> LOWELL.

> Her freezing heart, like one who sinks
> Outwearied in the drifting snow,
> Drowses to deadly sleep, and thinks
> No longer of its hopeless wo.—IBID.

> The great King of kings
> Hath, in the title of his law, commanded
> That thou shalt do no murder.—SHAKESPERE.

"I WAS born and brought up in Ole Virginny. My mudder was a slave, and my fadder was a Member of Congress. I belongs to one of de fus' families—got good blood in my veins—say my fadder could make a speech as smart as any-body in the city of Washington. My mudder was only fifteen year ole when I was born. She was a house-servant, but only light work to do; use to sew for missus, and tend de chil'ren; use to hab good times 'fore I was born; but after dat, times was not so easy. W'en a missus hates a slave wuss'n pison, times ain't easy for de slave, s'pose ye know. My mudder was *berry* handsome—handsome as Rose dar—jis' sech soft, shinin' hair and eyes, and skin as white as mos' anybody's. I can remember how she looked when I was a little fellow tumbling in de dirt, or in de porch wid massa's *oder* chil'ren—his real ones, I mean. She used to sing so beautiful—all de people lul to hear her sing—put de fretfullest baby to sleep wid her singin'. 'Spec' she was happy and kerless for a w'ile; but by time I got ole enough to notice, she use to cry more'n she laugh. She would sit and sing, holding missus' baby in her lap—her own would be put out to black nigger to nurse—and de tears a-rollin' down her cheeks all de time I was cuttin' up and rollin' 'round in de grass.

"You see, missus was awful cruel to her. W'enever massa was away in Washington City, w'ich he'd be months at a time, she'd whip her, and starve her, and freeze her, and ebery-t'ing she could do, 'cept to kill her outright. You see, missus wasn't berry handsome, and my mudder was; my mudder could read and write, too, and was rael ginteel; and missus hated her 'kase her husband liked her so well. Ef he hadn't favored her beyond the rest, and give her presents, and sot her up 'fore his own wife, I don't s'pose missus would 'ave got so bad. She used to try to make her husband sell her 'way down South; but he wouldn't do it—swore he'd sell hisself fust; and the more lies she told 'bout de poor slave-girl, and de more trouble she tried for to get her in, de more massa took her part. I don' blame Missus Jonsing now so much as I did once—but 'twas wrong, all round, and dat's a fact.

"Woll, you see, my mudder she lub massa berry much—she *lub him* orfully. W'en he'd been gone and come back, and she heard his voice 'fore she seen him, I've noticed her pressin' her han's to her heart, and gettin' faint-like, and then lookin' so happy—dat's w'en I was a growin' boy, and she were more'n twenty year ole. She nebber tell him how bad missus use her—how her back all scarred up with whipping, and her feet froze wid bein' kep' out one col' night all night. She was 'fraid massa would sell her, rudder dan see her used so bad; and she'd take it all, sooner'n be sold 'way from him.

"Woll, missus she find out way to make slave-girl more misablum still. She quit a-whippin' and a-starvin' her, and took to gibbing it to *me*. She hoped to make my mudder run away wid me, and nebber come back no more.

"My mudder was proud of me. She teach me to read and write all she knew; she made my clothes nice, and keep me clean, and w'en massa come home from Washington City, she'd fix me up, and contribe to hab me 'round, so he'd see how much I growed, and how bright I was; but he didn't seem to keer—only to be put out about it; and den she'd cry ober me nex' time we was alone togedder, 'cause he didn't want to see me 'roun'. I s'pose he didn't like to see me 'roun', when he was kissin' his *oder* chil'ren, and showin' 'em de nice presents he'd brought; but my mudder was a foolish slave, and it made her feel bad; and de fact is, 'twas all wrong all 'roun', anyhow.

"Woll, missus she treat me so bad, I got thin and trembly, and was all de time in a kind of scare; my mudder use to set and cry ober me at nights, w'en she could get me wid her, w'ich wasn't often, and sometimes she talk to me—oh, real bad—'bout Missus Jonsing; her eyes would shine till I was scared, and would begin to cry, and ask her not to look so; but I felt some dreffful bad feelings in my own heart, and once I told her I was goin' to kill missus when I got big enough. Den she try to hush me up, an' say I mus'n' t'ink such naughty, wicked t'ings But I did t'ink 'em.

"Woll, one day, I was ten, 'lebing year old, missus got oberseer to whip me for breaking a dish, and he happen to jerk my shoulder out of j'int, and den, I tell you, my mudder, she couldn' bar it no longer; she took me in her arms, and went before missus, and gib her sich a talking to, missus turned as w'ite as a ghost, and she had her out to de whipping-post less'n no time, to have 'de sass took out of her.' So, w'en we bof got well enuff to crawl aroun', my mudder she took me, one night, and we run away. I t'ink she t'ought she'd go de right way, and she'd get to Washington City, and tell massa how t'was, and beg him to sell her an' me away. But she got lost in de woods; dar was snow on de groun' de second night we was out; she gib me all de biscuit and meat she had in her pocket, I 'spec', and we wandered 'roun' and roun', days and days, and she put her petticoat ober me ob nights; and one night she sung and sung so sweet to me, dat I stop crying and fell 'sleep, t'inking of de angels, and de next mornin', when I woke up, my mudder was dead.

"Yes, she was cold and dead, sure enough; and dar I set and hollered and cried, till bym-bye some men who was a-huntin' come 'long, and dey found us, and took me out de woods; and 'bout a month after I wer' sent back to Missus Jonsing—but my mudder nebber troubled her no more.

"Missus wasn't quite so bad to me after dat, but she nebber liked me berry well. I was a right smart boy, so spry and knowing, they couldn' help having me 'round great deal. I use to wait on table and on company. I got lots of complemens and kicks both. I kep' up my readin' and writin' w'enever I had a chance, and I larned a little cypherin' from the new oberseer, who took a fancy to me; and massa tol' me once, mebbe I'd get to be oberseer myself some day. I was always kind o' quiet for my age, and the older I growed the quieter I got. You see I was t'inking of suthin more and more since my mudder was dead. Sometimes missus would ask me what made me so sullen; if I wasn't well took keer of and comfortable. I t'ink she was kind o' 'fraid of me. I use to look at her, w'en I stood 'hind massa's chair at table. She was a proud-looking woman, but she wasn't handsome. Sometimes, w'en she'd meet my eyes, she look kind of startled; 'spect dar was more in 'em than I meant myself, for all dis time I was t'inking, t'inking.

"Tell you, my frien's, w'at I was t'inking about: *I'd made up my mind to kill my missus.* Don' be so scar't, Rose. You see, I'd got it fixed up that I ought to do it. She'd killed my mudder, or de same, and w'en one pusson kills anodder de law hangs 'em. Woll, I knew, in course, I couldn' prove she'd killed my mudder, so I was bound to take de law in my own han's. You see, I *felt* so, and you can't expect poor, ignorant black folks feel t'ings right; t'was wrong, berry wrong, but fact is, ebery t'ing was wrong, and I couldn' get it right, nohow.

"Woll, Missus Jonsing, she got so she couldn' bar to have me 'roun' de table, and she got massa to gib me kind of assistant's place to de oberseer; and so I hung 'round, in and out de house, till I was 'bout twenty-two year ole; and still I hadn't had no berry good chance to do what I meant to.

"Howsumever, dar was anodder reason. Dar was a girl in de house dat I'd got to t'ink a heap of. She was right young and pretty. I wanted her for my wife, and she t'ought a good deal of missus, and I couldn' somehow bring myself to do de job, w'en she was 'round. I t'ought a *great deal* of Chloe, but she didn't seem to keer for me. She was berry sprightly, and I was so quiet-like, she didn' take to me. Last I found out she was belonging to young massa, missus' oldest son, jis' a year older'n me—my half-brudder he was, if he wouldn' like to be tol' of it. So den I made up my mind for certain.

"'Fore long, I had a chance. Massa and his son bof went to political meeting, over in de town, to be gone all night. 'Twas bright moonlight—bright as day—but I wasn' going to wait. She always kep' her door locked, but de window was open, for 'twas a warm night, and I climbed up on de roof of de porch, and got in de window as still as a mouse. I had an ax in my hand. I could see all about. Missus was sleeping on a bed. 'Long side de bed, on de floor, lay Chloe; she was sleeping, too. De bed stood out in de room, so I could step 'round de oder side, and not wake Chloe.

"My head was as hot as fire, and my heart as cold as ice. I raised de ax Jis' den Chloe riz right up like a sperit, and looked at me. I reckon she couldn' scream, she was so scar't; she raised her hand, as if forbidding me, and de ax kind o' sunk down. I couldn' kill missus, and she lookin' at me wid dose eyes.

"'Ef it 'twan't for *you* I'd do it,' I muttered; and den I jis' gib up, and turned 'round and went out de window, jumped down, and stood still a minute. I 'spected Chloe'd tell on me, and den it would be all up wid me; anyways, I didn' want to stay no longer. I'd made up my mind to run away, w'edder I did or didn' make out w'at I wanted. I had de key of de stable, and I'd got a hoss out in de lane, waitin'. So I stood jis' a minute, and den I fled, and I nebber see'd de ole plantation sence. I could write so well I'd writ myself a pass, and I rode dat night and de nex' mornin', w'en a couple of w'ite men met and stopped me. I showed my pass, and I got to Norfolk someways, and I had money, and paid my passage to New Orleans on a vessel w'at was going right away; and I've had all kinds ob times sence den, but nebber no good luck. I don' belief Chloe eber tol' on me, for I see de paper myself w'at massa advertised me in, an' dar wasn' not'ing said 'bout dat; but I got took up for a runaway, somehow, at las', by somebody as was hard up, and mus' sell somebody else's niggah, 'kase he'd none of his own. I was sol' by a man dat hadn' a speck of right to me, to a hotel-keeper in New Orleans; but I was 'fraid of bein' found out in dat conspicurous situation, and made myself so 'tickalerly disagreeable, dat he sol' me to Massa Bell—and dat's how *I* come down to Lousianny, Miss Rose, sartain."

CHAPTER IV.

CHRISTMAS.

Hark! hear the bells, the Christmas bells! Oh, no! who set them ringing?
I think I hear our bridal-bells, and I with joy am blind.—ALDRICH.

For, borne from bells on music soft,
That solemn hour went forth from heaven,
To stir the starry airs aloft,
And thrill the purple pulse of even.

Oh, happy hush of heart to heart!
Oh, moment molten through with bliss!
Oh Love, delaying long to part
The first, fast, individual kiss!—OWEN MEREDITH.

And had he not long read
The heart's hushed secret in the soft, dark eye
Lighted at his approach, and on the cheek,
Coloring all crimson at his lightest look?—MISS LANDON.

Capricious, wanton, bold and brutal lust
Is merely selfish; when resisted, cruel.—MILTON.

IT was late Christmas morning before any one stirred on the Fairfax plantation. There were no children at the old mansion-house, to waken with the first crow of chanticleer, and drag papa and mamma out of bed, to look for mysterious treasures dropped by their patron saint through the dark watches of the night; and everybody, white and black, had kept Christmas Eve with such fervor that Christmas Morn took them unawares. When the drowsy creatures began, one by one, to creep from their resting-places on cabin-floors, a sense of pleasure stole into the dullest brains. No work, no care, no punishment—nothing but eat and play; not for one day only, but for a week. They must enjoy themselves now enough to last them a whole year. The oldest negro, thrusting his white wool out-of-doors to wish merry Christmas to his next neighbor, was as much of a child as the radiant, rollicking, funny little grandchild darting between his legs, his ebony countenance suffused with the consciousness that he was going to have 'lasses with his hoe-cake for breakfast. There is no doubt but that the 'lasses with which that pickaninny besmeared himself, gave him as much joy as little Florence Bell's wax-doll, cornucopias and miniature tea-set gave her. It is those who are contented who are the richest.

Old Zip, being wide awake himself, resolved that no laggard should slumber longer; so he took his fiddle, and marched up and down the negro-quarters, playing and singing vociferously:

"Old Zip Coon, berry fine feller,
Plays on de banjo, coon in de holler."

"Berry fine fellow—ho! ho!" said a young darkey, scornfully, as the musician came up to him—"but I show him a trick or two!" and, turning back into his cabin, he brought forth a bran-new banjo, and began playing a bran-new tune, which Zip had never even heard, and which drew out the settlement, as the smell of clover draws bees.

"Wah did you get dat?" asked the old fiddler, with evident jealousy.

"Bought 'em," said the young competitor, thrumming away triumphantly.

"Banjo berry good for common niggers; but banjo ain't fiddle,"—and Uncle Zip resumed his playing with an energy which extinguished the new tune, and compelled the banjo to fall into rank and play second fiddle.

The shrill squeal of a fat porker soon blended with the music, as a couple of men entered a pen in the rear of the cabins, and seized the victim which was to be offered, a smoking sacrifice, to the day's festivities.

The grand feature of this day's frolic was to be a barbecue in the edge of the woods which skirted the plantation. Even the house-servants, such of them as could be spared, were not averse to joining in the wild novelty of this favorite sport, which was to begin at noon and end at midnight, and was engaged in by the hands of several of the plantations, each of which contributed its share to the furnishing of the feast. As they had slumbered until long after sunrise, there was no more than time for the women to bake the breakfast-cake, wash the children's faces, and get their own finery in order, and for the men to get the necessary "traps" together, by the appointed hour. The weather was propitious—still and bright, and just cool enough to be exhilarating.

In the center of a cleared space, which ran a little way back into the wood, the ceremonies began by kindling a huge fire, in which the tamarack-branches crackled and the pine-knots glowed, in a manner especially delightful to these dark children of the sun, who loved both the heat and the light. The luxury of toasting their shins was enjoyed with the most delightful laziness by the elders of the frolic, who shook their heads, rolled their eyes, laughed queerly, and made brief observations or told fantastic tales which taxed even their own wonderful credulity. All those who were not singing or dancing or fiddling, had enough to do in watching the motions of the men engaged in the important work of getting the feast rightly to "doing." Ebony babies rolled around like balls in the dry grass, and older urchins lugged small branches, with tremendous efforts, adding fuel to the flames, in the center of which began to deepen and vivify the hot logs which made the reliable foundation of the fire, before which sticks were set up, from which were suspended two huge "porkers," to be roasted whole, after the fashion of a barbecue.

Musical as the sweetest strains of the violin, was the continual splutter and sizzle of fat which began to drop from these. It filled all senses with rich anticipations. Under its inspiriting influence, the young folks began to dance with a vigor fully equal to their performances of the previous evening; while there was a much larger crowd and a fuller band of music. Uncle Zip's fiddle had been reinforced by two banjos and a tambourine, to say nothing of a tin-pan and a *kettle*-drum. And the music thus produced was of no mean character. Rich, lively, melodious, full of golden rhythm and delicious sensibility, it moved the African blood to responsive beats; it was simple and natural as their own feelings, and as gay: while it had about it an originality distinct as that of the race from which it emanated. All the splendor of their native clime is in the golden melodies of the negroes.

Although the roasted porkers were the principal item in the bill of fare, there were accessories. In a large pot, which swung over a small fire of its own, some score of chickens were giving forth a savory odor. They were under the superintendence of a Dinah who understood the art of stewing fowls. Let not the inquiring reader trouble his mind as to the means by which these delicacies were obtained; they may have been raised by some provident resident in the negro-quarters, or they may have been taken surreptitiously from the hen-houses of masters—it matters not.

There was also another rare dish, upon which was concentrated all the care and skill of the best cook in the party

Two or three enterprising persons, instead of engaging in the dance, the night before, had gone forth secretly, and their skillful hunting had been rewarded by that daintiest of all game, in the estimation of the colored people—an opossum. Stuffed with a stuffing compounded by the cook aforementioned, rolled in leaves and grass like a mummy in its swathings, and buried in ashes among hot stones, "possum up a gum stump" was expiating his folly in having been so foolish, notwithstanding his reputation for discretion, as to fall into the hands of the enemy. There were also some fresh fish, caught that morning in a creek which wandered through the woods at some distance from the spot, and just brought in by the exultant darkey who had secured them, which were put to bake in the same primitive manner. Eggs there were by the bushel—let us not be inquisitive, either, as to where they came from; and two or three women, as the crisp brown skins of the porkers announced their arrival at the stage of perfection, went busily to mixing up corn-dodgers, which they set up to brown on pieces of board before the fire, or laid upon hot stones. For drink, there was a caldron of coffee—for on the Fairfax plantation, the slaves had an allowance of coffee through the holidays—a jug of whisky for the men, and plenty of molasses-and-water for the pickaninnies.

No wearisome formality presided, like a garlanded skeleton, at this feast. When all was done, stalwart carvers brandished huge knives, with which they sliced off savory and unctuous portions of the roast for one and all; children lay on their backs, devouring "chicken-bones," and screaming to "mammy," for more. There was much shouting and laughing, grabbing from each other, chasing after the stolen morsel, and screams of merriment smothered in rich mouthfuls of good things—there was, withal, a great plentitude of eating. Neither appetites nor capabilities for fun were at all delicate.

The shining faces of the urchins shone still more with grease and delight. The girls shrieked and giggled, and the beaux kept them shrieking and giggling. Grotesque, wild, uncouth, like the creatures themselves, was their mirth; but it was sunny as the sky, beaming with good-humor, broad and pleasant, good to look at—not a touch of malice, not a sign of quarreling, not a case of downright drunkenness. Oblivious to the scars of the past and the toils of the future, these children of the sun basked in the pleasure of the present.

It was nearly dark as the feast was finished; the young people were too full of supper to care about recommencing the dance immediately; there were plenty of remnants to make out a second-feast when appetite should demand. As the twilight deepened, the fire was made to burn the more brightly; far up in the bright blue heaven the Star of Bethlehem glittered over the wild, fantastic group, as hopefully as over those fairer and finer creatures gathering to places of more refined enjoyment.

Far away into the forest flashed strange gleams of light, chased by stranger shadows. Birds and beasts, in wonder and trouble, flitted deeper into the recesses of the wood, in search of their accustomed repose. Quaint stories were told, and listened to with open mouths, and big, credulous eyes.

It was at this hour that the party was honored by a visit from the bridal party. Jim and July had been married in the afternoon, as Rose was obliged to attend her young mistress to a ball in the evening, and could not be spared except through the day. She and Hyperion were neither of them with the party now, having other duties to perform. But they had stood up at the ceremony, and had helped eat the cake and drink the wine furnished for the occasion.

All giggling and radiant, the new-married pair, attended by a group of house-servants, came to receive the congratulations of their friends, and to bestow a patronizing glance upon the barbecue.

July was resplendent in a white dress, white cotton gloves, a string of mock-pearls about her neck, and a wreath of silver flowers about her head. Her hair was long enough to braid, though "kinky" and coarse. She was a good-looking mulatto, though nothing approaching to Massa Bell's Rose in beauty or grace. Jim wore a gorgeous waistcoat, had a sprig of flowers in the button-hole of his coat, and also sported white cotton gloves. The bride received the attentions of the company with little tosses of the head and affected airs, well satisfied to be the observed of all observers.

"Mighty sorry yer didn' get here soon 'nuff to have a bit o' 'possum," said one of the proud hunters who had added that animal to the feast.

"Oh, we's had cake and wine," replied July, carelessly; but Jim, who liked 'possum as much as his neighbors, looked rather sorry too.

"Yer ain't too proud to take a cup o' coffee, if ye *are* a bride, I s'pose," said one of the women, offering that beverage to the new-comers.

"Nor to dance a right smart break-down," added Uncle Zip. "Come, Jim, lead out de bride, and I'll play ye de libeliest tune eber you danced to. Boys, be sure you keep time; play libely," he continued to the banjos, etc.

The fiddler's arm must have ached, as well as the legs of the dancers, by the time that jig was through; for it was as "lively" as he had promised.

After two or three dances, and having exhibited themselves to the universal admiration, the bride and groom departed, amid the good wishes, jests, and broad sallies of their entertainers.

High blazed the bonfire, loud rose the music, and gayer

than ever grew the frolic, as the evening deepened into night.

In the mean time, Christmas festivities were not confined to the colored people. Colonel Fairfax and his family dined with a neighbor. The dinner and its after-amusements were prolonged into the evening; but at dusk, Philip excused himself, to return home, finish his preparations, and make himself happy, by escorting Miss Bell to a ball which was given in a village a few miles distant.

This ball was to be a very select and brilliant affair—a private ball, indeed, given by a number of young gentlemen who invited their friends themselves; and just such an occasion as is especially enjoyed by young Southern people, who are very fond of dancing *festas*.

Philip went, in the family-carriage, for Miss Bell. Hyperion had consented to take Jim's place as driver, Jim being "berry pertickelerly engaged" that evening at home—a service he was not loth to perform since he knew that Rose was to accompany her mistress, who would need her aid in dressing, after arriving at the scene of festivities.

Mr. Philip found Miss Virginia well and in good spirits. After a few words of greeting, and many injunctions from her tender-hearted mother about her health, and not to allow the child to take cold, nor to over-exert herself, and to the driver to be careful, etc., all of which was eagerly promised, the young gentleman helped his partner into the carriage; Rose, with a huge band-box in her lap, took a seat beside the coachman, and they drove rapidly away.

Only those who have been similarly situated can appreciate the happiness of that brief ride to the unacknowledged lovers, who felt and thought so much and said so little, and who were so surprised, when the carriage drew up before the illuminated hall, to find that they were at the end of the drive

"How do I look?" asked the young lady anxiously, as her waiting-maid put the finishing touches to her dress, before one of the mirrors in the dressing-room.

"I nebber saw missus look so well before," whispered Rose—"it's trute, Miss Virginny; you do look oncommon han'some. Dar ain't a lady come in dis room yet, can compare—dat's so."

"You flatter me, because you love me. I suppose I look well to *you*," answered Virginia, in a low voice; yet she could not help looking pleased, and hoping that she *did* appear to the best advantage—for was not *he* to approve or disapprove?

If Virginia had been as vain as she was beautiful, she would have felt that she was destined to be the belle of the ball. Her dress was very becoming; and anticipations of enjoyment added unusual brilliancy to her always handsome features. Her slight figure seemed to float in a rose-tinted cloud; her attire being a very full and fleecy robe of the finest texture over a skirt of pink silk; a bandeau of pearls on her rich and elaborately braided hair, a few flowers in her bosom, and her fan and handkerchief costly and dainty. When she joined her partner at the door, she knew well that he was pleased with her, by the admiring glance which he could not forbear; the faint flush which rose to her cheek added the crowning grace to her loveliness.

Breathing the perfume of flowers, bathed in light, floating to delicious music, the hours of that brilliant ball stole swiftly away with Virginia. She was admired, and overwhelmed with attentions.

Perhaps a curious feature of the scene, to a stranger, would have been the crowd of dark faces at the dressing-room doors, which opened into the dancing saloons. The maids who had attended their mistresses, were privileged to peer 'n upon the festivities; and a group of eager, delighted countenances, of all shades of color, were visible at each.

Foremost among these, and almost pressed into the ball-room by the crowd behind her, was Rose, enjoying the triumph of her young lady with pure delight.

"By gracious! what a handsome girl!" exclaimed a tall, dark gentleman with whom Philip was conversing, as his eye suddenly fell on Rose.

"Which one?" asked Philip, his thoughts full of a certain young lady.

"There, in the door—a slave, I suppose. A superb creature! The handsomest mulatto I ever saw!"

"Yes, she *is* pretty," responded his companion, carelessly; "she's Miss Bell's waiting-maid, if I mistake not."

"Oh, ho! is she? I'm going to visit Judge Bell to-morrow. I have business with him—one reason of my being here at this time."

Philip Fairfax was not especially delighted with this information. The gentleman had been attentive to Miss Bell, had danced twice with her, had made himself very agreeable to her; and he was a person to be feared as a rival—considerably older than Philip, but more self-possessed, a good talker, elegant in his manners, aristocratic in his bearing, known to be wealthy, and one of the first gentlemen in New Orleans.

But, for the present, the gentleman's eyes were fastened upon Rose. She wore the dress which she had coveted for a wedding-dress—the corn-colored tissue with crimson trimmings. Her soft, glossy black hair was tastefully braided; that indescribable grace, which no thoroughly Caucasian blood could ever emulate, pervaded every movement and curve of her form; her clear complexion looked that of a rich brunette, in the lamp-light; while the luster of her eye, the sparkle of her smile as she watched her beloved mistress, gave a beautiful animation to her face. She was, indeed, dangerously handsome—not handsome only, but refined, gentle, womanly also; touched by that pensive grace which makes the vivacity of her race so charming, by contrast with the previous moment.

"A superb creature!" murmured the gentleman to himself.

Yes, a *creature*—a slave—that was what that beautiful woman was.

Again the gentleman danced with Miss Bell. She had met him at her father's house the previous year, just after her first return from school. He was a stranger to many of the company, being only a visitor in the village, and was one of the most distinguished of the guests. Virginia was as naturally flattered by his attentions, as Philip was naturally annoyed.

"Give my respects to your father, if you please, Miss Bell, and tell him I shall do myself the pleasure of calling upon him to-morrow—that is, to-day," he added, laughingly; for it was two o'clock when he bade her good-night.

Philip stood by and heard it, and saw the young girl's smile; and it was, perhaps, under the influence of the passing jealousy aroused, that he gathered courage, during the drive home, to decide his fate—to utter the important words, to receive the important answer.

Very tired, but very happy, was Virginia, as she sought her chamber in the first gray light of the expanding morning. Her heart was in such a tumult, soul and sense so thrilled and startled by a new bliss and a new reality, that there was a prospect of her not getting to sleep at all. She, who had gone forth half-trembling with a vague expectation of a crisis impending, had returned from the ball—*engaged.* Yes, "engaged," she whispered to herself, blushing, even in the quiet of her room; that epoch so interesting to maidenhood had come, had passed—she was actually engaged. Philip, on the way home, urged alike by love and jealousy, could no longer refrain from putting into words the question which had trembled in his heart so many days. And Virginia had answered it according to the prompting of her feelings, earnestly, joyfully. The momentary pleasure she had taken in the admiration of the distinguished stranger, melted away like mist before the full sunlight of this real passion. Her lover had no reason for jealousy; he went to his dreams, contented. If the driver, in gallantly assisting the maid to the ground, had found a chance for a sly kiss in the starlight, it was no more than the happy couple they attended upon had also found opportunity for—that first, shy, blissful kiss which seals the betrothal, and is kept forever as a precious memory.

It was with the recollection of that kiss burning in her cheeks, that Virginia joined the group around the late breakfast-table, which was not served until high-noon. Her mother was too busy to observe it, and the young girl's conscious looks passed undetected. She made haste to cover her own joyous secret, by giving her father the message of Mr. Talfierro.

"Talfierro! you don't say so! the devil!" growled the Judge, evidently less pleased than troubled; at which his daughter was surprised, for she remembered that he had been a favored guest the previous season. "I did not expect him so soon, by several weeks," he added, in a kind of apology, seeing Virginia regarding him. "However, it's all right. We'll make him welcome."

"Everybody is welcome, during the holidays. The more, the better," said the wife, as she passed the Judge his coffee.

"Yes, yes, of course," he replied, recovering his cheerfulness. "Well, my daughter, I trust you did credit to the family, last night—your first ball, eh?"

"Dat she did, massa; dat she did indeed, sir," answered Rose, with emphasis, she having come into the room with a bouquet of flowers, in time to overhear the question. "De handsomest young lady dar, by all odds. Dar's more'n one t'ought so—Massa Philip Fairfax for one, and here's his complemens, brought by 'Perion, and dese yere flowers, out de hot-house."

Virginia blushed so violently as she took the bouquet, as to fix the eyes of her mother suspiciously upon her; however, she had nothing serious to fear from the scrutiny, for she knew that Philip was a favorite with her parents, and that there were none of those hateful financial difficulties in the way, which disturb so many matches otherwise "made in heaven."

Hardly was the midday breakfast over, before the promised visitor appeared. But Virginia had ample time to attend to her toilet for the dinner, before she was summoned to the parlor, as her father and Mr. Talfierro had a long business-talk in the library, while she was dressing. In the mean time, Rose had very provokingly been called away, just in the midst of arranging her mistress' hair, to bring cigars and sherry into the library, when there were plenty of other servants who might have done that service just as well. It was very provoking of papa very—and Philip expected every moment

CHAPTER V.

SCIPIO'S STORY.

Look out upon the stars, my love,
And shame them with thine eyes,
On which, than on the lights above,
There hangs more destinies.
Night's beauty is the harmony
Of blending shades and light;
Then, lady, up—look out, and be
A sister to the night!—PINCKNEY.

Oh, Miss Minny, but I'm 'feared we'll have to part—
I've done broke my banjo, and you've done broke my heart.
NEGRO MELODIES.

THE same company that had listened to Johnson's story, on Christmas Eve, were gathered again in Maum Guinea's cabin, the night after the ball. She had treated them to a supper of roast fowls and sweet potatoes, with pound-cake and coffee for dessert; the fowls she had bought with her own money, and Mrs. Fairfax had given her the other things.

The supper was cleared away, the fire flashed up cheerfully, and the whole company joined in singing song after song, accompanied by a banjo played by Scipio, the good-natured fellow who had congratulated Jim on ridding the world of the devil. Hyperion sung some songs which his ready ear had caught from the parlor—fashionable airs which had not yet descended to the kitchen; hymns, also, of that vigorous and exciting character liked by the race, were given with great fervor, and when they were sung, Maum Guinea joined in with a clear, high voice that thrilled a person through and through but to hear.

When the music was exhausted, the stories began. Again Maumy arranged the "cuts" in her hand, and all drew, except Johnson, who, having told his story, was "out of the ring." The lot fell to July.

"Laws-a-massy! I ain't nuthin' to tell," she murmured, quite overcome by the idea. "Nuthin' nebber happened to me, 'cept gitting married, and you all knows dat."

"Wa'n't you nebber sold?" queried one of the group.

"Laws, yes, two, t'ree times; but dat ain't nuthin'. Fust time, I was a baby, and can't 'member nuthin' 'bout it; den I was sole to a lady to play wid her chil'ren, and she brought me down to Lousiany; and den she died, and missus bought me, and allers keep me."

"An' so you nebber did nuthin' but git married, hey, July?"

"No, nuthin' nebber happened to me, 'cept when I see a spook one night in de garden. T'ought I was clean gone *den*, sartain."

"How dat spook look, July?"

"Laws, I don'no how it look; I didn' stop to see. All I see was suthin white, and heerd it moanin'! 'Spec's it was missus' chile as died a long time ago."

"Oh, my!" ejaculated several, with fearful glances out of the window.

"S'posin' 'twas," said Maum Guinea; "sperit of little innocent chile would do no hurt, I'll warrant."

"Don't talk 'bout ghostesses," pleaded an apprehensive fellow, who looked big and stout enough to vanquish a score of the dreaded phantoms.

"Woll, July, ef you hain't got de gift of tongues, spokin of in de good book, course you can't be 'spected to use 'em," said another. "We'll hab to draw ag'in—dat's so!"

The lot this time fell to Scipio. He gave a desponding groan, shaking his head and making all kinds of contortions.

"I's in de same fix as July," said he, "only I ain't eben got married."

"Sho! Scipio, 'tain't fair," remonstrated Johnson; "I's told mine, and now de rest wants to back out."

"No, certing, 'tain't fair!" cried several.

"It's de solum, blessed trute, dough, dat I hain't no more history'n an alligator. I don' know who my mudder was, who my fadder was; w'edder I's got a blood-relation on de face of dis yearth, w'at name my own maumy gib me, w'ere I cum from, nor w'ere I's going to. All I know is, might as well laugh as cry. I's a happy nigger, naturally. Don't make no difference to me w'edder I was hatched out of an alligator's egg, or w'edder I had member Congress for *my* fadder, long's as I've 'nuff to eat, don't have to hurt myself workin', and nuthin' don't happen to my banjo—yah! yah! yah!—

> "Oh, if I was but young ag'in,
> I'd lead a differen' life;
> I'd take my money and buy me a farm,
> An' take—Rosa for my wife!"

And flourishing his hand across his beloved banjo, he bowed to Miss Rose with a gallant air.

"No you wouldn't," said Hyperion; "gib you to un'erstand, Mister Scipio, *I's* got a word to say about dat."

"Oh, ho! has you?" quoth Scipio, resignedly, while Johnson drooped his head on his hand and looked steadily into the fire. It was plain the young lady had plenty of admirers.

"Come now, Scip, tell suthin," pleaded a girl by his side.

"Woll, I s'pose I can tell a lie, if I can't tell truth?"

"But we 'greed to tell true stories," said Johnson.

"Oh, gorry, that'll go hard—'gin de grain," said Scipio, with another contortion. "Howsomeber, I'll try, an' if it makes me sick, Rose dar 'll have to take car' o' me. Woll, de fac' is, I was born onlucky. I got more w'ippins w'en I was a young'un, dan would 'ave sarbed massa's hull plantation, if dey had been properly diwided. Yer see, I was allers getting into trouble—standin' on my head 'stid of my heels, as a boy oughter; if missus send me of an errand, I nebber get back, 'cause it allers happened so many cur'us 'tings to keep me—couldn' raise no chickens, 'cause I 'tole so many eggs; and if dar was comp'ny to dinner, I allers upsot de dishes and drop de gravy 'bout on de carpet; an' I kep' de little pigs squealin' awful, and lame de turkies t'rowin' 'tones at 'em; so I got lots of w'ippins, and dey made me *smart*—dat's so—and I hain't got ober it yet.

"Woll, I was such a bodder, massa sen' me to be sold. I kicked and hollered dreffful, for I t'ought bein' sold was wuss 'an bein' w'ipped—yer see, I was but half-growed den, and I'd heerd de niggers talk 'bout being sold down to de rice-swamps, w'ich I t'ought was in de bad place 'bout w'ich Aunt Dinah used to pray and sing on Sunnays; an' I kicked so, dey tied my legs togedder, just as Cuffee ties chickens to take to market, and put me in a wagon and drove me to town; and I looked 'round, and t'ought wasn't so bad as dey'd make b'lieve. I see lots o' t'ings berry interesting, and w'en dey come to big room w'ere dey was a-sellin' niggers, up on a high place, I gets up purty good spirits, and was berry quiet and perlite, 'specially as massa said he'd t'rash all de skin off me, if I didn' behabe myself fust-rate. W'en dey put me up dar, and de feller begun to turn me roun' and praise me up, I t'ought to myself: 'Gorry, I guess I's some punkins, arter all!' and w'en I see a good-natured lookin' gentleum a-steppin' up, and lookin' at me purty much as if he'd a mind to buy me, I giggled, and put my t'umb on my nose, much as to ask him to please take me; and he smiled, and turned to de feller w'at was a-hollerin' me off:

"'Tricky?' 'quires he.

"'Oh, he's chock-full of life and sperits,' says de oder; he's bilin' ober wid health and strength—*he'll* nebber be one of de sullen kind,'—and de gentleum took a fancy to me, it 'pears, for dey struck up a bargain widout much trouble

"He was a mighty nice gentleum, and he wanted me for a kind of body-serbant like, to wait on him 'bout de house and go wid him 'way from home; and I like him, berry much indeed, berry. But I was born onlucky. Gorry, didn' I play him tricks, till he didn' know w'at he was about? He didn' like to hab me w'ipped, and he uses to keep a little orse-w'ip, and wollop me hisself, w'en I was outrageous; but I 'spect he didn' lay it on hard enough. I made him more trouble dan my head was worth—dat's so. I kindle de fire in de liberary wid de paper he'd been a-writin' on; I tip de inkstan' ober t'ree times a week reg'lar; I cotch my toe in de carpet ebery time I bringin' in de glasses, w'en he hab gentleum wid him; I 'teal his newspapers w'at he put away berry karful to make kites of; I tar' my clo'es and dirty 'em so, I neber fit to be seen w'en I was wanted in de parler; I puts massa's cologne on my own wool, and tries to shabe myself wid his razer, and get found out by cutting my face orful. He threatens to send me to de w'ippin'-post, and to sell me to de rice-swamp; and I allers so sorry, and promise so hard, he puts it off till nex' time. And so I grows up wid troubles enough ebery day to make my wool as w'ite as a sheep's; but it didn' pervent my keeping fat and comfo't-able, 'kase, as I said, it's better to laugh dan cry.

"But oh, lordy! w'en I got to be a nice young feller, and was full-growed, and had got ober t'aring my clo'es and tripping my feet in de carpet—w'ich I ain't quite recobered from yet, seein' as how, if I go to back out perlite, as a serbant oughter, I's sure to cotch my heels, dey is so uncom-mon long—w'en I'd get ober *dem* troubles, oh, lordy! den's w'en de *ser'us* troubles begun. Ladies and gentleum, has you eber been in lub? Dat tender sentiment is ondescribable, and I shan't agitate yer feelings by dwelling on it at dis time. Lub, ladies and gentleum, lub, is like a snappin'-tortle—ye'd better let it alone, or ye'll get caught 'fore you know it."—here Scipio paused a moment, his hand wandering tenderly over the strings of his banjo, while the girl next to him hitched a little closer and regarded him admiringly—he was evidently lost in retrospection.

"Woll, next house to massa's—he libbed in de city of Charleston, dose days—was a girl w'at allers set my heart to palpitatin' so, I was sure I was gettin' de St. Witus' dance, or suthin of de kind. Ah! my stars! but Dinah was a flirt! She use to wait for me to be openin' der side parler winders 'fore she shook her duster out ob de side winders; and Sunnay afternoons, w'en she'd got her fixins on, she use to walk by, berry slow, and cast look out de corner of her great black eyes, till I 'clare I couldn' stand it. I learn to play de banjo purpose to gib her serenade of a moonlight night—and she use to lean out de garret winder, and drop hollyhocks and roses down, jes' like w'ite ladies does under similar circumstances; and den I go home, happy as a pickaninny in a tub of 'lasses, and t'ink so much 'bout her, nex' day, dat I make more mistakes'n eber — hand massa his slippers w'en he ask for his cigars, put his coat on wrong side out, and show visitors into de dinin'-room, 'stead of de parlor.

"One Sunnay ebening I knock at de basement door of her house, and 'quire for Miss Dinah; and w'en dey show me in de kitchen, dar sat anodder gentleum, a-puttin' on airs and t'inking hisself mighty nice, 'cause he'd got a ring on his finger and a great big gilt chain ober his west. Yer oughter see dat girl dat ebening, w'at a coquette she was; smiling at me an' den at him, and makin' herself agreeable to bof of us, and we a lookin' at each oder, and speaking so dreffu. perlite, 'twould have excruciated you to see. Woll, t'ings went on so, for a monf or more; ebery ebening I was out, I called on Miss Dinah, and dat ar' rascal was allers dar too and daytimes she was allers gibbing me 'tickler 'couragement, out de winder and in de back porch.

"One night, de moon was like a silber doller, and eberyt'ing was lubly as a rose, and I took my banjo and got ober de fence 'tween de two gardens, and begun to play berry sweet under her winder, and I heerd her raising it, and jest as I turn my face up to kiss my hand to her, she empty a pitcher of water slap in my face. Den I heerd her giggle; den I heerd somebody outside de fence giggle too, and I looked and seen dat imperdent darkey peeking tru' and larfing at me. Gorry! I couldn' stand dat, no how! I flings my banjo at his head, and den I jes' gib one jump ober de fence, and I chase him, and cotch him, and I gib him such a pounding as he nebber got before; but de wust of it was, de watch come along and put us in de watch-house, and massa had to pay to get us out. He ask me how I came to be dar, and I up and tol' him de hull story, and he larfed at me, an' didn' scold—jes' said I 'musn' place my 'fections on de fair sect—dey was like eggs in July—berry onsartin. Yah! yah!

"Woll, I found de fair sect berry onsartin, indeed—leastwise, Miss Dinah. She nebber speak to me arter dat, 'cause I pounded her fine beau half to deff; an' mebbe it's best she didn', for massa died of yaller fever dat berry summer, and I was sold wid de rest de serbants, soon arter, and I'd had to bid Dinah a long farewell, any how—

> "Oh, far'-ye-well, far'-ye-well,
> Far'-ye-well, my Dinah,
> I'm goin' down to New Orleans,
> Far'-ye-well, my Dinah.

"Woll, I've had seberal different kind of times sence den, but trouble don' hurt me. It rolls off my min' like water off a duck's back. If I haven't got a wife, I've got a banjo, and dat never scratches nor bites, and is allers agreeable."

"Laws, Scipio, some females wouldn' scratch or bite," suggested the fair one by his side.

"Dasn't trust 'em," was the grave response.

"Better stick to yer banjo," muttered Maum Guinea.

"Ho! yes! ye'd better stick to yer banjo," said a woman of middle-age, the housekeeper from the Bell plantation; "w'at's the use o' wife or chil'ren, w'en you don' know w'en dey may be took away. I's had a husband, and four chil'ren, but I hain't one now."

"Was they took away?" whispered July.

"P'raps, if I draw the cut nex' time, I'll have to tell ye Scipio, play and sing 'Uncle Gabriel,'" she continued, as if to change the subject.

So Scipio began one of their favorite banjo-songs:

"Oh, my boys, I'm bound to tell you,
Oh! oh!
Listen awhile and I will tell you,
Oh! oh!
I'll tell you little 'bout Uncle Gabriel;
Oh, boys, I've just begun.
Hard times in ole Virginny.

Oh, don't you know ole Uncle Gabriel?
Oh! oh!
Oh, he was a darkey Gineral,
Oh! oh!
He was chief of the insurgents,
Way down in Southampton.
Hard times in ole Virginny.

It was a little boy betrayed him,
Oh! oh!
A little boy by the name of David,
Oh! oh!
Betrayed him at the Norfolk landing
Oh, boys, I'm getting done.
Hard times in old Virginny.

They took him down to the gallows,
Oh! oh!
They drove him down wid four grey horses,
Oh! oh!
Brice's Ben he drove de wagon,
Oh! boys, I'm getting done.
Hard times in ole Virginny.

There dey hung him and dey swung him,
Oh! oh!
And dey swung him and dey hung him,
Oh! oh!
And dat was de last of de darkey Gineral;
Oh, boys, I'm just done.
Hard times in ole Virginny.

"Tell us *your* story, Sophy," said Rose, when the chorus died away.

"Hush! not to night—dar ain't time. You and I mus' be going back 'fore long."

"Sophy," continued Rose, half under her breath, "did *you* ever hear of black folks rising up and murderin' their masters? You know I can read, and I come across a little book once, hid away in Missus Bell's bureau, and it told—oh, it told such a drefful story."

"Hush!" cried Sophie, sharply, and glancing out the window, and around the room, as if fearful that the "walls had ears;" her face was blanched to a kind of yellow white, and she shuddered visibly. "Musn' talk 'bout such t'ings, honey," she said, more calmly, a moment later. "Dey's bad, berry bad, and our massas wouldn' like to oberhear sech talk—we'd all be punished, like enough."

"I believe you do know suthin, Sophy—I've t'ought before," continued Rose, searching the countenance of the woman earnestly.

Rose was bright and intelligent, could read faces, and had

gathered up many curious bits of intelligence already, young as she was.

"Don't you be tryin' to find out w'at you no bisness to know," was the evasive answer. "W'en my time comes to tell my story, mebbe you'll find out some t'ings I've heard, and some I've seen. Come, Rose, we'd better be going."

"W'at a sleepy-head dat July is," exclaimed Rose, rather contemptuously, as she discovered that personage was sound asleep on Jim's shoulder. "I could stay awake t'ree hours yet."

"S'pose you could, sake of bein' wid 'Perion," replied Jim, laughing; "but July don't have to keep awake to be wid me -yah! yah!"

"Oh, you get out!" cried the company.

"I's willin'," he returned, shaking his bride by the shoulder "'specially as we's all goin' coon-huntin' to-morrow night and will have to keep wide awake den. Good-night, ladies and gemmen."

Well pleased with the promise of a coon-hunt, the party broke up, leaving Maum Guinea to the desolation of her solitary cabin.

There was no necessity for Hyperion's gallanting Rose home, as Sophy was fully capable of accomplishing that duty without his help; but he could not be made to realize it; so Sophy started on ahead, well aware that the young couple could dispense with her very close attendance; and so smartly did she trudge along that she gained the gate at the foot of the avenue fifteen minutes before the sauntering lovers overtook her. The Christmas holidays were halcyon days for them.

CHAPTER VI.

A HUNTING PARTY.

I will sing thee many a joyous lay
  As we chase the deer by the blue lake-side,
And the winds that over the prairie play
  Shall fan the cheek of my woodland bride.—HOFFMAN.

Mine are the river-fowl that scream
  From the long stripe of waving sedge;
The bear, that marks my weapon's gleam,
  Hides vainly in the forest's edge.
With what free growth the elm and plane
  Fling their huge arms across my way,
Gray, old; and cumbered with a train
  Of vines as huge, and old, and gray!—BRYANT.

Cursed be the heritage
  Of the sins we have not sinned!
Cursed be this boasting age,
  And the blind who lead the blind
O'er its creaking stage!—OWEN MEREDITH.

SATURDAY was cool and cloudy—a delicious day for hunting; and a party of ladies and gentlemen, consisting of the Bells, Fairfaxes, Mr. Talfierro, and one or two others, concluded to celebrate Christmas week for that day, by a grand hunt. A good many of the colored people were engaged in a similar manner; several went with their masters to assist in the labors incident to the occasion; and parties of negroes also went off by themselves in search of their favorite game of coon and opossum. The wood, in the edge of which the negroes had held their barbecue, was one of those dense forests peculiar to Louisiana and Florida, filled with tangled thickets, vines, dangling mosses, treacherous swamps; open ground in many places, where the hunting could go on without so much difficulty; in others, dark and impeded by underbrush, with an occasional lagoon, or creeping stream. It was the place of places for the hunter; he could have his choice: shy deer, fierce catamount, artful wild-turkey, tempting birds and water-fowl, or vulgar coon. There was one objection to the company of ladies—the nature of the ground would not permit of riding; and they were supposed hardly fitted to endure the fatigues of an expedition on foot. But the two who accompanied this party scorned that plea Virginia Bell was an accomplished pedestrian and an expert shot; while Kate Burleigh, her friend, was a wild, dashing creature, as fond of hounds and hunting as the men—who carried a knife in her belt, and handled her rifle as easily as the best. The two together felt themselves equal to a catamount, and it is a question if Kate would have fled from a bear, even, without a trial for the mastery. However, they did not intend, in case of over-weariness, to be a drawback to the ambition of their escort.

Four or five miles in the wood was a lovely sheet of water, along whose margin the magnolia dropped its fragrant blossoms, in their season; and which at all times was fragrant with the spicy pine, and beautiful with aquatic plants. Here there was always a boat moored, and fishing-tackle prepared; and the ladies proposed, upon reaching this spot, to take to the water, recruiting themselves by angling for fish, while their comrades went on as far as the game or inclination led. Each of them had a trusty slave to bear her rifle, and to row the boat, when they should reach the lagoon, remaining in attendance upon their wishes during the day. Johnson was Miss Bell's attendant, and Kate had a servant equally trustworthy.

It was the intention of the party to lunch on the banks of the lake—perhaps to dine there also; for if game was peculiarly tempting, they might remain out deep into the night.

Colonel Fairfax took Hyperion, Jim, and two or three stout negroes with him, and half a dozen dogs; Judge Bell was similarly attended: there was Philip, and a couple of his young friends, and Mr. Talfierro, who was, at present, a guest of Judge Bell's. As the whole company, with rifles and hounds, plunged into the deep shadows and flickering lights of the wood, they were in high spirits, the day promising so especially well.

"Haven't seen you for some time, Judge," remarked Colonel Fairfax to his neighbor, as they found themselves jogging along, side by side, the young people in advance, and no one near them, except Hyperion, who was just behind, but quite unheeded by them. "I suppose your work was finished some time ago—sugar ready for market?"

"Yes; got along very well this season; but did not have more than two-thirds the crop I had last year. I was disappointed, for I had made my calculations upon having a better one. Unlucky for me, *this* season in particular."

"That's a fact; we're all on short allowance this year. The sugar-crop is an uncertain reliance, anyhow. One tip-top season, and then two or three poor ones, generally."

"I shall have to begin planting in a week or two," said the Judge.

"Got to plant this year, eh?"

"Yes, I've ratooned two seasons. So I had to save a part of my cane for planting, which reduced the product still more. However, I hope to come out all right next time."

"Is your guest, Mr. Talfierro, from New Orleans?"

"Yes, that is his home," answered the Judge, growing a little moody in his manner, despite of his ardent love of hunting, which usually exalted his spirits to the highest exhilaration.

"His appearance is very prepossessing."

"He's a great favorite; and I like him, myself, very much—still, I didn't care to see him, at this time. Fact is, he holds my note for five thousand dollars, due a month ago, and I haven't a thousand dollars ready money. My crop fell short of my expectations."

"Of course he will wait. You are good for the amount, and it wouldn't be kind of him to press you for it. He can afford to take the interest and wait for the principal."

"Well, I thought he would do so, and I didn't give myself much trouble about it. But he's rather close in business matters, after all."

"If that's the case, you'll have to sell some of your negroes."

"To tell you the truth, Colonel, that's just what he wants me to do. He wants to buy from me."

"Then where's the difficulty? You can spare two or three or four of your field-hands, as well as not, I should think. An easy and economical way of paying the note that bothers you so."

"I expect I shall have to do that—sell some of my negroes—but I'll have to find other buyers, and that will give me some trouble. Mr. Talfierro has no plantation, and does not want working negroes. The truth is, Colonel, he's taken a fancy to Rose, and he wants *her*."

"Sho!" ejaculated his friend.

Neither of them noticed the convulsive start, the sickly pallor of the mulatto-boy, trudging along within ear-shot of their conversation.

"He's bound to have her."

"What does he offer?"

"Oh, the most extravagant price—twice as much as the girl's worth. If he wasn't rich and unincumbered, he wouldn't think of being so foolish. He'll give me four thousand dollars for her, and wait my convenience for the balance of the note."

"Four thousand! a fancy price. She'll never bring you

more than half that, again—perhaps not half. I should think you'd be tempted."

"Well, I *am* tempted. But I don't like to sell Rose. She's a house-servant. I've had her a good many years; and the worst of it is, my daughter is so much attached to her Virginia would cry her eyes out, if I were to dispose of her favorite maid."

"Girls cry easily, Judge; you mustn't give too much weight to their tears; they dry up soon, fortunately. She's a nice girl to have about one's house, Rose is—good-looking, bright and tidy. But four thousand dollars is a big price; she won't bring it many years. She's in her prime now—healthy and attractive."

"Yes, Talfierro swears she is the handsomest mulatto he ever saw. He's really quite bound to have her."

"You've got another young girl growing up—that Chloe of yours—can't she learn to take Rose's place in waiting upon your daughter? She'll soon learn to like her just as well."

"Chloe's a nice girl—smart and tidy. But Virginia seems to be peculiarly attached to Rose."

"Well, if you can afford to humor her in the fancy, I suppose it's all right. But girls' hearts are not easily broken; don't be too tender of 'em, Judge. They're like India-rubber: they take impressions, but they don't stay,"—and the Colonel laughed easily. "Have you noticed, Judge, the danger there is of you and I being brought into family relations? Say neighbor, what do you say to that?"

"I *have* been a little suspicious lately, Colonel, but haven't thought much about it, either. Well, friend, I'm agreed,"—and the neighbors shook hands, laughing and well pleased. "They're a fine couple, if I do say it. Couldn't either of 'em do better."

"If Miss Virginia has a lover t take up her thoughts,

she'll soon be resigned to Rose's loss," continued the matter-of-fact Colonel. "Four thousand dollars would buy her lots of wedding-finery. However, it's not for me to advise you, neighbor Bell."

"I suppose Virginia could be reconciled, but—but—the fact is, I don't just like to sell that girl. She's very much attached to all of us, and she's so—so young—and—" here the speaker hesitated, ashamed of his own natural impulse of virtue and humanity.

"We can't afford to humor the feelings of our negroes, Judge; it's a bad idea. They're a careless race, and don't suffer much from sentiment. I suppose Black Eagle, my pet horse, felt badly, when he was taken to strange pastures last year, but I was obliged to sell him. You know that the girl will, in all probability, be well treated, and have an easy time of it. She will be doing very well, very well indeed. Like as not, she'd be eager to go, if she knew what the state of the case is. Better ask her."

"I think not," responded Judge Bell, shaking his head.

"There! they've started something—a deer, I do believe," cried his companion, and the two hurried on; while the slave, who had heard every word which they uttered, followed with a dragging step, carrying the basket on his arm as if it weighed a thousand pounds.

Trudging along over knolls of sand, checkered by the lights and shadows playing through the trees; and through hollows tangled with vines and long, dry grass; catching their feet in the bare roots of palmettoes, washed out of the loose soil, the eager hunters now hurried on, silent and alert, rifles ready and eyes on the watch. Virginia kept up well with Philip's easy stride; she had taken her light rifle now from Johnson, who had hitherto relieved her of its weight. Kate kept with Colonel Fairfax, of whose skill she had a high opinion, and all pushed forward, each one emulous of the chance of the first shot.

As they glided along in silence, the faces of the lovers were brilliant and eager; they almost forgot that they were alone together, with soft mosses beneath their feet, and bright birds twittering in the branches above them, with the cool breeze of the light clouds kissing their cheeks at intervals, and all the soft, low noises of the deep forest about them; they were good hunters, both of them, and they would have forborne the sweetest opportunity for whispered words, in this moment of anticipation, to have seen, in the deep shadows before them, the starry eyes of a deer.

"Here is a track," whispered Philip, stooping down and pointing out to his companion where the light hoof of some passing animal had recently cut the dewy grass.

"And here is the mark of his horns against this tree," responded Virginia, showing where the bark had been rubbed up, on a water-oak near by.

"I declare, Miss Virginia, you are as sharp on a trail as an Indian," murmured her lover, admiringly. "Let us go on in this direction. I see the track again, here, and here."

They stole along, their hearts beating so loudly that they fancied almost the distant game might hear them. At that moment the baying of the dogs which attended the other members of the party announced that they were on the trail: the couple paused to listen. For a time, they heard only the sighing of the wind in the pines, or the soft dropping of dew or withered flowers from the tall magnolia trees; then the baying of the hounds again, the crack of a rifle, and the next instant they heard a rush in the underbrush a little to one side of them; and, turning, saw a noble buck standing disconcerted and motionless at thus being suddenly confronted by enemies, as well as pursued. That brief pause gave Philip time to swing his shot-gun into aim and fire. The deer tossed his head defiantly, and dashed away, right past them, for the hounds were behind him.

"Too bad," murmured Philip, and they started in pursuit. The deer sought the covert of a close thicket not far away; but that, which was small, was already nearly surrounded by dogs and men; and he suddenly turned, retraced his steps, and dashed by them again.

As his form stood out a moment, well defined, on a slight rise of ground, Virginia fired, and, by the stagger of the buck, as he bounded off, he was evidently wounded.

"Your shot told, Virginia," cried Philip, and he dashed on, in hopes of getting another chance himself.

A mighty tumult resounding through the woods proclaimed that the game was being closed upon. The negroes yelled, the hounds ditto, the men shouted; and the barking, screaming, the cheery cries, and the quick discharge of two or three guns, proved that the buck was brought to bay. Following the noise, Virginia reached the spot where the splendid game lay dead, scarcely a moment later than Philip. To her was given the principal honor, for it was her fire which had first wounded the deer and disabled him from successful flight.

"I will hang his antlers in the hall, in commemoration of the feat," said Judge Bell, patting his daughter proudly on the head.

Elated with this successful beginning of the day's sport, the party began to realize that they needed a little rest and refreshment before again taking up the march. They were not far from the lake, where the ladies proposed to await the return of the others, and to its banks they all now repaired, to partake of the lunch which the servants had brought with them. A cloth was spread upon the grass, under an oak, whose farthest branches were mirrored in the lake; and around this gathered the company, waited upon by their house-servants, while the rest of the negroes lolled in the shade, at a respectful distance. The murmur of the water, just rippled by the breeze, darkening and brightening as the fleecy clouds swept overhead, made pleasant music in their ears, giving an extra relish to the cold ham and fowls, the biscuits and claret, which formed the lunch. The plainest viands have an unwonted charm, when partaken of by a tired hunting-party in the open air, and here were plenty of delicacies, as well as substantials.

"What is the matter, Hyperion — are you sick?" asked Virginia, near the close of the repast, as he came near her to offer her the wine. She had been watching him for some time, concerned for him, as he looked so ill and haggard, performing his duties by force of will, and without a particle of his usual vivacity.

"No, not berry. Nuthin' much."

"Shall I tell Rose you had the blues to-day?"

Even that magic name awoke no sparkle on the dull face.

"T'ank you, missus, you berry kind."

Nobody else noticed the sudden and singular change which had come over the favorite slave—the pet boy—the pinched look of the nostrils, the contracted lines about the mouth and eyes, the listless movements.

"Isn't it perfectly charming here?" exclaimed Kate, as the two ladies found themselves alone, an hour later. "I could stay here forever."

"Oh, yes, very beautiful; I always loved it," answered Virginia.

Nevertheless, she would have liked to have been with Philip at that moment, if her physical endurance had been equal to a whole day's hunting.

"Come, boys, get out the boat, and row us across the water."

The slaves obeyed; the little boat was drawn up where the ladies could get into it; they took seats, and the rowers lazily dipped their oars, with just enough outlay of energy to keep the boat in motion. The fishing-tackle was not found in very good order; but they caught two or three scaly prizes, which they avowed their intention of having for supper.

Dreamily the boat flitted to and fro, amid broad-leaved plants; the young ladies talked, as girls will, much nonsense and some poetry; they dipped their hands in the water—fair hands, which floated, like water-lilies, drawn along by the current of the boat; they sung, and chattered; they laughed, they watched the wild-birds; and all this time, Johnson and Hyperion, silent, preoccupied, melancholy, rowed them whither they listed, not once striking up their usual merry boat-song of—

"Gineral Jackson mighty man,
  Waugh, my kingdom, fire away—
Fought on sea, and fought on land,
  Waugh, my kingdom, fire away."

"W'at de matter wid you, 'Perion? Needn' tell me-dar's suthin done gone wrong," remarked Johnson, as the two, having safely landed their fair voyagers, were now obeying further orders by gathering up dry underbrush to make a fire.

"Don't ask me, Johnson, *don't*. If de worst happen, you'll know it soon enough; and if it don't, no use fretting."

"Hope notting bad won't happen to *you*, ole feller," said his companion, earnestly; everybody liked Hyperion, and Johnson had experienced so much trouble himself, that he knew it was no light matter which had come over his friend.

"'Tain't *me*," was the brief reply, and that was all the *valet* could be induced to say.

"Give us a roaring, dancing, beautiful fire, Johnson; it's getting dark, and there's no signs of the hunters yet. We are going to surprise them with a glorious supper, when they get back. Are there dishes enough in the baskets, boys?"

"See what we have killed! Did you think we were so skillful?"—and Virginia held up half-a-dozen birds which they had shot in the last hour, while the boys were preparing the fire.

"Go, get the choicest part of the venison, Hyperion—some for broiling, some for roasting; and you, Johnson, find some stones to bake the fish in. Is there plenty of pepper and salt and wine, and are there any sandwiches left? Oh, here's biscuit enough to last a week, and all kinds of nice things. Maum Guinea knows how to calculate the appetites of a hunting-party. Hurry, boys, we're bound to have a grand feast."

Darkness came down over the forest; but the fire blazed high and bright. The cheeks of the young ladies glowed with excitement. They trilled merry snatches of song, as they assisted in the preparations going on for a supper in the woods.

There was danger of the haunch of venison being over-roasted, for it was full nine o'clock before the cries of the hunters announced their return. They came, making their way through the night by the aid of blazing pine-knots, which they bore aloft; and they were not sorry, as they gathered about the beacon-fire on the lake shore, to see the cloth laid, and to receive a hospitable invitation from their fair friends to stop and sup. The birds were done to a turn, the fishes rolled out of their leafy coverings, white and tempting, the venison was all that it ought to be, considering who killed the game; seldom was an impromptu feast more keenly relished than by the famished hunters, who had returned laden with the trophies of the day's sport. The dogs looked on with asking eyes, and were rewarded for their excellent services by many a sweet bone and dainty morsel.

While they were yet at supper, several negroes passed, with guns and axes, in a high state of excitement.

"Oh, massas, we's treed a coon!" they shouted exultingly, as they hurried by.

Philip, and two or three of the younger gentlemen, were not as yet so wearied, but that they concluded to join the negroes, and be in at the death of the coon. Snatching torches, and heedless of the remonstrance of the ladies, though promising not to be away over half an hour, they joined in the pursuit of the poor little worried coon.

"Dar, dar, he's in dat tree, sure 'nuff; I seen it move, and de dogs is barking all round it," cried a darkey, exultingly.

"Whar's de ax?"

"Needn' cut um down," cried another. "I see him berry plain, right in dat crotch up dar, and I's gwine to shoot um."

"Shoot away!" shouted Philip, laughingly, without much confidence in the skill of the negro, who blazed away with his old gun, and was answered by a cry which thrilled the group with horror—not that of a poor coon, in distress, but of a human-being.

"Good heavens! you've shot a man!" exclaimed Philip.

Groans of anguish descended from the tree; they waved their torches, but could see nothing distinctly, for the thickness of the branches. It was the first impression of all that they had come upon some negro runaway, who had been skulking in the deep forest, and who had hidden in the tree, fearing discovery by the hunters.

The teeth of some of the negroes began to chatter, and their eyes rolled apprehensively; they had heard strange tales about these refugees, and knew not what desperate character they had chanced upon.

"Oh, Lordy! Lord be mussiful to me a sinner! Oh,

Lordy! I's killed! I's clean gone killed, no mistake! oh, Lordy!"

"That's Uncle Zip's voice, as sure as I'm alive," said Philip.

"It's Uncle Zip!" echoed all.

"Zip, is that you?" called Philip.

"Oh, laws-a-mussy! Oh, Lordy! yis, its me!"

"Are you much hurt? Can't you come down?"

"Oh, I's killed, sure 'nuff! Oh, no, I can't come down. I's shot right in de shoul'er—can't stir, oh—oh—ouch!"

"Well, you are in a bad box, old fellow—no mistake," said Philip. "Boys, how shall we get him down?"

"We's hab to climb up dar, and try if we can luf him down easy," was the suggestion, which was finally adopted.

Two stout negroes climbed the tree until they came to the wounded man, about whose waist they tied a rope, and let him down as gently as possible; but not without much groaning and crying from the poor old fellow, who was really in a good deal of pain.

"How came you up in the tree?" inquired his young master, after he had given him a little brandy from a flask in his belt.

"Oh, massa, I don' want to tell," was the whimpering reply.

"Gorry, I knows," cried one of the negroes; "it's a bee-tree."

"Oh, ho! oh, ho!" cried the others.

Now, it was a well-known fact among his neighbors in the negro-quarters, that the old fiddler had been enjoying, for some weeks, an unfailing supply of honey. They had suspected that he had discovered a bee-tree; but, if so, he had no idea of sharing his prize; the selfish old rascal kept his store of sweets to himself, much to the envy of his friends. They had kept watch on his proceedings, in hopes of tracking him to his treasure; but he had been too sly for them. And here he was now, caught in the sweet trap in this cruel manner. When his companions averred that it was a bee-tree, he groaned more terribly than ever.

"Cheer up, Zip," said Philip, kindly; "you're not killed, by any means; you'll be all right in a week or two."

"Oh, oh, Lordy! 'tain't dat, massa. I don' mind de shot so much, dough my shoul'er hurts awful; but dey'll 'teal all my honey."

"Never mind your honey, my boy. You've paid pretty dear for your bee-tree. Let it go, and be thankful you're not killed outright."

"Oh, massa, I can't play de fiddle no more berry soon—can't play de fiddle on New Year's, nohow; and it hurts awful. But dat ain't de worst. Oh, massa, wish you'd tell 'em let *my* bee-tree alone."

"Well, well, the boys shan't have your honey. But it'll be all gone before you're able to come here again. You'd better be got home now, as soon as possible."

Several of the negroes were obliged to abandon the pleasure of capturing the coon, and assist in carrying home poor Zip, whose chief grief was in the discovery of his treasure.

"Oh, my bee-tree, my bee-tree! Boys, let my bee-tree alone!" was the burden of his moans, as he was assisted back to his cabin.

The party by the shore now hastily broke up; Colonel Fairfax hurrying down to see to the dressing of the negro's wound, and to send for a surgeon, if necessary. It was high time for the sport to be ended, the hand on the clock telling Sunday morning before any one was in bed. By the flickering fire which faded and expired in intensest darkness, before the gray of dawn took the place of its uncertain glimmer, all night, like an animal of the forest, crouched Hyperion.

CHAPTER VII.

SOPHY'S STORY.

God works for all. Ye can not hem the hope of being free,
With parallels of latitude, with mountain-range or sea;
Chain down your slaves with ignorance, ye can not keep apart,
With all your craft of tyranny, the human heart from heart.
LOWELL.

And on the lover of her youth,
She turned her patient eyes,
And saw him, sad and faint and sick,
Beneath those alien skies.

She saw him pick the cotton-blooms,
And cut the sugar-cane—
A ring of iron on his wrist,
And round his heart a chain.—ALDRICH.

From the hearths of their cabins,
The fields of their corn,
Unwarned and unweaponed,
The victims were torn.
By the whirlwind of murder
Swept up and swept on,
To the low, reedy fen-lands,
The marsh of the swan.—WHITTIER.

HARDLY had Maum Guinea dished the breakfast on Sunday morning and sent it to the house, before the door of her cabin opened, and Hyperion entered, looking so changed from the saucy and elegant *valet* he usually appeared, that she almost dropped from her hand the coffee-pot from which she was about to take her own allowance.

"Now, chile, you's sick, sartain; and you've come to look for suthin to cure you. W'at's de matter?"

He dropped into the chair which sat by the little kitchen-table, and leaned his head into his hand without making any reply.

"W'at's de matter, chile? speak!" she said, very kindly, for he was a favorite with her—perhaps he reminded her of some one of her own kin, whom she had some time cared for and loved.

"It's all *here*," he said, at last, pressing his hand on his heart.

"W'at is it, honey? Tell Maum Ginny, and mebbe your heart'll feel lighter. But drink dis coffee, fust—'twill kin' o' set you up, and gib you stren'th."

"I don't want nuffin' to eat or drink; my throat is choked up wid such a lump, I couldn't swaller a mouf'ful, Maumy."

"Woll, now, jes' speak right out, w'at de trubble, darlin'?"

"Oh, Maum Ginny, dey're talkin' 'bout sellin' Rose."

"Sellin' Rose!"

"Yis, I heerd 'em myself. Massa Bell, he's offered four t'ousand dollers for her; and he's hard up for money, and Massa Fairfax he say—'Sell her, sell her!'"

"Oh, dey wouldn' sell Rose. Miss Virginny wouldn' let 'em." She tried to speak cheerfully, though her hands trembled as she pushed the dishes about, pretending a carelessness she did not feel.

"Dey spoke 'bout dat; and dey said, 'Miss Virginny soon get ober it'—Miss Virginny would get ober it, but *I* nebber should, Maum Ginny,"—he raised his eyes to her face with an expression which pained her corded and scarred old heart, albeit it was used to torture.

"Who wants to buy her?"

"That gentleum from New Orleans we see here yesterday, —dat berry proud gentleum wid de di'mond buttons in his shirt,"—poor Hyperion had noticed, with the appreciative eye of his calling, the glittering brilliants which bedecked the splendid gentleman.

"Has he got a wife?"

"No"

"Curse 'em!" exclaimed the woman suddenly, drawing her tall form up, while her eyes flashed with vivid fire, "curse 'em, I say! curse 'em all—buyer, seller, de whole w'ite race!"

"Oh, Maumy!"

"Don' you curse 'em, chile? Ain't dar dark spot in your bosom, jes' as bitter as gall? Oh, dey'll sell our chil'ren, w'en dey wants money! Massa Bell better sell his own girl! She ain't so good nor so purty as Rose. *She* wouldn' bring four t'ousand dollers, ho! ho!"

"Oh, Maumy; how you talk!"—the young mulatto-man had not yet become so familiar with secret and long-suppressed feelings like these, as not to be startled when he heard them uttered. "But I wish I was a w'ite man."

"Oh, yis!" scornfully, "you'd be a human bein' then, you know."

"I could help myself—I could do suthin. Now I can do notting—notting at all—my hands is tied. I laid out in de woods las' night—all night, t'inkin' about it. De stars shone like de glory hallelujah, de lake kep' whisperin' till I'd most a mind to jump in, and not hab to t'ink so hard any more. Oh, how I did wish I had four t'ousand dollers to go and gib Massa Bell, and take Rose and marry her as we's promised to each oder. But I hadn't no money—I could nebber earn any —not if I work my fingers to de bone all my life, I won't have any money, 'kase it's all massa's, and I b'long to him. I can't take a wife, and hab her all *my own*, to take care of her and de pickaninnies, and be proud of dem, and feel der *mine.* I can't be notting—I can't hab notting—I'm a slave, Maum Ginny, dough I nebber knew what it meant, till I hear massa Bell talk yesterday. Oh, Lordy, how I wish I had some money!—if I had pile of dollers big dis room, I'd gib it all to buy Rose 'way from dat gentleum. Oh, I wish I had some money. Oh, Maumy, what shall I do?—my head is all a-fire."

"Don't take on so, honey; drink dis hot coffee, 'twill clar yer head," she urged again, coaxingly. "Leastwise, don't gib it up yet. I don' belieb Miss Virginny'll let Rose go. I'll go to her, myself, and tell her dis berry ebening—I'll go to Massa Bell, and I'll shake my fist in his face, and tell him if he sell dat girl 'way to New Orleans gentleum, he'll nebber prosper long as he lib. I'll scar' him out of it! Taste yer coffee, do, chile."

A drowning man catches at straws; and Hyperion, holding himself so high an opinion of the cook's character and influence, felt cheered by her promise to interfere in the matter. He drank the stimulating beverage which she pressed upon him, and felt his spirits rise into a degree of hope.

Judge Bell had not said that he was positively going to dispose of Rose; he had expressed reluctance to part with her, and if he could get Maum Guinea, Miss Virginia, and perhaps young Massa Philip to intercede for her, she might be saved from the fate which threatened her — she might some time be his wife, as Philip and Virginia had promised. How willing would he be now, to wait a year, or two years, if he could be certain that she would then be his! Would he not even be resigned to giving her up entirely, if he could know that she would never fall into the hands of that diamond gentleman?

The Sabbath is a day not particularly observed for its religious character upon extreme southern plantations. Some of the Creole planters work their slaves alike upon that and other days; but generally it is kept as a kind of lazy-day. But during Christmas week, it was holiday like the rest; the sound of a banjo, accompanied by lively singing, came from a cabin not far from Maum Guinea's; the ambitious young performer having it all his own way, now Uncle Zip had been laid up by that unfortunate mistake which had caused him to be treated no better than a coon.

"He Zip Coon now, sure 'nuff," said one darkey, shaking with laughter when he heard of the mistake; "guess he won't want to sing 'Cooney in de holler,' any more—he holler loud 'nuff hisself,"—at which piece of humor all his hearers ya-yahed in their soft, hearty way. A negro can laugh as easily as he can breathe; and as for his wit, he has not arrived at that stage of development, including the morose, envious, analytic, comparative, sarcastic and irreverent, in which wit comes into play. A negro is seldom witty—it is only the gold-colored descendants, infused with the tingling sharpness of the alien blood, who are ever known to be more than good-naturedly humorous.

"He's had honey on his hoe-cake ever since frost come," added another. "Sarved him right, setting up in his bee-tree like a bar', so cross and selfish."

"Woll, he won't eat no more *dat* honey, boys; 'kase I staid behind las' night, and took a bucket and brought it all 'way; we'll have a time wid dat honey dis berry arternoon. Git my ole woman to bake us lots o' cake, and we'll jis' have a feas'—no mistake."

The sound of the banjo drew out the indolent creatures from their late breakfasts; woolly heads were thrust out of doors to see what kind of a day it was going to be, and little groups gathered about on the fences and the steps of the houses. Colonel Fairfax's plantation was considered a model by his neighbors; among other things, the negro-quarters were arranged with more comfort and system than was common. The cabins, all of a size, and uniform in appearance, were ranged down either side of a broad alley, with little garden-patches in the rear, and the alley itself serving as play-ground for the children, and hall-of-assembly for the whole population, during their hours of social recreation.

The banjo-player sat on the steps before the door of one of these huts, with an admiring crowd about him, singing in a rich voice, which it was a pleasure to listen to—

John, come down in de holler,
Oh, work and talk and holler,
Oh, John, come down in de holler,
I'm gwine away to-morrow.
Oh, John, etc.
I'm gwine away to marry,
Oh, John, etc.
Get my cloves in order,
Oh, John, etc.
I's gwine away to-morrow,
Oh, John, etc.
Oh, work and talk and holler,
Oh, John, etc.
Massa guv me doller,
Oh, John, etc.
Don't cry yer eyes out, honey,
Oh, John, etc.
I'm gwine to get some money,
Oh, John, etc.
But I'll come back to-morrow,
Oh, John, etc.
So work and talk and holler,
Oh, John, etc.
Work all day and Sunday,
Oh, John, etc.
Massa get de money,
Oh, John, etc.
Don' cry yerself to def,
Oh, John, etc.
So fare-you-well, my honey,
Oh, John, etc.

The words of this melody were certainly not marvelous for wit or elegance, but they were characteristic, and the music was delightful—when half-a-dozen voices joined in the chorus it was inspiring; to these homely, hard-worked, monotonous-lived creatures, it was their one great enjoyment

—the one expression of the oriental warmth and sunshine still flowing in the undercurrent of their sluggish blood.

The tinkle of the banjo fell on Hyperion's ear, as the blows of a whip fall on a naked back; he could not bear the torment; and making his friend Guinea promise to go with him that afternoon to Judge Bell's, he went away into the house to attend his young master, who was just rising after the unusual fatigues of the previous day.

"Heigho," yawned Philip, in dressing gown and slippers, seating himself before a fire which the chilliness of the day made desirable, "every bone in my body aches. I believe I trudged thirty miles, yesterday; had a splendid day, though! Bring my breakfast to my room, boy; I'm not going down this morning."

"What's the matter with *you?*" he asked, as Hyperion arranged the coffee, toast, ham and eggs upon a little table near him. "*You* had an easy time, old fellow—nothing to do but wait upon the ladies. What's the matter? Has Rose been giving you the mitten?"

"Oh, no, Massa Philip; de trute is, Massa Bell is talkin' of—of—" his lip quivered and his voice choked up so that he could go no farther.

"What is he talking of?" queried the young gentleman his curiosity aroused.

"Of sellin' Rose," sobbed Hyperion—and breaking completely down, he cried like a child.

"Whew!" said Philip, with a long whistle, "that *is* bad!" The "institution" under which he had grown up had not so murdered all natural sympathy in him, but that he, young man and lover as he was, felt a passing fellow-feeling for the distressed mulatto "boy."

"Oh, I guess that can't be so," he added, presently, sipping his coffee, "she's been in the family so many years. Miss

Virginia can't spare her. I don't see what Judge Bell should be wanting to sell Rose, for; he can well afford to keep her, and she's a good, obedient girl."

"Dat New Orleans gentleum offer a big price for Rose, massa"

"Aha! that's it, is it? Too bad! too bad! Ought to be shamed of himself!"

He went on with his breakfast, and seeing with how little spirit his *valet* was performing his light duties, he said, gayly:

"Never mind, boy, 'there's as good fish in the sea as ever was caught.' If they send Rose away, I'll keep a sharp look-out for some other pretty girl, that will suit you just as well."

"Don't want no oder," was the trembling reply.

It was evident that Philip Fairfax, with all his good feeling—his young, generous nature—did not regard the fact of a slave losing the object of his affection, and losing her in such a way too, in the same light which he would have viewed it, if somebody had come along and forced from *him* his right and title to the heart and hand of a certain fair young girl, who was dreaming of him at that hour, even with her prayer-book open before her. In the eyes of hard masters, slaves are brutes, to be worked as much as will "pay," like their horses and mules; in the eyes of kind masters, they are, at best, a sort of children, to be looked after and made to do their tasks. Philip was kind; he would have been sorry if his pet "boy" had complained of the toothache, or the loss of some trifling treasure; he was sorry for him now; but he did not take his case to heart, and judge it as he would have done his own—how could he? If he had done so, he would have pulled the key-stone from the foundation of the whole splendid theory of slavery.

"Oh, massa," pleaded the *valet*, throwing himself upon the indulgence to which he was accustomed, when Philip had finished his repast, and had fallen to whistling softly, looking out the window, and thinking about his betrothed, "won't you speak to Miss Virginny about Rose, yerself?"

"Yes, yes, I'll speak to her, if that'll satisfy you. But what good will it do? It isn't likely Miss Virginia will have much to say about it. Of course she will want to keep her dressing-maid, if it's possible. She'll coax her bear of a papa sweetly, without any asking, I'll warrant you. But if he's bound to make a good bargain, *I* can't help it, Hyperion, my boy. It's *my* policy to be as agreeable as possible just at present; it wouldn't look well for me to presume to interfere in family matters, already; don't you see? ha! ha!"—and he laughed softly.

This was too reasonable to be denied; and it was not the province of a slave to argue with his master—so Hyperion held his peace.

Late in the afternoon he and Maum Guinea set out for the Bell plantation. He had promised Rose to visit her, Sabbath evening. Sophy, the housekeeper, whom we have before mentioned, had invited both them and Maum Guinea to take tea with her, in her kitchen; it was her turn to "treat," she said; they had accepted her invitation with alacrity, knowing they should have a good time; for Sophy was only inferior to Maum Guinea herself, in the art of cooking, and being stewardess of the establishment, she could afford to give them a fine supper upon so important an occasion as Christmas week.

As they knocked at Sophy's door, the young man's heart sunk and felt cold within him. He had not seen Rose since this awful shadow had fallen between them; he did not know whether she was yet apprised of her danger; he did not know, he almost feared, that the girl might want to accept of the brilliant lot in store for her, as the favored slave of so wealthy and handsome a man, with whom she could lead a life of idleness, and be decked out in all the finery her tropic taste coveted. Yes, Rose herself might choose it! All kinds of fears pressed upon him, until he felt sinking, and leaned against the casement for support.

It was his affianced herself who opened the door. She knew they would come to Sophy's first, and she was already there, waiting them. How handsome she looked! So gay, so happy, so proud—for she was dressed in her best, and her mistress had given a new brooch for a holiday present—a great, gold brooch, with a bit of paste-brilliant in the center which sparkled with the rise and fall of her shapely breast.

She knew she was looking well; her lover almost shrunk before the blaze of her beauty; there was just that dash of coquetry, that bewitching coolness, showing through sunny breadths of smiles, which a handsome woman can afford to assume, and which it requires no refinement of schools to teach her—it is her nature, white or black, rich or poor.

" She don'no nuffin 'bout it yet, dat's clar," whispered Maum Guinea, in an aside as they entered, " and don't you tell her any t'ing just now. You and she be as happy as yer can, once more, anyhow; and perhaps it'll all be right yit. I'll go out and speak to Massa Bell w'en I gets a good chance."

Happy! Yes, even with all that dark doubt of the future, the mulatto-man experienced a perhaps even more intense pleasure in the society of the woman he loved; his eyes followed every movement of her lithe form; he smiled at all she did and said; and if he did not talk much, Rose knew that he felt much, for she read the language of his eyes.

It was so pleasant in Sophy's large, light kitchen. She had invited Johnson, and two or three others, also; her guests were sitting about, laughing and talking so naturally, that Hyperion began to feel as if he had had a bad dream, and was just waking up to his every-day experience.

The table was drawn out in the middle of the floor, and a coarse white cloth covered up all marks of its uses in cooking; two or three kinds of sweetmeats, in glass dishes, graced the board; and a plate of butter, a luxury at the South. A turkey was basting before the fire, and the odor of white-flour biscuits came from the bake-kettle on the hearth, blending with the matchless fragrance of coffee; these, with the sweet potatoes roasting in the ashes, were to make a supper worthy of the times, and all the more keenly relished, since it could be enjoyed but at one portion of the year.

It was already well understood among their friends that Rose and Hyperion were "engaged," and were to be married if their owners would allow. With jest and merriment they were placed side by side at the table. The unusually luxurious fare, and the natural good-humor of the company, made the occasion one of great delight. Even Maum Guinea was cheerful, hoping in her heart for the best. Rose found the "merrythought," or, as they called it, the "wish-bone," on her plate; and she and her lover made their wish, pulling the bone apart to decide whose wish was to be fulfilled.

"I've won—I've won!" cried Rose, gayly, while her companion's hand fell heavily down, and his face wore a look of disappointment at which all the young people laughed.

He did, indeed, feel deeply disappointed; for he was not above the superstitions of his people, and placed great faith in all such matters as this. What he had wished for may be easily inferred.

"What did you ask fur, Rose?" queried one of the party.

"Oh, I ain't goin' to tell, 'cause if I do, I shan't get it. It breaks de charm."

"Oh, do tell! you'll get it, all de same."

"No, I shan't. Mebbe I wished for a silk dress to wear wid my new breas'-pin, and mebbe I didn't. I shan't tell."

Another pang shot through her lover's heart at these laughing words. She had wished for a silk dress, the foolish, giddy thing, and perhaps she would have one sooner than she expected.

After supper, Maum Guinea slipped out, and was absent half an hour, while the rest of the company sat about, laughing and singing, the girls helping their hostess to wash up the dishes and put the room to rights. The work was all finished, and the party gathered about the firelight in a half-circle, when Maum Guinea returned.

"He's partly promised—I'm pretty sartain it'll be right," she whispered in answer to the mute question in Hyperion's eyes.

The words pierced through him, like arrows of sunshine, with a sharp joy. He had so much confidence in the woman that he felt almost free from apprehension; he squeezed Rose's hand, so that she cried out, to the jest and amusement of the rest; he immediately began to talk, to tell funny stories, and to sing his best songs in his "happiest manner." Rose grew very proud of him, he was so witty, such a splendid singer—her eyes glanced triumphantly from him to the company, as much as to ask, "Who has such a nice young man as I has?"

When he had exhausted his sudden flow of jollity, the visitors began to press Sophy for the story she had partly promised them. She seemed reluctant, but finally said:

"Woll, woll, we'll draw cuts—and if it falls to me, I'll tell my story."

To their satisfaction the lot fell to her.

"Suthin about yerself, you know—suthin true, the way we agreed."

"If I tell you any thing 'bout myself, you must all promise to nebber, nebber tell to noboddy what you hear in dis room to-night."

"Oh, we won't nebber tell," they exclaimed, eagerly, their eyes beginning to expand with curiosity, and a kind of delicious terror of they knew not what.

"You mus' promise on de Bible," she said, rising and bringing an old, well-worn copy of the New Testament. "'Cause I's never told dis story afore, and if you should let it out, you might git me into trouble."

Each one laid his hand on the book, and promised not to tell, and then they gathered closer, almost trembling with eagerness to hear a story so important that it must be kept such a profound secret.

"Dar'll be some terrible things in it; but you musn't get scar't. It's passed and gone now, w'atever it is. Set up clost, fer I mus' speak low. Wouldn' like to be oberheard, nohow."

In a kind of half-whisper, enough in itself to make what she said impressive, and which chilled through her susceptible audience like a breath of north wind, Sophy began her story:

"I was born in Southampton county, in ole Virginny; I lived on massa's plantation all de time; I was kind of kitchen-girl, and done chores, and learned to cook, and w'en I was fifteen I was married. Me and my man, we had a cabin of our own, and lived togedder berry comfortable. Massa's farm was a tobacky farm. My man's name was Nelson. He was good to me; t'ought mighty sight o' me, and w'en I had my fust baby—laws! he was de tickledest and de most sot-up nigger you eber saw. Ah, Lord-a-mighty, don' I recolleck dat yit?

"He was good to me; but somehow anodder he got into trouble wid oberseer purty often; I 'spect he was sometimes a little sassy. You knows some hosses and oxen dey hab to be drove, and whipped, and scolded more'n oders, to make 'em go de ways dey's wanted—dey's kind o' stubborn. Woll, so it was wid Nelson. I 'spect he'd got some notion in his head 'bout not liking to be ordered 'roun' so; and our oberseer was mighty cross man, allers knocking niggers about.

"One day, w'en my baby was 'bout t'ree months ole, I'd got done de work at de house; 'twas summer ebening, and warm, and I'd come home to cook my man's supper, and nuss my baby. Troo' de day I hab to leave my young'un wid all de rest, in care of old brack woman too ole to do much work. Dey keep de babies in a kind o' pen, w'ere dey could crawl 'round widout much tendin'—I could go and nuss it once in a w'ile—woll, I come here at night, and got his supper ready for him, and den sot down in de door to play wid my little one. I felt berry nice dat time, 'kase de head-cook had gib me piece of cold chicken and rice-pudding for my man, for helpin' her right smart wid de big dinner fer company: and I was t'inking w'at a treat it would be to Nelson. But Nelson didn' come home. He usually got home by dark, summer days; but de clocks strike nine, ten, and he didn' come. I began to stop singing, and to feel dreffful oppressed 'bout breathing. I t'ought mebbe it was because de night was so warm Little Sam was soun' asleep, so I laid him down on de bed, and started off to look for my husband. Suthin took me right straight to de corn-house; and as I came clost to it, I hearn somebody groanin'. I *knew* 'twas him, and I flew and tore open de door, and dar he lay. De oberseer had gib him awful whipping—awful! and den, here de weather was so warm, he'd jist turn de salt and water over his back, and let him lay.

"I helped him up and got him home; he didn't eat no cold chicken nor no rice puddin' dat night. Massa scold de oberseer for whippin' Nelson so hard, 'kase he was one of his best hands, and he couldn't go to work ag'in fer most two weeks. After dat he let my husband alone fer a long time; but dar wasn't any good feeling between de two. I use to beg Nelson not to aggrawate him, 'cause he was a bad-tempered man, anyhow, and he wouldn't gain nothing but blows and cusses by going contrawise to him; but he was spunky too, Nelson was, and once-and-a-while de fire would blaze up dat he tried so hard fer to keep down. I knew he did try, for *my* sake, 'cause I begged him so hard.

"Our Sam was a beautiful pickaninny: so round, and fat, and shiny, and so full of fun. W'en he got big enough to roll around and kick, to laugh, and, bym-bye, to holler 'Pop, Pop!' w'en his fadder come home, den Nelson grew more happy-like. He lubbed his boy so much, he forgot his bad feelings tow'd de oberseer; he didn't set no more of ebenings glooming over de whipping he got. Massa liked him berry much, 'kase Nelson had more sense'n most niggers, and he use to get him to do all de pertikeler jobs 'bout de farm. Sometimes he'd gib him few shillings silber; den Nelson he'd buy suthin for his boy, and he got him a red calico frock—real turkey calico—the purtiest you eber see.

"One day I was up to de house wid Sam; Nelson was pickin tobacky in de field. Sam was goin' on two year old and use to play about de yard or kitchen w'ile I was working 'round. I'd jist dropped de taters I was peeling, and run out to see w'at he was doing, w'en I met massa and a strange gemman walking through de yard, and dey stopped to look at my boy, and dey praised him up wonderful. He had on his red dress, and I wan't surprised dat dey t'ought him a right smart, purty chile; but I didn't t'ink notting farder, for 'tain't often, yer know, dat masters sell little chil'ren 'way from der mudders. Bym-bye I heard de gemman say, kind of low:

"'I'll give you five hundred for him—not a cent more.'

"My heart jumped right up in my mouf; I went and picked my boy up, and stood a-looking at 'em, wild-like.

"'Sophy,' says massa, kind of laughin', but shamed-like, how'd you like to give up your boy to this nice gemman here? He'd be took good care of—jest as good as you could give him.'

"'Oh, massa!' dat was ebery word I could say; but I didn't belieb him den, 'kase he was a kind of laughin', and I t'ought he was tryin' me for a joke.

"'I've partly promised him to dis gemman; so you may wash him up and get him ready, for he's got to leab in two hours, in de stage.'

"'Oh, massa, I can't! I can't!'—I kind of screamed it out, which made him a little angry, for he spoke more sharp.

"'Pshaw!' says he, 'don't be foolish, Sophy. He'll be well treated. You see, dis gemman has got a girl has lost her baby, and she wants anodder, and she'll be extra kind to it. *You'll* hab anodder in a month or two, and den you won't mind de loss of dis so much,' and he laughed. 'One'll be 'nuff for you to take care of; don't be selfish, my girl. Go and get de boy ready, and bring him back here; and be spry 'bout it—ain't no time to spare. I'll show you de girl as is to keep him, and you'll see she's a nice pusson.'

"'Can't I take him down to de field to bid his pap good-bye?' I asked.

"'Dar won't be time; besides, it'll only make you both feel wuss. W'en your oder baby is born, you won't miss dis. Come, Sophy, be spry.'

"I went to my cabin wid my boy. I tried to get out a little apron to put on him, and to wash his face and hands. But I was too weak; I jist staggered to de bed, and set down and cried ober him, and kissed him. T'ree, four times I tried to get up, for I knew massa would be awful mad; but I *couldn't*, and dar I sot w'en he come after us.

"'W'y didn't you bring him up to de house? De stage is going by in a few minutes. You don't behave yourself berry well, Sophy,' says he, and he takes my boy out of my arms, and walks out of de room wid him—and dat's de last I eber see of Sam.

"I sot dar, kind of stupid; and bym-bye I heerd de stage-coach coming 'long de road, and it stopped afore de house. I tried to get up, but I was too weak. Den, w'en it started on again, I flew out like a wild creature, and up de lane to de gate, jes' in time to see it whirlin' ober de hill—and dat was all. I guess I kind of fainted, till I come to, and heerd old Bess, de head-cook speaking to me, and she put her arm round me and lifted me up.

"'Nebber mind,' says she, 'you'll get use to it. *I's* had five sold away, in my time. Come, I'll go back to your cabin wid you. I's got a little sperits here will rewive you up.'

"'Nelson! Nelson!' was all I said.

"'Yis, he'll take it harder dan most men would. But he'll get ober it. Don' fret, honey. Eberybody has trouble. Las' year, massa hisself had a purty little girl die; your baby ain't dead; cheer up, honey.'

"'I wish it was dead,' I muttered.

"She took me in de house and made me drink some brandy, and staid wid me as long as she could, till she hed to go back and get supper. Den I sat alone, t'inking what Nelson would say w'en he came in, and his boy gone. It didn't 'pear to me as if 'twas so; I'd git up and look in de bed, see if Sam wasn't dar, fast asleep—den I set down ag'in, and wish my husband nebber would come home.

"I heerd him comin' along, whistlin', and he puts his head in de door, and calls out:

"'Sam! Sam! here's poppy cotched a squirrel in de fence. Come, Sam!' Den he looked at me, and says he, 'Is he asleep?'—den, for de fust time, I bust out a-cryin', and he let de squirrel drop, and looks round sharp, and says: 'W'at's happened?—is de boy hurt?'

"'Oh, Nelson, massa's sold him, and dey's took him far away.'

"He dropped down on de step 'sif he was shot, and nebber spoke. I crawled up to him and leaned my head on his shoulder, and dar we sot 'most all night. He didn't say much—he wasn't no great talker no time—and all he t'ought not eben I could tell. But arter dat he was changed berry much. He was so silent and stubborn, I was almost 'fraid of him; but he did his work well—nobody complained of him.

"Well, w'en my next baby come along, I felt a little happier. It was a boy too, and I 'spected Nelson would get over his trouble, and take to de new pickaninny He did. He was softer to it dan he'd eber been to Sam; he never spanked it, nor got fretted wid it. But de did'nt seem to play wid it so much, and he nebber come home whistlin'—ef I heerd him whistlin' far off, w'en he turned into de lane he allers stopped. 'Peared like as if he was allers afraid, w'en he opened de door, he shouldn't see no pickaninny dar. He was still, and hard-working, so dat eben dat ugly oberseer couldn't find much fault wid him.

"Dan was a likely boy, too—we called our second, Dan'l, after de good man in de Bible, who was took up from de den of lions, as de hymn says—jist as pert and healthy as little Sam had been. He was a favorite wid white and brack folks, jist as bright as a dollar, and so full of funny tricks. We tried not to set our hearts on him, for he'd be sold away too; but it 'peared as if de harder we tried not to, de closter he grew to us. We knew de smartest chil'ren sold de fust.

"Well, frien's, Dan'l was spared to us till he was nigh six years old; and den massa had a bad crop, and a hard time, and he was getting more slaves dan he could 'ford to keep and Dan was sold, wid a hull lot more, large and small.

"I asked massa to sell us 'long wid our child; but he so so much store by Nelson, he didn't want to part wid him 'sides, de cook was gettin' ole, and I mos'ly took her place. So our boy went away, and we nebber knew whar, nor w'ed der he be dead or libing now.

"Massa sot great store by Nelson, and it was sorry times for massa dat he did. Berry fine to like him, 'kase he honest and work hard; but he was a-playin' wid fire, w'en he sole *his* chil'ren away. My man wasn' like some niggers; he couldn' b'ar everyt'ing, and nebber seem to feel it. He couldn't laugh and sing, and take t'ings easy, no matter what happen. He didn' like knocks and whippins, and raising chil'ren for market, like as they was chickens and pigs.

"I wonder if dar's anybody 'round?" continued the story-teller, after a moment's pause. "Set up closter, my frien's, and fust let me look out a minit,"—and she went to the door, peered forth into the darkness returned, and resumed her narrative in a half-whisper:

"Not long after Dan was gone from us, Nelson begun to go out nights. He'd steal away after I was in bed, and wouldn't come in, sometimes, till nigh daylight. If I asked him whar he was, sometimes he'd say, huntin' coons; and ag'in, fishing, but he never brought no fish home, and I didn't believe him. 'Peared to me dar was suthin pertikeler on his mind, but he wouldn't tell me what it was. Sometimes, when de oberseer had gib him a kick or a blow, he'd speak of it at night, and laugh in such a strange way, it made my flesh creep. I didn't know what to make of Nelson. Dough he was my own husband, and good to me, and we'd bin faithful to each oder, and lubbed each oder better'n most men and wives, I didn' understan' him, in dose times. But I knew he was troubled, and I lubbed him all de more. I knew he had only me, now Dan'l was gone, for we'd had no more chil'ren, and I tried to be a good wife to him. I nebber scolded him for staying out, but tried to get him as good breakfast as I could; and I didn't pry into his business, only to say dat I wish I knew what was on his mind, 'kase I might comfort him. Den he'd shake his head, and say I shall done know all when de right time come.

"T'ings go on dis way five or six months. One Sunnay he go ober to neighbor's farm, in de woods, to have a fine time, roasting a pig, wid some der hands. De niggers all like barbecues, and I was glad he was going—t'ought 'twould cheer him up a little. So he starts off a little 'fore noon, and 'twas two o'clock at night when de door opens, and my husband speaks in a whisper, telling me to get up and dress myself, and be ready, 'for mighty t'ings are to be done in de land.'

"Scar't and trembling, I got out and slipped on my frock, not knowing but de judgment-day of de Lord was at hand W'en I was dressed, he come in, and six men wid him. De moon was just going down, and shone in de little square window, so I could see der faces. Dey looked awful—all scowling, and der eyes burning: and dey had guns and big knifes. Nelson had de big butcher-knife w'ich I used in cooking, sharpened up. I begun to cry and pray, when one nigger. I knowed him well—'twas Nat Turner, over to Travis', dat all de brack folks t'ought was a prophet—hushed me up. Did yer eber hear of Nat Turner? Yis, Ginny, *you* has—I see it in yer face. Nat Turner, he spoke in a clear, awful whisper, dat went straight tru' me, and he says: 'De work of de Lord begins dis night. I've seen it in de heavens—I've read de signs of de times: dar's been wonders in de sky, and drops of blood on de corn. De Holy Spirit has bid me arise, and prepare myself. I am to slay mine enemies wid der own weapons; de black spirits contended wid de white in de heabens, and I see de blacks victorious. Cheer up, woman. Your chil'ren shall no longer be sold from your bosom, nor your husband lashed at de whipping-post. I am come to repay. "Vengeance is mine, I will repay," saith the Lord.' Oh, Lord-a-mighty! he looked so turrible when he was a-talking; he said many more things, which I can't tell you as he said 'em. 'De Savior has ordered it, dat I be de liberator of my people—dat I lift 'em out of de hand of de oppressor. Dis night, we will begin His work. Not one white man, woman or chile, will we leave alive in South ampton county; we will conquer it, as did Washington in de Rebolution. W'en de Lord say unto us, "Smite!" den will we smite. We will not torment 'em wid de scourge, or wid fire, nor defile der women, as dey have done wid ours. But we will slay dem utterly, and consume dem from off de face of de yearth.'

"'Oh, Nelson,' said I, clinging to him, as dey begun to go out, for de moon was sinkin', and dey were in haste to be off, 'w'atever you do to massa and missus, don't kill little Katie.'

"'Yes, we must not spare one—not one—not de baby at its mammy's breast,' he said, shaking my hand berry hard. 'Good-bye, Sophy. We'll be back after you, w'en it's all ober. Keep quiet. Don't let on you know anyt'ing. You shall be rich and happy—no more a slave. If de worst comes to de worst, fly to de Dismal Swamp. Dar will be frien's dar.'

"I still hung on to him. 'Don't murder Katie,' I whispered, 'I love her.'

"'So do I,' said he, 'but de Lord's work must be done.'

"I was just like ice, wid fright and horror. When dey went out, I stood shivering in de dark. Purty soon, I t'ought I heerd a scream, but I wasn't certain; den, in a few minutes more, I heerd 'em go to de stables and take out all de horses, and ride away. I darsn't stir, till mornin'; den, wid de first light, I heerd old Dinah screeching wild and loud, and going out, I met her coming from de house, wringing her hands, and her eyes sticking out. 'Come! come!' she says; 'Oh, Lord-a-mercy! Oh, Lord-a-mercy!' I knew already, but I kept still, and run after her into de house. Dar, just dragged from der beds, in der night-clo'es, was massa and missus, stone dead, der throats cut, like as dey were pigs, and de carpet soaked full of blood. I jist gib one look, and run into de little bedroom off deyr's, war I knew Miss Katie slept. Oh, Christ! I see it now! I nebber shall forget it! Ebery night, w'en I wake up in de dark, I see her, jest as I see her den—dat beautiful chile—lying in her purty bed, murdered—her dimpling t'roat all cut straight across, and de blood gluing her shining curls to her neck and cheek. She was so sweet and kind, Katie was, and only ten years ole. She was like my own pickaninnies to me. She'd allers been fond of me, 'kase I took care of her w'en she was baby, de first year I was married. Dar she lay, de innocent—no mudder, no fadder, to straighten her little limbs, and wash dat cruel blood away. I sot down on de edge of de bed, and held her hand, and cried ober it, and kissed her poor little face. De whole plantation was awake, and takin' on awful. Most of de men had jined de insurrectioners, and gone off, and de women was hollerin' and prayin'. De oberseer was dead too, and I felt glad when I heard it. But I couldn't feel glad when I looked at little Katie. I t'ought over how I felt when I found my husband, most killed with whipping, and de salt brine on his bleeding back—w'en I heard de stage-coach rumble away over de hill wid my little Sam—w'en Dan'l was took away—w'en I had been flogged myself—I t'ought of all our wrongs and hardships, and I couldn't blame my husband—I knew he b'lieved he was doin' de Lord's work—but I wished dey had spared dear Katie.

"Dar was an awful time after dat," continued the narrator, her voice rising, but still in a whisper, high and sharp. "Oh dar was an awful time. All Mr. Travis' family was murdered too; and de're niggers joined ours, and dey rode on to de next plantation; dar dey killed all de white people, and got more help, and dey went 'round about to ebery house, all night, all day, all next night, all next day—for eight-and-forty hours de work went on. At ebery place de slaves rose up, and aided dem; they murdered de're own masters and missuses, and be berry chil'ren dey played wid. Dey b'lieved Nat Turner was a prophet, and de time of der deliverance was at hand. Yes, dey b'lieved it. Dey obeyed him, w'at he told 'em. All de dark spots slaves hide 'way in de're hearts, and say nuthin', come to light den—all de fires break tru' de ashes den, and blaze up turrible. Do you t'ink it was right, my frien's?"

"Yes," said Hyperion.

"No," said Rose.

"Well, de most of 'em t'ought it was right, w'edder it were, or not. Liberty is sweet, even to poor brack slave—and in Virginny dar's plenty of white blood mixed wid ours, you all know. Dey murdered der own fadders, der own brudders and sisters, no doubt, many times; but w'at were dese, more dan oders, 'cept to make 'em feel more spiteful.

"We waited in fear and trembling; praying and crying, we waited. Oh, dose were awful days!—awful for de poor white women and chil'ren, dat had fled for de're lives, w'en dey heerd w'at was going on. Dey were hid in de woods, night and day. I saw 'em myself, lots of em, w'en I went off to hear what I could hear. I pitied 'em—more'n dey'd ever pitied *me*. I took meat and bread to some dat were in Travis' woods, wid de're chil'ren most starved.

"I begun to t'ink that Turner was sure 'nuff a prophet—dat new times was coming for poor brack people; I begun to dream of undependence and liberty, such as had been our masters', and if it hadn't been for little Katie, I'd have felt joyful enough to sing hymns of triumph. I could sew, and I took one of her white dresses and made her a little shroud, and put her in a box—for nobody come to bury the dead, and we women dug a grave and put her in. Some de foolish nigger-girls dey help derselves to missus' jewelry and fine clothes, and put 'em on, and dance and cut up; but I made 'em put 'em back and behave derselves—leastwise, till dey heard how matters was going.

"So we waited. At night we would see ghosts and hear turrible cries. Some of us didn't dar' to go near de house, 'kase of de corpses dar. And I, after little Katie was buried, didn't want to go nigh. De dead bodies begun to corrupt, for 'twas hot August weather; but we women-folks couldn't bury 'em. So we waited—Oh, Lord-a-mighty, yes!

"'Twas four nights now, and I was lying awake in my cabin, thinking over things so fast I couldn' sleep, and the latch raised softly and Nelson come in. I was so 'fraid of sperits, and awful things, I'd kept my lamp a-burning, and I could see how tired and sad he looked.

"'It's all up, I'm afeard,' he said, in answer to my first question. 'We got along well enough, till they stopped agin our will, at Parker's—we ought to have pushed on to the village before they heerd the news there; but we didn't. The whites got after us. They've scattered us, now. I come back here, in hopes of finding Nat and getting wid him again —I'd have some hopes, if I could get wid him.'

"'Oh, Nelson, what'll we do?' I cried; but he looked so worn and fagged, I wouldn't tell him how hea·vy my heart was; I sot some milk and potatoes on the table, and he eat like a starving man.

"'Sophy, I must go,' says he, as soon as he'd done eating

"I begged him to let me go wid him, w'atever happened but he wouldn't hear to it den; he said I'd be a drawback, 'kase dey might get wid Nat, and get to fightin' de whites ag'in, and den women-folks would be in de way.

"'You jest hold your tongue, and don't let on dat you ever knowed what was goin' on; and you won't be harmed,' says he. 'If I don't get back for you—if it's a failure after all, and de Lord widholds His help—den, if you don' hear from me, jest wait your chance, ef you have to wait a year, and run away he fus' opportunity, and make your way to de Dismal Swamp—it's only twenty-five miles from here, and you'll find frien's, dar!'

"He wrung my hand most off, and I clung to him like a burr, but he broke away, and went out into de night, and I crept back into bed to purtend to sleep, as if nothin' had happened. De next day many white men rode up to de house, all armed wid swords, pistols and guns; and dey buried massa and missus, and dey dragged off every colored man dar was, w'at had nothin' to do wid de troubles at all.

"After that, dar was white men all de time riding ober de country and soldiers 'way from Norfolk and Richmond, dev come to help put down de blacks. Oh, Lord-a-mercy! dem was awful times!

"Dey done and gone and butchered our people widout judge or jury—hundreds and hundreds was shot, which was a mussiful death, quick over But shooting was too good for any but de innocent—dem dey suspected as having had any-t'ing to do wid de insurrectioners, dey hanged, and whipped, and burned—yes, burned—oh, Lord!" here the story-teller drew in her breath with a strange, inward gurgle and shriek, which made every one of her auditory jump to their feet and sink back again.

"Dey burned Nelson," she continued, after several moments of silence. "I'll tell you how 'twas. You see dey came, great lot o' white folks one day, and dey took me, and dey tell me my husband was arrested, and in Jerusalem jail; and dey say if I 'fess w'edder he was guilty or not, and tell all I know 'bout Nat Turner, dey wouldn' punish me, dey'd let me be in peace—but if I didn' tell every word I knowed, dey would whip me till I couldn't stand. I tol' 'em, I shouldn' say nothin' agin my own husband, and I didn' know nothin' 'bout Nat Turner—I'd never see'd him but once, and I didn' know nothing 'bout him, good or bad. I knew w'at was comin', and I prayed deep and still to de Lord above to pity me; but I wouldn' tell on Nelson. Dey stripped me stark naked, tied me up, and whipped me till I was most dead; but I wouldn't 'fess. I fainted away, and dey throw pickle on me, and left me; and next day dey come back and tie me up ag'in and whip me on my raw back, and den dey turn me round and whip me t'odder side, till I was raw all round. I kin show you de scars, dey're on my breast, dey're on my back. But my lips was shut, only I screamed at fust; till I got beyond dat, and passed away to anodder world—a hell of misery, where it 'peared to me I'd lived a hundred years, wid devils yelling 'round me, and red-hot fire a falling on me all de time. So at last dey give me up, 'kase dey t'ought I was dead anyhow. But I come to; de old cook, who was so ole and foolish dey let her alone, she nussed me up; and dar I lay, day arter day, so sore I couldn' stir, wondering what dey'd done wid Nelson. It 'peared as if de wish to hear 'bout him, to walk to de village and see him, if he was still in jail, gib me strength to get well. It was t'ree weeks before I could crawl; den I set out, and crept along as best I could; it was fifteen miles to Jerusalem, whar de jail and court-house was, and it took me nigh two days to get dar. I asked de jailer let me see my husband; he swore at me, and giving me a kick, told me to 'cl'ar out! I'd never see him again, till I see him in h—!' I asked him w'at dey did wid him; he wouldn' tell me, but I found out afterwards, one way and 'nodder, dough some folks was 'human enough not to want to let me know. Fust dey tried to make him 'fess, as dey did me, by flogging. Dey tied his han's and feet, and bent his knees up to his shoul'ers and fastened dem wid a stick; den dey rolled him on de floor like as he was a bar'l, and dey lashed him more'n two hundred times. W'at you s'pose he t'ought of? S'pose he t'ought of Sam and Dan'l, s'pose he t'ought of blows and kicks—woll, woll! it's over now, nigh onto thirty year. Dey kept him in jail 'bout two weeks; and he had his trial; and dey proved on him, dat he was a ring-leader—dat he was Prophet Nat's right-hand man, and dey was going to hang him; but de mob got hold of him, and dragged him from de officers, and swore hanging was too good for him—and so—that's what become of Nelson!

"'Spect I was kind o' crazy-like for a w'ile—next thing I knew, I was lyin' on little Katie's grave. Ole cook found me, and made me eat; and in two or t'ree days a change come ober me—I was kind o' lifted up out o' my misery. It come into my head dat Nat Turner was in de woods clost by, and dat he would starve to def. You see dey hadn't found him yet, and dar was hundreds a lookin' for him. De whole country was in a trimble; women couldn't sleep a-nights, nor men lay down der guns til Prophet Nat was found.

"It come into my mind to carry him food, and I made a pocket in my dress, and put in bread and 'taters, and went a-wanderin' roun' night and day, purtendin' I was getting yerbs and fire-wood. Dar was lots of white folks, eberywhar keeping watch, all de time, on ebery road, and in de woods. Once I heard a whisper, just a short piece off—it was day-time, den, and de whisper called me—'Sophy!' and I looked sharp and saw a man's face, peering out of de ground, as it were, and I see in a minit it was Nat Turner's, and I answered him low-like—purtending to pick up sticks! 'W'at is it, Nat? I see ye—can I help you any?' And he answers back—'Come to-night, and bring me food—I'm starving—don't speak now, pass on.' So dat night, I went ag'in, berry cautious, and I found him, whar he'd dug a hole beside a log, and crawled in, and hid de place wid leaves and bushes, and I gib him suthin to eat, and told him what had happened to Nelson, and all de news I could—and he tol' me if I ever see his wife, to tell her 'bout him; and I darsn't stay but a minit, for de woods was full of men, night and day. In dis way, I brought him food two, t'ree weeks; once I went, and he was gone.. Nex' day I heard, he'd been taken, and was in prison. Den we was told he had been seen, and driven out, but had escaped. Ten days later, dey rea'ly cotched him, and den I knew 'twas all up wid him. De mob tried to kill him on de way to jail; but he had his trial and was hung.

"When he was hung and dead, dar was rejoicing in de land. De white folks breafed free ag'in. He died like a man—Oh, he was a prophet, sure 'nuff, Nat Turner was; but he couldn' overcome dis yere wicked worl'—de time wasn't ripe.

"I went to see his wife, arter he was dead. She'd been a

purty cre'tur, young and bright, wid good white blood in her, too. They'd just been whippin' her cruelly to make her give up her husband's papers. I tol' her w'at I'd done for Nat in de woods, and she t'ank me heartily.

"Bruised, and beaten, and sore, no money, no home, no massa or missus, no chil'ren, no husband—woll, I hung 'round de ole cabin a spell, and den I starts for de Dismal Swamp. I couldn' bring myself to hire out to Southampton people, and nobody claimed me yet; dough I heard de relatives of massa and missus was comin to 'tend to de property, which made me hurry off de faster. So I foun' my way to de Dismal Swamp, and I live dar one whole winter, wid a band of run-aways; and de hunters got on our track one day, and dey cotched me, and put me up at auction and sold me—and I'm a libin' yet.

"Sometimes I wonder if I should know Sam or Dan'l if I should meet 'em down in Lousianny—dey's growed big men now. But all I's looking forward to is to lay my poor, scarred body in de yearth, and go up to glory, see if I can find my husband dar."

It was some time after Sophy finished her story before any one felt like speaking. Then they all promised her faithfully never to repeat what they had heard—and slaves, it is proven, can keep a secret.

No one could rally his spirits enough for a song or jest; the young people stole out; Hyperion gave Rose a squeeze, and a kiss which had something so earnest in it, that she neither giggled nor frowned; and he and Maum Guinea turned silently and walked slowly home beneath the eternal smile of the midnight stars.

CHAPTER VIII.

ALLIGATOR STORIES.

"Strange stories they tell,
By exotic fires,
Of the monsters that dwell
Where the pyramid aspires—
Of the uncouth crocodile,
God of the ancient Nile."

The alligator, swimming in the lonely lagoon,
Strains his dull ear to catch the banjo-tune.
NEGRO MELODIES.

PHILIP was hardly sorry, upon second-thought, to hear that Mr. Talfierro was after a slave-girl instead of a wife, for that gentleman was reputed immensely wealthy, and had just that incense of fashion and family hanging about him as would have made him a formidable rival with the parents, if not with the daughter. If Mr. Talfierro had offered to cancel his claims upon Judge Bell, by a proposition for the hand o his child, the old gentleman would hardly have had grace to withstand the temptation of so brilliant an alliance, even if the girl's fancies did seem at present to be fixed upon another object.

But this dangerous person seemed to be so confirmed in his bachelor habits, that not the sweetness and beauty of Virginia had any deeper effect upon him than to draw out his most graceful compliments; and against these she was well fortified by the assurance of somebody else's devotion.

Talking the matter over, that Sunday evening, in a sly nook of the deep-windowed parlors, the lovers came to the conclusion that it would be safe for Philip to ask the father's consent to their engagement, upon the very first opportunity; and this opportunity occurred immediately.

Judge Bell was in the adjoining library, and wanted the help of Philip's younger eyes in finding a certain book upon an upper shelf; and while Mr. Talfierro listened to Virginia's piano in the parlor, her lover "screwed his courage to the sticking point," and very manfully and handsomely, asked the approval of the father to confirm the betrothal.

Contiguous estates, fair fortunes, neighborly proximity, and an amiable, promising young gentleman, were not to be slighted; and the Judge had no objection to offer to the suit of the elated lover.

When Virginia glanced up from her singing, at Philip's return to the parlor, she saw, by his gay smile, that the matter had been favorably settled.

And now, indeed, her heart overflowed with happiness, as a bird's breast overflows with song; she could no longer keep silent the bliss within her; but when she sought her chamber that night, and found Rose waiting to undress her, she confessed to her faithful attendant the blushing story.

"Oh, I am so happy, Rose. We will have a splendid wedding! And you shall be married the same evening. Yes, I've set my heart upon that, as one of the accessories—to have you and Hyperion married at the same time. You see you will belong to the same family then—and it will be so nice—you to wait upon me, and your husband upon my—" here she stopped short, with a vivid blush, and made haste to let down her hair to cover her confusion.

"I's much obliged, missus, I'm sure," answered Rose, looking equally happy. "Hope you won't hab *berry* long engagement—don't see no use in your putting it off *berry* long."

Virginia laughed at this *naive* betrayal.

"It'll take me some time to get ready, you know. Philip is anxious enough, seeing there is no particular reason for delay; but I'm going to take time to have everything right. One can be married but once, you see—and it ought to be done properly. There will have to be so much sewing, and so many preparations. And I'll have to take a trip to New Orleans, to do my shopping. Oh, won't it be delightful—buying the dress and veil, and ordering bonnets and gloves. I can be ever so extravagant, and papa won't grumble; for it will be the first wedding in the family; and he'll see the propriety of having it in style. We shall have to make our needles fly, Rose; this nice, cool weather is just fit for sewing, and I must have dresses of everything pretty. When I go to New Orleans, I'll buy *you* a wedding-dress, too. What shall it be, Rose?"

"I don' hardly know—I t'ink I should like a real sweet pink—but I'd rudder ask 'Perion w'at *his* taste is, 'fore I decide for sartain. You's berry kind, Miss Virginny,"—and she cast a gratified look upon the young lady, as she tucked up her hair in its little lawn cap.

Utterly unconscious of the danger which hung over her, the slave-girl curled down on the floor beside her mistress' bed, her usual place of repose, as glad with pleasant anticipations as the heiress whose fair hand seemed to have power to confer so much delight.

Both awoke from their cloudless dreams as only the young and careless can awake. Virginia went to breakfast, to be smiled at more fondly than usual by her mother, and to be slyly rallied by her father, to the discomfiture of her appetite, and the risk of upsetting her cup or meeting with some other table-accident.

There was a great dinner in the afternoon, and music and dancing in the evening. Virginia was so busy with dressing, receiving guests and entertaining them, that she could hardly dispense to Philip his share of favors; which almost made him wish that the holidays were over, and he had her to himself in the usual peace and quietness of those spacious parlors.

Rose, too, was very busy, waiting upon ladies, happy and animated, enjoying the occasion even more heartily than the guests. She was in her element, smoothing out handsome dresses, flying at the bidding of this and that elegant lady, listening to the music in the hall, bringing refreshments to the parlors, and always finding time to admire her own lovely young mistress, and exalt her above all others.

Once, passing through the hall, after dancing had commenced in the evening, she encountered the handsome gentleman from New Orleans, who had been at the Judge's so much within the last few days. There was no one near but the musicians, who could hear nothing but their own accords, and when he paused, she paused too, thinking that he wished some service.

"Rose," said he, with a smile, "did you know you were mine?"

She gave him a startled glance; she did not comprehend him at all, and thinking finally that he was attempting a jest, she smiled too, replying:

"How is dat, Massa Talfierro?"

"I bought you—are you glad? You will have easy times with me," he answered, much delighted with her apparent acquiescence in the bargain, for he was a fine gentleman, of delicate susceptibilities, and hated scenes.

"Laws, massa, might a made a better choice," she replied lightly, and glided by; she was used to be jested with by gentlemen, and the idea did not occur to her that he was in earnest.

Such a fact would require time to make an impression upon her; if she had been told by the Judge himself, she would have been incredulous at first; she knew she was a favorite; and she no more dreaded leaving her *home*, than one of its own children dreaded it.

Now the Judge, in finally consenting to the bargain, and still before the papers were signed, had requested the girl's purchaser to convey the news to her himself; as he had a kind of impression that there would be rebellion, or at least, tears and remonstrance; and Mr. Talfierro, secure in his good opinion of his powers of pleasing and persuasion, had been willing to do this.

It was true, as a general thing, that girls in Rose's condition were not over-scrupulous, and that they were delighted with change and novelty—willing to go, whenever sold, if the new master were more liberal than the old.

He took it for granted that Rose had understood him, and that, like others of her class, she was careless of change, and satisfied with her lot; and he returned to the Judge with the intelligence of her saucy acquiescence.

"She's a spirited creature—she can give jest for jest—she'd as soon try the world in a new place as a kitten or a dog," remarked her expectant owner.

"I'm really glad she took it so quietly—I hate a fuss," responded the Judge.

In the mean time, while music and feasting went on in the mansion-houses of the plantations, it was kept up with more vigor if less grace in the cabin, and out in the open air. Far and wide resounded the tinkling banjo and the merry violin, answering each other from one estate to another, while the light of bonfires never died out. Coons and opossums fell daily victims to relentless pursuers, and their lifeless bodies were offered a savory sacrifice at the barbecues which were nightly held.

Hogs which had become wild in the woods, and no longer belonged to any one in particular, were lawful game—chickens, wherever they could be bought or stolen, and all the small prizes of the forest which the negroes could trap or hunt. Seldom had there been so merry a Christmas time as this, some of whose events we are recording The planters generally had cut and ground a tolerable crop, and were disposed to humor the slaves who had toiled eighteen hours out of the twenty-four, during "grinding-season." The weather had been propitious; not a rainy day, so far; the air cool and bracing, the days and nights calm and bright. The whole country, black and white, seemed determined to enjoy itself to an amount of social pleasure which should atone for any degree of isolation or privation during the year.

The light and music which streamed from Judge Bell's mansion, on Monday night, was reflected back from the fiddle and bonfire which made echo in a distant part of his plantation. A group of negro men, field-hands the most of them, were gathered around a huge fire, at which an opossum and a pig were roasting. There were no women present, and consequently, no dancing; but one of them had a fiddle, and with the universal love for music which characterizes them, they interspersed their wild and often silly stories with songs and melodies, some of them merry as the leaping fire, and some of them plaintive and touching beyond expression.

This group of revellers was composed of some of the smartest and most skillful of the out-door slaves—the most of them good hunters and fishers—who had been off for a day's sport, unencumbered by those who could not aid them to advantage.

They stretched their brawny limbs about the fire, delighting their sensitive shins with the warmth, and talking in uncouth accents, laughing musically, watching the pig roast, and also the pumpkin, and carefully attending to the 'possum, wrapped in leaves and gently baking amid ashes and heated stones. According to their own statements, some of their had had wonderful adventures, the most of which had never extended beyond the swamps and woods of their own plantations. But they were full of reminiscences of turkey-hunts and "painters," and strange experiences of alligators—some of the latter stories bearing evident marks of having descended from their Congo mothers, in the original shape of crocodiles, here softened down to our less formidable tribe. A *fetishish* and hobgoblin air had some of these remarkable traditions, grotesque and ridiculous, with not enough reason in them to pin the airiest faith to; but they were delightful to these vivid, untrained imaginations, and perhaps the wild-rolling eyes and big-mouthed credulity of the hearers were all in keeping with the stories.

One told about a turkey-hunt in which he took the most conspicuous part; but, as hunting wild-turkeys requires more caution and delicate skill than seemed to be in his organization, perhaps he exaggerated his personal importance. His auditors swallowed his story as good-naturedly as they would have done the wild-turkey itself; and after it was finished, the negro with the fiddle sang a favorite song of the plantation-lands in Louisiana and Georgia, the chorus of which is a curiously-correct imitation of the peculiar cry of the turkey-cock when he calls to his distant mate—a soft, guttural, resounding utterance—and in the chorus the whole party joined—

"Chug-a-loggee, chug-a-loggee, chug-a-loggee chug!"

"Look-a-heah, niggas! S'pose an alligator come out of de cane-brake as big as dat cypress log dar—guess you wouldn't sing chug-a-loggee!" said a "boy" who had just dropped into the circle.

"Wha' for?" exclaimed half a dozen of the darkies in chorus, as they sprang to their feet and rolled their eyes in an extraordinary manner. Each one, standing as immovable for the moment, as a post, still rolled his eyes so as to catch a full view of the entire vicinity.

"Yah! yah! Ef you ain't the skeeriest niggas in dis parish!" exclaimed the "boy," as he fairly exploded with laughter at the statuesque figures before him.

"*Alligator!*" he suddenly screamed, in a frightened voice, as he bounded up in the air and started back.

"*Alligator!*" frantically screamed every darkey, as they disappeared in the darkness like shadows over the greensward.

"Yah! yah! yah! Oh, gorra mighty! Yah! yah! yah! Dis nigga will jes' die wid larfin'! Yah! yah! *Alli*—yah! yah!—*gator!* Yah! yah!" and the black joker rolled over on the ground, in his explosive enjoyment of the fright he had caused. He first tumbled head over heels, like a coon tumbling from a tree; then ran his head into the ground; then "fetched up" against a tree, to steady himself. Suddenly, he listened:

"Hark! W'at's dat? It's something *sizzlin'!* It's de pig, sure!"—and he went forward to the fire, to find the pig fairly frying before the hot embers.

"Dis'll *nebber* do! Pig spilin', and de niggas gone! Oh Lord! dar's de 'possum cookin' like an old shoe. Niggas! Hoo—oo—oo—oo!"—and his rich voice died away in the darkness like a retreating song. Presently a shadow flitted in the distance—then another, and soon all the negroes were again before the fire. Seeing the imminence of the crisis, every one hastened to relieve the burning pig and 'possum. When all was right again, they sat silently down. At length one of them said:

"Conundibus, wha' for you cry out '*alligator!*' when dar's no alligator 'round in de winter?"

"Yes, dat's just what *I* wants to know,' said another.

"It's my 'pinion de circumstances is mighty s'picious"

said a third darkey. "Dar's de tail ob dat 'possum *clean gone!*"

This brought them all to their feet again. The 'possum-tail gone!—that was a calamity! Conundibus was a rascal, that was clear. The darkies approached him threateningly With a wild "Yah! yah! yah!" he disappeared in the darkness, whither the others dare not follow him. Muttering their odd and wild imprecations upon "de young dog," who was "eber cuttin' up de feelin's" by his practical jokes, the party was soon laughing and jabbering like a set of parrots, over their now thoroughly-cooked feast. Pig was taken from the spit and placed on a great sugar-pan, which served as a platter; potatoes were raked out of the hot ashes; 'possum was carefully laid upon an old earthenware dish especially reserved for the delicacy. Its tail was gone! and Conundibus was voted to be a "berry serious rascal." When all was ready, the violin struck up a clear, ringing air, and the negroes, standing around, joined hands as they uttered in concert a wild chaunt, half song and half recitative, which it is almost impossible to put into words:

	By de dark lagoon,	(*Recitative.*)
	Huah! Huah! Huah!	(*Chorus.*)
	By de cane-brake's track,	(*Rec.*)
	Huah! Huah! Huah!	(*Cho.*)
	By de cypress swamp,	(*Rec.*)
	Huah! Huah! Huah!	(*Cho.*)
First voice.—	De darkness sleeps—	(*Tenor solo.*)
Second "	De winds make moan—	(*Bass* ")
Third "	De waters dream—	(*Soprano* ")
Fourth "	De stars keep watch.	(*Alto* ")
	Hark! Hark!	(*Staccato chorus*)

(*Violin plays a plaintive melody, imitating a woman's song.*)

First voice.—	My wife is dar, ober dar!
Second "	My mother is dar, ober dar!
Third "	My sister is dar, ober dar!
Fourth "	My true love is dar, ober dar!
	Hark! Hark!

(Violin plays a low but joyous strain, which dies away on the strings.)

By de dark lagoon—
By de cane-brake's track—
By de cypress swamp—
Huah—huah—huah!
Huah—huah—huah!
Huah—huah—huah!

This last chorus was prolonged until it seemed to melt into the still air. The singers then all shook hands, and the feast began. In a moment all was a bedlam of enjoyment. Song dance, joke—each followed rapidly, even as the negroes eat of the pig, potatoes and hoe-cake; for, let the spirit of fun be ever so exuberant, it did not, for a moment, stay the feast.

"*W'at's dat?*" suddenly exclaimed one of the darkies astride of the cypress-log, having a pig's leg in his hand, while his well-filled mouth almost stopped his utterance.

Instantly all was still as death; then all eyes opened wide as shutters—all mouths gaped—each negro's arms and fingers stiffened at his side, and knees perceptibly quaked.

"De debbil hisself!" shouted the darkey from the log, and, with a wild "whoop!" he disappeared in the woods.

"De debbil! Oh! oh! oh!" was heard on all sides, as the darkies vanished in the darkness, leaving the feast deserted. Then there came slowly forward—what was it? An alligator, apparently; yet it walked *erect*, as if standing on its tail. The monster came slowly forward, uttering a noise something similar to a pig's grunt, until it stood by the deserted feast. It walked around the board, passed through the fire, knocked the embers aside, and, finally, bent down before the feast. The breast between the fore-legs parted, and the head of Conundibus looked out, his cheeks fairly wet with the tears of his suppressed laughter. Then he protruded his hand to seize a morsel of the delicious pig, and was in the act of bearing it to his mouth, when—crash, crash, fell the blows upon his alligator's head. It was the turn of Conundibus to be frightened. He burst from the skin, to find one of the darkies, armed with a club, ready to dash out his brains. His sudden appearance, however, apparently from the very monster's bowels, caused the assailant to stagger back in horror. Conundibus, throwing the skin over on the stupefied negro, made for the woods, while the thick recesses were rendered fairly jubilant with his laughter.

But his laughter proved his frolic's ruin; for the negroes, secreted in the darkness, sprang out, and soon had him prisoner. They dragged him forward to the fire, to find the fellow with the club carefully examining the hollow skin, to be assured there was not another darkey within its ample hollow. The capture of the "serious rascal" revealed all, and although the darkies had had their feast almost spoiled, so clever was the trick that they soon forgave the joker, and the feast went on. Alligator stories became the theme of discourse as the pig continued to disappear.

"Whar did you get dat big skin, Conundibus?" said the negro whose club had so nearly finished the apparition.

"You jes' tell me wha' for you come back to see dat I *wasn't* an alligator—you jes' tell dat afore I answers any interrogums," said Conundibus, anxious to learn how it was possible for any negro to get his courage up to the point of assailing "de debbil."

"W'y, you see, I t'ought it was only de old cane-brake alligator waked up from his snooze jes' for to get sunthin' to fill his stomach aside ob stones. I t'ought he jes' *smell* pig, and come out ob de mud, and he so stiff he couldn't walk, so he come along on his tail. I knowed 'twasn't de debbil, 'cause *I* saw de debbil once, and he was a horse, wid a cow's head and a chicken's tail, and had a church bell on his back. *Dat* I *knowed* was de debbil; and so I knowed dis yere wasn't

de debbil widout he been habin' children. T'inks I, if he *been* habin' children, I better kill 'em, else de family get *so* big dat ebery nigga's house must have a debbil in it—yah! yah! yah!"

Conundibus half-suspected his friend (John Cottontop, as he was called, from having something on his head that was neither hair nor wool, but looked like a black cotton ball) knew that the apparition was not the devil, nor the old fabled cane-brake alligator, who was supposed to have haunted the swamps on the plantation for many a generation. Cottontop was not considered remarkably brave, for he always *would* run at the cry of "*alligator!*" and would make others run; yet, it was a fact, that John was one of the best alligator hunters on the place—that he killed more of "the varmints," and made more money from the sale of their oil and skins, than all the rest of the negroes put together. The truth in this case was, John had first run, as was his failing; but the thought of oil and hide always would give him courage again; and, in this instance, having caught a glimpse of the apparition before he ran, he had returned to bag his game in the usual way, by hitting it on the head from behind.

Conundibus proceeded to narrate his adventure in obtaining this particular hide:

"You see, darkies, de alligator, which isn't so plenty as dey used to was, is goin' off like de Injins—nobody knows whar; but I believes," he said, with a knowing shake of his very woolly head, "I believes dar is a hole *somewhar* dat goes in de groun', and dat de alligators, and Injins, and deer, and 'possums goes in and finds anodder place better'n dis, 'cause dar isn't no niggas nor poor whites dar to pester 'em. *Dat's* my most perfound comprepinion."

"Your what?" said Cottontop, greatly interested in the deep insinuation of the philosophic Conundibus.

"Oh, look heah, nigga: I can't gib you sense any more'n de oberseer can give your head good nigga's ha'r!" was the rather tart reply. Cottontop was silenced.

Conundibus proceeded: "Woll, dis yere old 'un wouldn't clear out wid de rest. He staid behind and cum ashore ebery night las' year, to stick his nose in massa's groun', out of 'cause he couldn't help it, I s'pose. I war down in de swamp by de lower bayou one Sunday, you see—you needn't roll your eyes so ober dar, you nigger preacher wid de fiddle—one Sunday, jus' to see whar de light cum from perhaps, or whar de dark went to ebery mornin', when what should I see but dat alligator dar, trablin' aroun' on Sunday like a gentleum wid a big chaw of tobac' in his mouf. By golly, I struck out ob dem woods and across to de houses in a hurry, and jes' let de boys know it. So we went back, and dar he war, sure enough. We tried to head him off, but de smart old fox would go towards de bayou anyhow; so we kept pesterin' him, and makin' him snap his tail like a whip, until he had knocked de bark all off on it—you see dar it is all gone. I knowed if he got in de water he was gone for good, so I jes' got straddle his back. You know when a nigger gits on an alligator's back, dat dey jes' stops, and swells up and blows like a bull, dey gits *so* mad. So de ole feller stops, and de way he stirred up de groun' was a sin. De shadow of his tail knocked two niggers down, and he struck out his face for anodder nigga's heels, and almos' kotched 'em Gosh! dat nigga wouldn't been a chaw tobacker for de beast You see *I* was de boss ob dat boat, 'kase I was on deck—yah! yah! and de critter couldn't shake me off. De ole fool didn't know enough to lay down an' roll ober. He got blowed all out wid his fussin' 'roun' to get me off. De boys put out both his eyes wid de pike-spear; den I took de spear and put it right under dis foreleg yere, and dat did de job for him. He jes' lay right out and whined like a dog, and den died. Dat's all."

"Who got de ile?" said Cottontop.

"I didn't stop to see *dat* dirty work!" said the story-teller, with a kind of mock dignity. "De boys dragged de beast up to de houses, and arter de skin war off I jes' took it. Dat's all."

"Dat ain't nuffin. I's killed a houseful of 'gators, I has," said a short, thick-set, scrubby-headed looking darkey, celebrated chiefly for the quantity of pig he could eat and the big stories he could tell. "I's made 'em carry me across de lagune *many* times. "I's got an alligator bridle to ride 'em wid. I's got an alligator skin at de hut on rockers, and ebery one ob *my* pickaninnies was brought up in *dat* skin. I's got—"

"Look-a-heah, Pluribus, you isn't got one t'ing. You isn't got a piece of pig about you, have you?" said Conundibus. The injured Pluribus could only be silent, and in two minutes more was fast asleep on the greensward, literally surfeited with the pig he had devoured.

"I don't b'lieve w'at dat nigger say about ridin' de alligators across de bayou," said Cottontop. "I once heard tell dat de mails on de Mississip was carried up and down by boys on de alligator's back—dat dey went so fas' you could only see a streak through de water; but I don't believe dat, nohow, 'kase I *knows* de beast is de slowestest critter dat eber did live. Why, I'll tell you: once I was goin' across de bayous in de oberseer's skiff, to de ole rice plantation W'en I got to de bayou, dar was jus' about two hundred little alligators creepin' aroun', jes' hatched out in de sand. De ole alligator was out on de mud. I went ober to de old place, staid dar all night, come back nex' day, and de old alligator had made only jes' about twenty rods, dat's all

But, I tell you, dey is great in de water! I jes' went ober der holes in de skiff, and I b'lieve dey could beat me wid de best boat. I once took ole massa and anodder gentleum ober to see de ugly beasts in der holes. Oh, de Lord! De gentleum was so skeered dat we pulled ashore, and he got sick a-hearin 'em beller, and grunt, and splash."

"Cottontop, w'at you kill so many alligators for?" said one of the listeners.

"None of your business!" said the apparently offended negro alligator-merchant, for such he was; and to his hand was the growing scarcity of "the animals" owing more than to any other cause. The fellow hunted them chiefly in the winter with great success pecuniarily. He would travel around in the daytime and discover where the creature had buried itself for the winter's torpor. The spot was always indicated by a round ridge on the surface of the ground. Having marked the spot, he would return at night, build his fire, open the mound, cut off the alligator's head, open and disembowel him. The fat of the ribs and flesh he would "try out" in his pans, and before morning would return loaded with skins and oil. The skins he sold at a good price, for fancy leather, and the oil he disposed of at a very paying rate, for machinery lucubration. In this trade he had amassed a snug sum of money, and was, therefore, quite a "respectable darkey"—notwithstanding the negroes, for some reason, did not like the manner in which he had procured his wealth. It was whispered around among the slaves that Cottontop had twice offered his money to the old master to induce him to give Maum Guinea her freedom. The superstitious blacks believed that his wish was to get rid of the old cook; but, if such an offer had been made, it was from the negro's knowledge of the negro's heart—because he read in the old woman's face the secret of her agony and penetrated the dark shadow which rested upon her soul.

The small hours wore on, and one by one, the black revellers fell asleep by the fast-dying embers. As Cottontop concluded, the fiddler arose, took his violin down from the bush, from which it hung in safety, and, one strong stroke across its strings started the black assembly suddenly into life. Each black arose, and in a moment, standing there before the almost expired fire, they formed into the mystic ring of clasped hands to chaunt again their wild chorus:

> By de dark lagoon—
> By de cane-brake's track—
> By de cypress swamp—
> Huah—huah—huah!

The words rolled out on the air and died away in the distance as if speeding on their way to other lands—as if to pursue airy paths to far Africa, to awake on the banks of the fabled streams of Negro-land the responsive

> Huah—huah—huah!

at once the revelation of the slave's misery and his hopes of the future.

When the grey streaks of morning pencilled the east, over the low lagoons, the Cypress-swamp barbecue was among the the things of the past—only capable of sending one pleasant thrill to the negro's breast as its memory was recalled.

CHAPTER IX.

THE FUGITIVES.

And the nightingales softly are singing
  In the mellow and moonlighted air;
And the minstrels their viols are stringing,
  And the dancers for dancing prepare.

None heeds us, beloved Irene!
  None will mark if we linger or fly.
Amid all the masks in yon revel,
  There is not an ear or an eye—
Not one—that will gaze or will listen;
  And save the small star in the sky,
Which, to light us, so softly doth glisten,
  There is none will pursue us, Irene.
  Oh, love me, oh, save me, I die!—OWEN MEREDITH.

These lovers fled away into the night.—KEATS.

VIRGINIA was in her chamber, standing before the mirror, clasping a pearl necklace about her throat. Her cheeks were flushed, and her eyes brilliant with delight; for it was New Year's morning, and on the little pier-table were various parcels which she had just opened—the gifts of parents and friends. The handsomest of these was the necklace—sent by Mr. Talfierro as a bridal as well as New Year's present, with his compliments and congratulations — the Judge having informed him, on the previous day, of the approaching marriage of his daughter. Philip's gift also was there—a richly ornamented guitar, which he had been to the village expressly to purchase, and which was the only thing he could find in the little town which he thought would please his betrothed. More elaborate and costly presents he intended to select upon his visit to the great city which he also found it necessary to make before the occasion of the wedding. There were books, and perfumes in fancy cases, dresses, and pretty trifles in profusion; so that the young girl had hardly known what to admire most, until the little parcel containing the pearls was unfastened, and then her delight was complete. Very charming it looked, glistening about the slender throat—fine and softly rounded, if not so fair as the jewels—the graceful pendants rising and falling with the motion of her breath.

"Mr. Talfierro is such an agreeable gentleman—so tasteful and generous," she murmured. "Look, Rose, what Mr. Talfierro has sent me," as she heard her waiting-maid enter, and caught a glimpse of her dress in the mirror. "Oh, I am so much pleased with it—it will be so pretty for the—the wedding," she continued, still looking in the glass at the fair reflection before her.

It was not until she felt the skirt of her dress grasped strangely that she turned and beheld Rose crouching at her feet as if overwhelmed with terror, her eyes dilated, her lips parted, and trying in vain to gasp out an articulate word.

"Save me! save me!" she presently sobbed or rather shrieked out.

"What from?" asked Virginia, looking toward the door, a half formed thought of a poisonous serpent or a rabid dog rushing into her mind; but seeing and hearing nothing, half fearing the girl had gone suddenly insane, so wild was her expression.

"Oh, Miss Virginny, *you* can save me, and you will!"

"Certainly I will," spoke the mistress, soothingly. "What is it, child?"

"It's him—it's dat New Orleans gentleum—your fadder has done gone and sold me to him."

"Sold *you*, Rose? Oh, I guess you are mistaken."

"I wish I was, Miss Virginny. But dey's bof told me now. Your fadder says so hisself. I's to go to-morrow airly,"—and sob after sob b oke distressingly from the dark, panting bosom.

"If papa has sold you, he has done very wrong," cried Virginia, flushed and indignant. "He knows I can not do without you!"

"In course you can't, Miss Virginny. Who'd do your beautiful hair, or your lawn dresses, I'd like to know!"

Poor Rose! She was thinking of Hyperion, of herself—of her faithful lover and her hated owner—but she felt instinctively, in that hour of desperation, that it would be in vain to appeal to "white folks" on common grounds of sympathy, and she grasped at the idea of her being useful and necessary to Miss Virginia, as a drowning man grasps at a straw. The momentous question of the slave-girl's fate resolved itself into the critical problem of "who would do her missus' hair, and clear-starch her muslins."

"At this time of all others, Rose! So much to plan and do —and all the sewing and embroidery. I shall just tell papa flatly that I can not and will not get married, if I am compelled to part with you."

"Oh, do! do tell him, dear missus," and for a moment a gleam of hope shone over the beautiful, wild, imploring face, like sunset out of a summer storm-cloud; but it was swept over by a second gust of despair, as she added: "Ah! ah! he tell me de papers done been signed."

"Well, we'll get them *un*-signed then," said Virginia, resolutely. "I'll ask Mr. Talfierro himself; I'll appeal to his gallantry. *He* certainly can not have as much need of a lady's-maid as I,"—and she half-laughed in the midst of her irritation. "If he wants a housekeeper, he can find plenty, more fit than you; while I can not possibly dispense with you. I have learned you to do every thing so nicely—and besides, I like you so much, Rose, dear,"—and a sense of gratitude and love filled her heart at the instant, as she remembered the faithful, untiring, affectionate attentions of the girl through so many years.

"Rose's heart would done break to be sold away from her own young missus,"—and the speaker pressed her hand on her heart, as if there were already a sharp pain there.

"Get up, Rose; and don't cry—at least until we see what can be done. I'd rather Mr. Talfierro had kept his pearls, than that he should have vexed me so. It does not seem like New Year's morning any longer—I'm so out of humor. However, we needn't fret, either of us. It can not be, and it *shall* not!"—and the young lady threw down the necklace with a very decided movement. "Look at my pretty presents, Rose, while I go speak to my father."

She went out of the room; but the girl did not look at the pretty presents—not the glittering of jewels nor the lustre of a silk robe glancing out of its wrapper of tissue-paper could light her eyes with a passing curiosity; she sat upon the floor, motionless, her hands folded in her lap, her glance bent upon the carpet, the rich tints and flitting changes of her brilliant countenance faded to a dull, dead yellow.

In the mean time, Virginia found her father alone in his little office-room. The family had breakfasted, and the compliments of the day had already passed; something of the pleasure which parents experience in bestowing good gifts on their delighted children still irradiated his countenance.

"Hey, puss, what now? Any thing wanting?" he inquired, as his eldest and pet child came towards him with some hesitation.

"I came to speak about Rose, father.

"Rose! Yes, yes, I expect a scene, Miss Virginia—but please be brief about it. The deed is done, and can't be undone."

He spoke a little nervously. It was evident that he did not feel as if he had been doing exactly the right thing. He knew, first, that the girl was a great favorite with his daughter, and that she would be very unwilling to give her up; and secondly, his conscience, as a man, was troubled, for he knew, much better than his child, the object of the purchase, and he could not *quite* persuade himself that the mulatto-girl, always modest and virtuous thus far in her young life, was just the creature for that kind of a sale. He had taken the liberty of disposing of her, body and soul, and yet, curiously, he did not feel entirely easy about so plain and common a business transaction.

The idea of modesty and virtue in a Louisiana colored-girl might well be ridiculed; as a general thing, she has neither; and who is to blame for it we do not propose to argue. It is doubtless a great blessing to the colored race that it is held in slavery for the salvation of its soul and the precious boon of its enlightenment; and if such a state of morals prevails in the far South, we suppose it to be only one of the branches of the above inestimable blessing. Rose happened to have grown up with more than her share of excellence for the reason that she had always been more of a companion of the young daughter of the house, than a common servant; and there had been no grown-up sons; and the family of Judge Bell lived quietly, and with more than the ordinary degree of refinement for that latitude. Thus, by reason of her seclusion, and her constant association with the ladies of a gentle household, it came to pass that the slave-girl Rose blushed as easily and kept herself as charily, as her friend and mistress Virginia.

"Well, papa, I don't see how I am to get along withou her. I shall never, never find anybody to take her place,"—and the young lady burst into tears

"It will be inconvenient for a while, I know; but little Dinah will soon be grown enough to do all that Rose does She's large enough, now, to make a very nice little waiting girl."

"She can't embroider, nor sew worth looking at; and I'll look like a fright with her at my hair—and now, just when—"

"It *will* be bad for you to be looking like a fright now-a-days, puss. But I guess we can manage that."

"Besides, father, I think it is cruel to send Rose off among strangers. She is such a timid thing—and so much attached to us. She seems distracted with the very idea. Indeed, indeed, papa, it makes me unhappy to look at her."

"I'm sorry for Rose, and for you, too, little one. I hate to part with her myself. She is honest and faithful—a good girl. It was only necessity that induced me. Girls of your age do not know what business-troubles are. To satisfy you that I was obliged to do as I did, I will tell you that Mr. Talfierro held my note for five thousand dollars; that he came here to collect it; that I had not the money; and that he offered to cancel the whole amount, in return for Rose. He seems to have taken a fancy to her; and he is rich and can afford to indulge his fancies. In fact, he is determined to have her. He went so far as to threaten the prosecution of the debt, if I didn't accede to his manner of settling it. Now, the girl isn't worth half that in market; it's a fancy price, and I could not afford to refuse it."

'I wish Mr. Talfierro had never seen us! I wish he had his necklace back. I don't like him a particle," cried Virginia, with girlish petulance.

"He has not done such a bad thing for you, my dear. I am so pinched for money this season, that if he had not done as he has done, I don't see how I could have provided you with a suitable outfit. Reflect upon it, Virginia. I should have been compelled to raise five thousand dollars. Now I am not only free from that, but the portion of that sum which I had managed to lay by, I can afford to use for your benefit. It will not be an unpleasant thing for you to take ten or twelve hundred dollars to the city to go shopping with. You can soon make another girl available, without the extravagance of keeping a five-thousand-dollar waiting-maid. Don't you see?"

"Yes, I see; but I'm sorry for Rose—I can't help it, father. She was engaged to Philip's man, and they seemed so attached to each other—it's not right to separate them. I had promised her she should be married at the same time with myself."

"Pooh! pooh! girls' nonsense! Soon get over it, both of you."

"I can't bear to tell her that she really has got to go," continued Virginia, lingering in the room, as if still hoping for a revokal of the sentence.

"The best way would have been to have said nothing about it, till the time came for departure. An hour would have sufficed to pack her trinkets. If I'd been wise, I should have thought of it."

"She couldn't have even said good-by to Hyperion."

"Well, the fewer good-byes the better, in such cases. They are excitable creatures, the whole race of 'em. They will wail one moment and laugh the next. I suppose they'll make a great fuss, and get over it all the sooner. You can tell Rose, for her comfort, that you will be in New Orleans in a few weeks, and then you will come and see her."

"You've no idea, father, how she seems to feel about it."

"Nor I *can't help it!* It's no use talking, now,"—he spoke more sternly. "Bid her prepare herself, and do not hint at the possibility of her remaining. Be decided, and you will save yourself a scene."

Virginia withdrew, and with reluctant footsteps sought her chamber. As she entered it, Rose stirred for the first time; raising her head, she looked in the tearful face of her young mistress.

"No use tellin' me de news," she remarked—and getting up, went quietly to arranging the room.

That day the Judge's family were to dine with Colonel Fairfax. The festivity was to serve as the introduction to that feeling of relationship and mutual interest natural to the present state of affairs. The betrothal of the young people was already avowed in both households. Philip had stimulated Maum Guinea, by a gold dollar, and still more by one of his golden smiles, to do her handsomest in the culinary department, and to Hyperion he had given warning to exercise his utmost skill. The dinner was to be succeeded by evening gayeties, to which a few more young people were invited.

The peculiar circumstances attending this little party kept Virginia in a pleasant flutter of anticipation. If it had not been for the sad, dull face of the girl who flitted about her with unusual assiduity, doing every thing kind and careful, but speaking little and shedding no tears, she would have been extremely happy. But she could not, in the selfishness of her own joy, quite shut out the distress of her slave. Her voice trembled when she addressed her, calling her "Rose, dear," and "her darling Rose," to testify her own unwillingness to give her up.

"Make me look as well as possible," she said, as Rose took down her rich hair to dress it for the *fête*; "I wish Philip not to be ashamed of me. Besides, it will be the *last* time you will dress me. It's *too* bad! I *hate* Mr. Talfierro!"

"So do I," whispered the slave-girl, under her breath, and

a single flash broke from under her drooping lashes, like the glitter of a dagger.

"Will you go with me over to Colonel Fairfax's, or will you stay here and be getting yourself ready for your journey?" asked Virginia, when ready to descend from her chamber, bright and beautiful as tasteful and loving hands could make her.

"I'd like to go 'long wid you, missus."

"I thought perhaps it would be better for you, and for *him* too, not to see him, Rose," continued her mistress, gently.

"Oh, no! no! I must see him, and Maum Ginny."

"If you wish it, you certainly shall. You can go over with us, and stay until we return. It will not take you long to arrange your little affairs here."

The slave-girl did not smile bitterly, with the mockery of the white nature, at the idea that people in her position, no matter how faithful their service, were not burdened by the accumulation of many effects—her whole being was preoccupied by one feeling, to the exclusion of every other less-absorbing passion.

When they arrived at Colonel Fairfax's, Rose went immediately to the cook's cabin.

"Oh, Mammy!"

The words burst out of her heart with a sudden cry; it was all she said as she sat down on the wooden stool by the table, covering her face with her shawl. The cook raised herself to her full height from over the savory dish she was preparing: her black eyes seemed to shrink into half their size and double their intensity, as she fixed them upon the drooping form before her.

"Ho! ho! I 'spected as much."

"Did you know it?" asked the visitor quickly, dropping her shawl.

"De curse is a-falling, chile."

"Oh, Maumy!"

"It always falls—sooner or later. W'at you got black blood in you veins fur? It's pizened—since the days of Noah, its pizened. It burns in our veins like fire—it's got de fire of de burning lake mixed up in it. When white blood runs wid dat, it's wuss still. Ho! chile, I knew well 'nuff w'at you'd come to."

"Does *he* know it?"

"Woll, he heard it. But he hoped ag'in hope. Hasn't lived as long as Maum Ginny, or he'd know better. *I* never hope nothing."

She went on with her cooking.

"Can't you save me, Maumy?"

"Me, chile?"

"You can do so many things, Ginny!"

"Can't make black blood white."

There was nothing said for the next few minutes. The cook was in all the hurry and bustle of dishing up a grand dinner. Her assistants were coming in and out, hurrying between the cabin and the mansion. She scarcely glanced at her forlorn visitor; but once, as she added the "finishing touch" to a spicy soup, she muttered:

"'Twon't spile *their* appetites any."

It was not until all the various courses had been sent in, and the dessert was on the table, that there was any quiet in the kitchen. Even then Hyperion had not come in, though he knew Rose was there; as it was part of his duty, on that day, to assist in the dining-room.

After the coffee had been sent in, there was comparative repose. But the cook did not dispose herself to conversation. She drove out the slatternly girl who came to wash up the kettles and pans, and went at that work herself with a vigor which soon put an end to it. Beyond offering a cup of coffee and a plate of dainties to Rose, she scarcely spoke; and when her tasks were finished, sat down without tasting of food, and stared into the fire. Rose did not feel hurt by her manner; she knew that her own grief was working in Maum Guinea's breast almost as powerfully as in her own; and indeed, she was herself in a sort of stupor, hardly realizing the passing moments, but only wondering when Hyperion would enter and speak with her.

The brief winter twilight had descended when he did so. Shadows lurked in the corners of the cabin, chased restlessly by tongues of light that seemed to seek to sting them, as the fire flashed up or sank apart. A vivid glare from the falling embers revealed the mulatto-man's face, as he opened the door and stepped in, opposite to Rose. It was full of gloom and despair. With a great sob, she rose and threw herself upon his bosom; and there, for the first time since she had learned her fate, tears came to her relief, and she wept out the dreadful weight which had oppressed her all day, choking her throat and burning her eyelids. He passed his trembling hand again and again over her wavy, silken hair; he had no words of comfort, for there was no comfort in the world for them. He could not say "peace, when there was no peace."

A long while they stood thus, until her weeping became less vehement. The sound of music reached them, thrilling through the darkness, from the brilliantly-illuminated mansion.

"Come, Rose, Miss Virginia wants you in de dressing-room."

"You come back here, chil'ren, fust chance you get," said Maum Guinea, as they went out.

After they had left, she stirred up the fire, put on fresh fuel, put various dishes to warming, made a fresh pot of coffee, and set the little table with a good supper. It was, perhaps, nine o'clock when they returned together, to have a few last words of endearment and farewell, with only their beloved "Maumy" for a listener. The time had come for her to express herself. Closing the door carefully, she spoke in a low, steady voice:

"Quit yer crying, chil'ren, and make up yer minds to *do something* Why don't you run away?"

They looked up at her in fear and surprise; her form seemed the expression of a concentrated will; her eyes were bright and resolute, as a panther's when her young are threatened by the hunter.

"I'd be afraid," whispered Rose, with a shudder.

"Would you be afraid, if *I'd* go 'long?" asked Maum Guinea.

"No, Maumy, not wid you and 'Perion."

"Where could we go?" asked the young man.

He had lifted himself up eagerly, and looked ready to meet the emergency; but it is not strange that he asked where they could go—they had not that dreaded, dreary refuge of the Dismal Swamp, to which many a desperate fugitive betakes himself; the country was open and settled; the river, a day's journey away. There was only the temporary refuge of the dark and tangled forest lying along the edge of the plantation; they might reach that, and if they escaped immediate arrest, might make their way, by night-journeys, to the river; and there would be the double danger of detection, and the great difficulty of securing a passage on any of the boats.

"I's got my plans, and they are doubtful 'nuff, too. But if you'd rather run the risks, than see Rose go off to New Orleans wid dat new owner, why, we'll try—dat's all. Don't make much difference to me whar *I* am. I's as well off here as I can be anywhar, now; but if it be a help and comfort to ye, to have my company, why, I'm goin' along. Dey may tear me to pieces, if dey want to—I'm going. I didn't t'ink I'd ever sot my heart on anyt'ing in dis yere world ag'in; but I've grown to like you two—'pears 'most as if you were my own; and if you want Mammy to go wid you, she's going. And now, we can't stand it to hide in de woods, 'less we eat something. Set down and make a good supper; ye'll need it 'fore we's tru' wid this."

She began to pour out the coffee as she spoke. They obeyed her with a kind of blind, bewildered obedience. Hope, too, sprung up, at her words; and those, whose dry throats had refused to swallow a morsel through the day, now ate with considerable appetite. She forced upon each the second cup of strong, stimulating coffee, and herself partook of the same.

"An' now," said she, as they concluded the hurried repast, "you bof go back to de house. Rose must stand 'roun', whar she will be seen; and you go to your master's room, 'Perion, and draw up your papers as a free colored man. You must write like Colonel Fairfax, and sign his name. You's pert at writing, and you can do it. Put on your silber watch and all your little fixin's, to look respectable, and take all de money you have. I hab a hundred dollars myself. It will buy our passage, if we get to de boats. I'll be your maumy—Rose'll be your wife. Den you get back here—I'll be ready."

Half an hour later, the three stood in the field running along beyond the negro-quarters. Maum Guinea had sent the young folks on first, remaining behind only long enough to cover the fire and fasten the door of her cabin, as if she had retired for the night.

"It's full ten o'clock; they'll be going home in two hours. You'll be missed den, sartain; but probably not before dat. 'Perion, did you help yourself to Massa Philip's revolver?"

"I did. But I wouldn't use it 'gainst any of *dem*. I t'ought of painters, or wolves, maybe, in de woods."

"And I have a knife," continued Maum Guinea. "Here, Rose, put dese yere biscuits in your pocket—mine is full. Come along."

She strode on as rapidly as if the sun lighted her footsteps, followed by Hyperion, dragging Rose by the hand, who had to run to keep up with them. Fantastic clouds, rugged and black, fled across the starlit sky—not more swiftly and violently than the poor fugitives beneath fled across the open fields. When they came to the edge of the great forest, they paused for a moment.

"Which way?" whispered Maum Guinea.

"Towards de lake," replied Hyperion. "Dar is a cave I found one day, clost by de water. W'en it begins to get daylight, I can find it, and we can crawl in dar."

"Oh, dear! w'at if dar were painters in dar, 'Perion?"

The young man pressed the trembling fingers of the timid girl—poor creature! so cowardly, so superstitious, so sensitive to cold and darkness, it was no wonder she trembled with fright and chilliness. The firm grasp of his hand reassured her, as they entered the gloomy wood. The real difficulties of the flight were just begun. Not a gleam of the dim starlight penetrated the shadows, except at intervals, where it would glimmer upon the water of treacherous marshes. Stumbling over logs, becoming entangled in brushwood, with nothing but instinct, as it were, to tell them the direction they should take, they made their way slowly and painfully; in doubt then, if they were really going toward the lake, but anxious, at all events, to get as far into the forest as possible, before the daylight should come to the aid of their pursuers. If they had ventured to light a pine-knot torch, they might have made much more rapid progress, and been sure of their route; but their flight might be already discovered, and the light be a snare to draw attention upon them. So they pressed forward, stumbling, crawling, running, as they could, through the thick darkness. After many hours of such journeying, they were rejoiced by coming suddenly upon the banks of the lake; they heard its soft ripple, and saw its waters flash back the evanescent gleam of beclouded stars. It would be in vain to search for the secret opening to the cave in such a night as surrounded them. Weary, and holding in their panting breath to listen for the dreaded sounds of pursuit, they rested upon a decaying log, waiting for the first gray light—they knew it could not be far distant. An owl in a tree overhead hooted dismally, as if in derision of their hopes and fears; at every cry of his, or the least twitter of birds in their nest, or the snapping of a twig beneath the light foot of some passing animal, Rose would cling to her lover, and his arm would tighten its grasp about her. The wind grew more chilly toward morning, and, despite her shawl, she shivered with the cold; for she was but a tropical plant, house-reared at that, tender and easily blighted.

Maum Guinea drew her knees up to her chin, and rocked herself to and fro to keep warm, and perhaps to keep down thought! Foolish fugitives! trembling in the cold and darkness. For what had they fled from comfort and plenty, from fire, food, kind masters, and easy service? Reckless, ungrateful, improvident creatures! Hyperion had spent his whole life on the Fairfax plantation; he had always been petted, done little work, and had especial indulgence. How had his masters wronged *him*, that he should repay them thus, by betaking himself off, at a loss to them of eighteen or twenty hundred dollars. The man had his own thoughts, as he sat there one long hour of that winter night. He had not studied Master Philip's mirror in vain. He knew that he looked as much like that dashing and chivalrous young gentleman, as one half-brother is apt to look like another. He did not know who his mother was, and Colonel Fairfax was not as proud of him as of his legitimate son; though he had always done him the justice to regard him as a fine piece of property. The Colonel had just given a festival of rejoicing over the betrothal of one son, and Judge Bell, that excellent citizen, had just sold this girl here by his side, to whom *he* was affianced, to raise the means of bestowing his daughter with becoming *éclat* upon that favored son.

That splendid reasoning faculty, developed to such a subtle degree of fineness in the brain of the pure-blooded white, had not as yet attained such power in this six-eighths mulatto-man; he did not deduce from these facts the overwhelming arguments which proved their righteousness to the entire satisfaction of the owners, at that moment engaged in bitter denunciation of his baseness—perhaps he did not reason at all; it was all passion with him, and not logic; he loved the dark beauty who clung to him in the shadows—he hated that rich gentleman who had come up from New Orleans to buy that which her love had promised to him; and under the impulse of these two wild passions, he had fled. Any one can read, at a glance, his want of wisdom and his wretched ingratitude; no one can blame the two gentlemen who denounce him with such harshness, as they stride up and down the portico, and wait for their horses to be brought by the first red streak of morning. We feel that they have been robbed and disappointed. One has lost two of his very best animals, and the other will have to meet a five thousand dollar note under intensely provoking circumstances. What is most conducive to the financial prosperity of a nation at once becomes right—and what is best for the financial interests of these two individuals is, of course, right, and they have our sympathy. No human understanding could be so dull as not to comprehend the excuse they had for impatience and occasional light-swearing; the deep chagrin and irritation which took the place of the jovial good-humor of the previous evening.

In the mean time, "the rain falls upon the just and the unjust"—the same red streak of dawn which shows them the road glimmering across the country, shows to Hyperion familiar scenery which indicates his proximity to the place of refuge. They travel along the edge of the water for a half-mile further, and then the man creeps on his hands and knees, passing under bushes and tangled vines, while the women wait and tremble, for it is growing lighter every moment. Birds begin to chirp and flutter, the soft, gurgling notes of the wild-turkey resound through the wood, a bar of gold is lifted from the eastern gates, and morning is let in—the bosom of the lake flashes rose-red; little frosty points glitter here and there on trees and clumps of dried grass—suddenly there is a great crash in the underbrush not a rod away, and Rose flings herself into Maum Guinea's arms, screaming:

"We's caught! we's caught!"

"Hush, chile," whispered the woman, sternly, "it's only a deer!"

Ah, yes! it was a beautiful deer coming to the lake for his morning draught; but at sight of the group he had startled, he bounded off, as startled as they—and Rose drew a long breath of relief.

The fright made them all nervous; it seemed to Hyperion as if there was a mist before his eyes which prevented his finding what he knew was there, while Maumy pressed in her arms the timid creature whose heart fluttered wildly against her own—keeping, at the same time, a keen glance wandering in every direction.

"Oh, 'Perion, I's afraid it's not here at all!"

"Don't say so, Rose; I know it is here, somewhere."

"Hark!" said Maum Guinea. "I hear a horn!"

Hyperion straightened himself up to listen.

"Yes," he replied, "they are in the woods now."

"T'ank de Lord! here is de cave! Quick, Rose, Maumy!"

The woman stooped down and crawled through the low opening from before which he had parted the dripping moss and dried vines. It was all darkness and uncertainty before them, detection and despair outside.

Hyperion quickly followed, replacing the door which nature had hung before the grotto, as carefully as possible. They crept back as far as they dared, and sat huddled together on the damp, cold rock which floored the cavern. All was doubt and night about them, though they could watch the gleam of day which pierced the curtain at the entrance. As the sun rose higher, there was more light about them; they could dimly discern their surroundings; so that Rose could convince herself that no crouching panther was near, to spring upon them unaware.

Dismal hours crept by like slimy snails. Fatigue overpowered the young girl, and with head on Maumy's bosom, she slept, her hand still clasped by her lover, whose eyes were fixed upon her face, constantly—a face delicate and pretty, even with the brilliant eyes shut in slumber, and in this wan light looking white and clear as marble.

It was afternoon when she awoke, quite ready to eat the dry biscuit, and the slice of ham, which Maum Guinea drew from her ample pocket. While they were partaking of this considerately-provided lunch, they heard sounds which arrested every faculty, holding it in strained suspense.

The horn which they had heard in the morning resounded through the woods, so close at hand that it seemed almost at the entrance of the cave.

It was followed by the voices of men, and the barking of a dog. By the shouts and excited conversation, it was plain that the party thought themselves on the track of the fugitives.

"Do you s'pose dey would bring dem turrible dogs?" whispered Rose.

"Never!" responded Maum Guinea, emphatically; "neider of our masters would do *dat*."

"I's got lead 'nuff here to kill a couple of bloodhounds," muttered Hyperion, grasping his revolver, while a fierce fire burned in his eyes.

"I'm not 'fraid of *one*," answered Maum Guinea, looking at her knife, "but massa wouldn't do *dat*. Dey don't keep 'em, and dey wouldn't be known to borrow 'em. 'Sides, dey don't want to tear dis yere purty flesh—'twouldn't be worf five t'ousand dollars, after de dogs had worried it,"—and she laid her hand on the girl's shoulder. "If 'twas only my ole bones, 'twouldn't matter."

"Dat cursed Bruno will hunt me out, dough," suddenly exclaimed the man, almost aloud; and surely enough, the next moment, whining and barking around their hiding-place, the dog came.

They heard him scratching at the vines, and then he bounded through the frail barrier, and ran up to them with a rejoicing look. He was a fine, large animal, owned by Philip, and had always been an especial favorite with Hyperion, whose liking he had faithfully returned. Totally unconscious of the peril in which he was placing his friend, he leaped around him caressingly, with quick cries of excitement and pleasure.

"Lie down, sir! be still!" said the man, in a low, stern voice; but the dog was too much excited by his discovery to obey with his usual alacrity.

In that time of danger, Hyperion would have shot down the animal, much as he liked him, but the report of the pistol would be yet more fatal. Maum Guinea, powerful and self possessed, seized the dog's head, and drew the sharp meat-knife which she carried, firmly across his throat.

"Poor Bruno!" murmured Rose, as he rolled over in death.

And then the trio waited in such suspense as is agony of itself.

The dog had so torn and trampled the vines which previously concealed the entrance, as to make its discovery an easy matter; and doubtless the men were close upon his tracks. A man parted the bushes, peered in, stooped, crawled through the opening, and stood before them, regarding the group with a curious and mingled expression. It was Johnson, of Judge Bell's plantation—they were discovered! Hyperion might have killed him, but he would have been compelled ultimately to surrender, and it was not in his heart to kill any one of his pursuers—unless it might be Rose's new owner. He looked in the agitated faces before him, and his eyes finally settled upon the girl's. She threw up her hands, imploringly:

"Jonson," she whispered, "*you* will not tell on us?"

"Good-bye, Rose; if you get off from here, don't forget Jonson."

He turned abruptly, and had just made his way out, and pulled the bushes hastily over the spot, when others came up, and they heard him say:

"Where's Bruno? I've been chasing him up, as he seems to be on track of suthin; but he's gone off in dat thicket now. 'Pears to me dat brush looks rudder suspicious. Dar ain't nothin' to be seen 'round here. Let's 'xamine dat brush-heap,"—and the party went away, leaving the fugitives another respite.

The sound of pursuit did not again approach so near them: but they had been too thoroughly alarmed to recover even the small measure of repose they had enjoyed through the morning. The afternoon wore away wearily. As the darkness began to close up the mouth of the cave, poor Rose's courage almost gave way. She was cold and hungry, thirsty and weary, her bones ached, and her flesh quivered; her mind was full of apprehension of wild animals which might be coming home to their lairs; she thought of Miss Virginia, and her pleasant chamber full of warmth and light—and again she thought of Mr. Talfierro, and nestling closer to her lover, borrowed from his superior strength and courage, energy to endure her trials.

When it was quite night, they crept forth, to drink of the waters of the lake, and to stretch their cramped and chilly limbs. It had been discussed whether they had better start that night, and try to make their way to the river, or wait where they were for a day or two, until the woods had been thoroughly searched, and the chase abandoned. As they had enough food to keep them from perishing, for a couple of days, and were now probably more secure where they were for the present, they decided to remain one day longer in their hiding-place. When they had quaffed the water for which they had been longing many hours, and eaten the one biscuit apiece which Maum Guinea distributed, they gathered branches of hemlock, and armsful of dry grass, which they carried into the cave, to make their damp resting-place more endurable. In order to break off branches where the disturbance would not be observed by any passing eye, Hyperion climbed trees, and selected them from the upper portions. It was a relief to them to have something wherewith to busy themselves, and they were almost sorry when their work was done.

A little while they sat on the bank, listening to the soft plash of the water, and looking at the dancing stars, glimmering like shivered diamonds in the bosom of the lake. Maum Guinea sat a little apart from the young couple, lost in her own peculiar reveries; while they, thus together, whose lips and hands could touch at will, were happy, despite the threatening circumstances which surrounded them.

"I t'ink we're going to have good times, 'fore long, Rose," whispered her lover. "If we get on a boat, and get safe to a free State, den we have no more trouble. We'll be married right away; and we'll keep house of our own—nobody only you and I and Maumy. Maumy will cook, and you will sew for ladies, and I will do—oh, many t'ings! We'll live right nice. No rich gentleum won't come for to buy you dar—we'll be married man and wife like white folks. And our pretty pickaninnies won't be sold 'way from us dar, Rose."

The girl laughed, and slapped his cheek; if there had been light, he might have seen the rich blood, which thrilled through her frame at his words, rush into her cheeks with a dark glow which had a beauty of its own.

So they talked and caressed each other, until the bitter reality of their situation was almost forgotten.

"Come," said Maum Guinea, after a time, "we must sleep what we can to-night; for to-morrow night, de Lord willin', we'll be marching for a better land dan dis."

Ah! a better land.

They crept back into the cave. The fragrant hemlock, and crisp, elastic grass made a comparatively comfortable couch; Maumy made of her bosom a pillow for Rose, and the three slept securely in their novel bedchamber.

"Oh, I's so tired!" exclaimed Rose, in her childlike manner, as the long hours of the succeeding day crept onward, with nothing to vary their monotony. "Maumy, don't you remember you partly promised to tell us a story 'bout your self? I wish you'd tell it now. Do, Maumy, I's so tired."

"Better not tell it, 'till we're safe away from dis yere country. 'Might make you low-spirited, chile; and you'll need all your courage."

"I'd rudder you'd tell it now. When we get 'way from here, I don't want to hear t'ings to make me sad—want to forget 'em. Do, Ginny! my head aches, and the time is so long."

"I never have tole it to nobody," muttered the woman.

"Maybe you'd feel better to tell it to *us*, Maumy."

"Ah! I never 'spect to feel better on dis yearth, chile. Folks gets where dar ain't any comfort for 'em, sometimes. But seeing I'm yer maumy now, sartain, and have took up my lot wid yours, whatever happens, maybe I'll tell it to ye."

She sat silent a few moments, as if making up her mind to the effort. Dew dripped from the dark rocks above them; the only light was the dull glimmer at the mouth of the cave; the dreariness of the place was indescribable, and her mood was just desperate enough to impel her to the narrative which hitherto had never passed her lips. With her two eager listeners gazing into her strange, expressive face, Maum Guinea began her story.

CHAPTER X.

MAUM GUINEA'S STORY.

Soft my heart, and warm his wooing,
What we did seemed, while 'twas doing,
Beautiful and wise;
Wiser, fairer, more in tune
Than all else in that sweet June,
And sinless as the skies
That warmed the willing earth, thro' all the languid skies.
SYDNEY DOBELL.

And closer, closer to her heart,
She held the little child,
Who stretched its fragile hand to feel
Her bosom's warmth, and smiled.

But she—she did not own a touch
Of that fond little hand—
Great God! that such a thing should be,
Within a Christian land!—ALDRICH.

"WHEN I was a little girl I lived on de banks of de James river. 'Twas a purty place, and we b'longed to a right nice family; we use to pride ourselves on our family. We held our heads mighty high 'kase we b'long to Massa Gregory. De house was big and han'some; dar was flowers all about it, and gardens, and de lawn in front run straight down to de river. I use to set under de big trees and see de water flow by, all blue and full of gold sparkles. Nebber, nebber do I look up to de Almighty's heaben above us, w'en it's bright and full of stars, but I minds de James river, and de days w'en I was a girl. I was a wild kind of a cre'tur—not bad, but full of fun and mischief; I was happy all day long; and I was so pert dey let me be, and didn' ask me to work not enough to hurt a chicken. Massa was a pleasant man; he 'lowed his slaves to l'arn to read, if dey want to, and to go to meetin'; he nebber whip 'em, 'less dey was awful bad, and prowoked him to it. Missus was a Christian lady, jest as sweet and pious as de Lord ever made. She took a liking to me, and she learned me to read de Bible, in her own room; and she taught me how it was wicked to do wrong, and w'at it was to be good and do right. I had no parents, dat I knew, and she sort of petted me and kep' me 'round her, doing light work for her, like sewing and such, and I had more'n half my time to myself. She dressed me nice, and taught me to be tidy and careful. I loved her so much, I tried to do jest as she wanted, but I was wild, and I used to play too much, and tear my frocks and lose things. Den she'd scold me so softly, it broke me down worse dan if she was ugly, and I'd cry and try to do better. Her eyes wasn't berry strong, and she learned me to read so well, I had to read de Bible to her mos' ebery evening, and always on de Sabbath day. I didn't like it, 'cause it was so solemn, and I'd rudder be in de kitchen, cuttin' up, or out on de lawn a lookin' at de flowers and water; but I wouldn' let on I didn' like it, fear I'd hurt her feelings. She'd t'ink it was awful if I'd say I didn't like de Bible. I *did* love it, only it was so sober, and I was so full of fun; and it use to make me feel pleasant and patient, and I was fond of hearing my missus pray, too—she use to pray for *me* well as for white folks, and for her servants as if dey was her chil'ren. She was so beautiful, I never tired looking at Missus Gregory; not dat she was young, for she was growin' past middle-age, but her face was so sweet, and she allers wore such fine lace on her caps and about her throat and wrists, and her cheeks were so pale and fine, and her hands so white, and she was so graceful and such a perfect lady. I've nebber seen her like to dis day.

"She tried not to make too much of any of her yearthly idols, but her heart was sot on her boy. Most while, w'en I was a growing girl, he was up North at college. He was an only chile, and fadder and mudder bof t'ought dar nebber was anodder like him. W'en his letters use to come, dey would read 'em so eager and laugh ober 'em; and bym-bye missus would 'teal up-stairs and read 'em again, and kiss 'em, and sit wid 'em in her lap, looking out de window and smiling to herself.

"One winter we was going to hab grand times at Chris mas, for young Massa Dudley was comin' home for good and all. He'd done got tru' wid school, and was comin' home a young gentleum. Missus was glad, 'cause he was not going back; and we was tickled, 'cause we t'ought dar would be gay times wid young massa in de house.

"De cook, she was busy for weeks. She took me in de kitchen, mornin's, and made me help her stone raisins and chop apples, and beat eggs and mix up cake—den was when I took my first lesson in cookin'. I liked to go dar 'cause de merry clatter of de dishes, and all de nice articles she was at liberty to use, made it pleasant; and she'd gib me bunch of raisins and piece of citron or orange for being good 'bout helpin' her. We made cake 'nuff for a weddin'; and mince-pies, and ebery t'ing nice dat would keep; and jest afore de day, all sorts of t'ings besides. 'Peared as if ole cook 'membered ebery dish dat massa Dudley liked 'specially well, and dat was good many, for w'en he'd been home of holidays he'd commonly been blessed wid a growin' appetite.

"Laws! day 'fore Chris'mas, w'at a lookin' for de stage dar was! Even missus couldn' keep 'way from de winder and little Peter, de waiter-boy, he sot out on top de fence on a little rise of groun', to be de first to tell de news. Dinner was nigh done bein' ready, and Dinah was beginning to fret; I'd gone and put on a clean frock to help wait on table, and missus had pulled de parlor curtains open fifty times, w'en Peter gib a shout, and we all run, and de stage come a-rollin 'long and stopped 'fore de house. 'Tain't much, to hear me tell de little pertickelers; but it was much to *me*, in dem days, and I's nebber forgot de smallest circumstance. W'en Massa Dudley sprung out de stage, light as a feader, de people dey all rushed 'round a-kissin' him and shakin' hands—ole nurse she hugged him right 'round de neck, and he laughed and was mighty good-natured, but hurried 'way from us up to de porch, where missus was standin' wid her shawl 'round her, waiting to welcome him home. *I* didn' speak to him, nor shake hands like de rest; and w'en dinner was on de table, I didn' like to go in de room to wait on it. He looked so *perfeck* w'en he sprung out de stage, dat I jus' shrunk away and didn' dar' to speak to him. Sassy as I was, and full of laugh and fun, I hadn' a word to say, but jus' stood back so he wouldn' notice me.

"I's a-going to tell you jus' how foolish I was; I shan't spare myself. W'en de bell rung for dinner, I went into cook's bedroom, off de cabin, and took a look in a little glass she kep' hanging dar. 'Twas de firs' time in my life I had t'ought 'bout how I looked. Ah! w'at a silly chile I was! as if it made speck o' difference to Massa Dudley how a nigger look! but I'd been sp'iled and petted, and I was jus' sixteen year ole, and nebber had felt serious, 'cept on Sundays, since I was born. I t'ought my pink frock was mighty purty, and I tossed my goold ear-rings for all de worl' as Rose tosses her's when she feels sperited and bright. I was proud of my hair, 'cause 'twas long enuff to braid, and real shiny; but w'en I looked in de glass I wished I wasn't nigger at all. I wished I was all white 'stead of part.

"Dey had a merry dinner—so much talk, so many t'ings to tell; and Massa Dudley, he tell such cur'ous stories he keep 'em laughing half de time. I could see how proud his mudder was. He was so glad to be to home, his eyes shone and his cheeks was red; he was as gay as a kitten, and he praised all de dishes, and eat 'nuff to satisfy ole cook, almost. I couldn' look up, hardly, I felt so shy, which was new for me; and w'en dinner was mos' done finished, he noticed me, and says to his mudder:

"'Who you got dar? a new girl? Bless me, if it ain't little Ginny grown up like a sunflower! She makes you a nice maid, don't she, mudder?'

"'Yes, Ginny is a great help to me. She's my right hand, said missus, and den I felt happy to be praised by *her*; but I darsn't look up, and young massa laugh, and say:

"''Twas right new to see a bashful darkey.'

"Woll, dey had a merry Chris'mas; nebber was a merrier Chris'mas on de ole Gregory plantation; young massa made de house as bright as a streak of sunshine; dar was company, and music, and feasting, till after New Year's. I had a good time waitin' on de company, and seein' all de frolicks, 'sides having presents and a share of all de niceties. I felt happy; but 'twas a queer feeling, not like I used to w'en I romped on de lawn and cut up all kind o' mischief; I was quiet and proper, so dat missus praised me, and was pleased de way I waited on her visitors.

"After dat I was more her favorite dan ever. She learned me to sew nice and 'broider, and I 'broidered pair o' slippers for her son, w'ich she wanted to give him; I read to her evenings, and it wasn't so tiresome to me den, 'cause de weader was cold, and I couldn' go a-rambling over de lawn and down de river, as I did in summer. I was so quiet and orderly, and read de Bible so willin', missus t'ought I was going to be good Christian girl, and she said I might jine de church if I wanted. But I said I'd wait till spring.

"Woll, it come spring. De flowers begun to blow open in de soft mornin's; de sky was full of pur'y clouds, de winds talk, de birds sing, and my heart—poor, foolish, colored-girl's heart—grow fuller and fuller, till I couldn' breaf no more in de house, and one warm night, just afore dark, I run down to de edge of de water, and stand and look at de little sparkles of sunshine not quite gone 'way on de ripples; and I heard somebody come whistlin' and singing to hisself along de bank. I wanted to run back, but I couldn' stir a step; my heart beat so hard, and I jus' purtended I didn' see him, and w'en he come close by I didn' look up at all; so he stops side of me, and says:

"'Look up, Ginny. I've been home three months, and I've never seen your eyes yet, you shy little thing.'

"I had to mind him; and I 'spect he saw right tru' my eyes what was in my heart, but I couldn' help it to save my life.

"'You've got han'some eyes, Ginny,' says he, 'dey're de softest and brightest ever I saw,'—and den he stooped, picking up pebbles and t'rowing 'em into de water, and bym-bye he asked me what I was looking at so steady, when he come along; and I told him I loved de James river, and I often come and look at de water w'en it was full of sparkles. He made me talk, and I got over bein' so bashful, and felt so strange and happy in his company, and he kep' his eyes on my face, and smiled so sweet, and we stood dar till it was quite dark, w'en he said:

"'I declar', you're quite a girl, Ginny—mudder is learning you too much. You must give me a kiss, Ginny, to pay for being so purty,'—and he put his arm around my waist, and kissed me, and laughed a little.

"I run away, frightened and happy too. W'en I got near de house, missus called me out de window to come up and read my evening chapter. I could hardly see de words, dey danced so, and I couldn' tell one t'ing I'd been a-readin' 'bout w'en I got tru'. I sot by de window, de Bible in my lap, and I got looking at de stars, and t'inking of Massa Dudley, and I didn' hear missus till she'd spoke to me twice.

"'Ginny,' said she, again, very stern for her, 'I see suthin to-night that displease me very much.'

"I hung my head, for I knew den she'd been looking out de window, and seen us togedder down by de river; I hadn' t'ought nor done nothing wicked, but I felt 'shamed and guilty for all.

"'Mind, Ginny,' she said, 'I don't blame *you*—it's my son dat's to blame if any thing wrong should happen. But I want to warn you. I shall speak to him also. You mus' remember what you've learned in dat Holy Book—if you sin you won't be ignorant, for I've taught you your duty. I want you to be a good girl and a Christian. God has made you of a different color and race from us; but he has given you sense enough to know what's right and proper. Some missuses is willin' der slaves should do wrong; but I am not. Be a good girl, and you shall have a worthy husband from among your own people one of dese days. Don't forget what I've said, Ginny.'

"Dear missus! she was almost a saint. I wanted to kneel down and kiss her hand, and promise to mind her faithfully, but my t'roat choked up, and I went out silent. If I'd followed her advice, I'd saved myself lots o' trouble. I did mind it for a while—but 'de heart is deceitful above all t'ings, and desp'rately wicked,' and I 'spect mine was one of de worst. Leastwise, it deceived *me*. What I was doin' 'peared to me right at de time. I wasn't sorry, I wasn't 'shamed—only I didn't want missus to know it. Dat spring and summer I was berry happy. I use to take my sewing and set under a great elm tree by de water's edge, singing softly to myself—never 'flecting 'bout de future—jus' as gay and karless as de birds overhead; only once-and-awhile I'd take fits of thinking, and den I'd be way down low-sperited.

"So one day I was sewing in missus' chamber. and I wasn't very well, and I got dizzy and couldn't sew for a little w'ile, and she took notice of me. I t'ink she was as angry as she ever 'lowed herself to be; and I t'ink she was more hurt at her son dan she was angry wid me; for I know she talked to him dat evening long time, and nex' day he went off to an uncle's, and didn' come back for a fortnight.

"I was dreadful hurt and grieved to t'ink missus 'spised me, and couldn't abide me 'round her any more. She didn' let me read to her, nor set in her room to sew; but made me go to Chloe's cabin, and dar I lived till my baby was born. 'Twas a little girl, most as white as anybody's chile. Missus nebber come to see it, dough she sent me nice t'ings for it to wear and for me to eat when I was getting well. Den it was I 'gan to 'flect on what I was and what I'd done. If I'd been like mos' niggers I shouldn't a cared a speck; I'd taken it easy and been idle and karless. But somehow I was allers deeper in my feelings dan most colored folks; and missus' teaching had made me more so.

"My baby was the purtiest little cre'tur that ever lived. I loved her. If I was to tell you a t'ousand times you couldn' guess how much I loved her. W'en she was asleep, I'd sit and watch her all de time; w'en she was awake in my lap, I'd look into her eyes and never get tired. She had such beautiful eyes—blue—yes, chil'ren, her eyes were blue as Massa Dudley's—and so soft and smiling; and her head was covered with little black shiny rings of silky hair; and, though she was dark-complected, she had red lips, and rich dimples in her golden arms and neck. Every body said she was a perfect beauty.

"I'd a been perfectly happy with my baby, only I wanted

Massa Dudley to see her, and he never come near us. She was born in the winter; and the first time I saw him after it, was when I was setting up at the window, quite well, and holding up little Judy, trying to make her laugh. He went by de cabin, wid his gun on his shoulder, going a-hunting, and he looked up and laughed, and asked me how I was getting along; but he didn't notice baby, only wid a queer, quick kind o' look, and den he hurried on as if he was 'fraid of something.

"I didn' see him to speak to him till spring-time come again; but I comforted myself t'inking how purty Judy was growing, and how we'd 'joy ourselves playin' on de lawn, in de grass, w'en warm weader come. So one day I was setting on de door-step of our cabin, and Massa Dudley come along, and dis time he stop and speak to us; it was jus' a year from de time he first spoke to me down by de river, and my heart was full, a-t'inking of it, 'fore I heard him coming.

"'You're better-lookin' dan ever, Ginny,' says he, wid his ole smile. 'You make a right nice maumy. Is dis your baby? She's a bright little thing. I'm sure Madam Gregory needn't have scolded us so for our naughty doings. Your baby'll sell for a t'ousand dollars by time you're ready to wean it. It's good property. Never seen a nicer darkey,'— and he laughed and chucked me under de chin, and went off whistlin'.

"It was a bright spring day, full of sunshine; but it grew suddenly dark to me—dark and cold. My heart grew cold. Yes, chil'ren, it grew so cold, it's never been really warm since. Only the feel of the children's soft hands in my bosom has kept it warm at all. I sot still till night, till ole Chloe call me in, tellin' me Judy would cotch cold. I went in and warmed my baby by de fire whar supper was cooked; I rubbed her little cold feet, and nussed her, but half my comfort in her was took away—done gone forever. I knew now, dat de purtier and de smarter she was, de more likely I was to lose her—de brighter she was, de more money she was worf! Den I had my own selfish trouble. I loved young massa—loved him jus' as well as w'ite folks love—mighty sight better dan de most. I 'dored the very yearth he trod on—and it broke my heart to hab him speak so to me. I oughter have 'spected it—I'd no reason to 'spect anyt'ing else. I knew I was a slave—a poor, ignorant colored person; an' dat I'd no business to feel hurt. Folks would have laughed to know I felt bad 'bout his speaking so. '*Course* he'd act so and feel so. I was a fool, and I knew it. I didn't blame him, 'cause I'd nothing to blame. I only loved him all de more, and wished he'd come about and be as kind to me as he used to be.

"But he didn't take much notice of me dat summer. I guess his mudder talked him out of it—'sides, he was 'way visiting good deal, and by fall it began to be talked on de plantation dat Massa Dudley was goin' soon to bring a bride to de ole Gregory mansion.

"Everybody but me was tickled 'bout it—de darkeys like weddings and merry times, and dey's allers pleased when sich t'ings are coming off. My heart was sore; but nobody knew nuffin' 'bout it. I was so quiet and humble—not sassy and set-up, like some of de girls—dat missus took me back into her favor. I t'ink she was sorry for me, dough she said nothing. I was 'round de house a good deal, sewing and waiting on her; but I couldn' keep my baby tru' de day; it was sent off, wid de oder babies, to de pen for ole Chloe to mind; I had it to sleep wid me nights, and I went to nurse it once or twice a day to de pen. I felt cu'ros 'bout my baby; I couldn' b'ar to have it 'sociate wid de oder little niggers in de pen. I made its clothes good, and it was always clean when I give it to ole nurse; but it would always get dirty rollin' 'round and playing wid de rest. Nobody knew how I felt about it, and Chloe would jeer me for keeping it so fine; but dey t'ought it was 'cause I could sew so nice, and oder women jus' had rags on der chil'ren.

"Some time in de summer, wid missus' advice and consent, I jined de church. De church was a great comfort to me, and I t'ink it relieved Massa Dudley's mind, too; he was glad to get rid of me so, for he knew I was of a terrible passionate disposition, and he hadn't cared to see me 'round much, after he'd got engaged to be married.

"'Read your Bible, Ginny, and be a good girl,' he says to me, kind of mock-solemn, wid dat naughty laugh dat allers make him look so han'some, but dat showed de Lucifer dar was in him—it was de day he was going off for to bring his bride home.

"I forgot w'at de good Book says about doing good to dem dat despitefully use you; my cheeks got hot, and my eyes flashed fire, for I t'ought he was kinder making fun of me, and de more I loved him, de more I couldn't b'ar it.

"'Give my respects to your wife. I hope I shall like her mighty well!' I answered back, so spiteful dat it sobered him down, and he shook his finger at me, and said:

"'Take car', Ginny! don't you go to being naughty—if you get ill-tempered, we may have to sell you!'—and he walked off so haughty, as masters can walk, w'en dey walk over brack people's feelin's.

"It didn't put me in a very good humor for seeing de bride. I kep' brooding over it all de week de family was away. I worked hard, dough, to keep from getting bitter, and I done my work right well. I made de bride's chamber look beautiful, and I helped Dinah wid de cake and fixin's, doin' almost better dan she. I'd been considered to hab good taste, for a slave-girl; I could draw patterns for embroidery, and my needlework was beautiful; so I sot to work to see how well I could make t'ings look de day dey was all 'spected back. I put flowers in de wedding-chamber and parlors, and set de table splendid—de butler he jus' stand back and let me fix it.

"Woll, I t'ink a woman is a woman, if she *have* got brack blood in her. W'en all was done, I went and changed my own dress. I made myself look jus' as handsome as I could. I had some corals missus had gib me, and I put 'em in my hair; I had a silk dress, and I put it on, wid some bows of red ribbon. I'd never worked enough to spile my hands, and I was proud of 'em 'cause dey was slender and soft. Den I dressed up little Judy in a w'ite frock, wid a string of beads round her neck and bows on her shoulders, and I brushed out her ha'r till it was all in shiny rings down onto her neck; I got a bouquet of flowers, which I intended to give to de bride when she come in de hall; and I waited wid de rest of de serbants.

"Dar was a great time when Massa Gregory drew up wid his wife; and after dem, young massa wid his bride. De whole plantation was a laughing and shakin' hands, and wishin' 'em joy, and ole Dinah was a-making herself very conspicuous, as usual. I stood back to see how de bride looked. I'd a burning curiosity to see if she was beautiful, and as much of a lady as my missus. Dey say jealousy makes people's eyes sharp. De minit I looked at her I knowed she was a cold-hearted, selfish kind of a woman, who'd married Massa Dudley 'cause he was rich and good family. She was 'bout nineteen or twenty; tall, rather pale, with gold colored hair and very delicate features. She was a good form, and would have passed for a beauty most anywhar; but *I* didn't t'ink she was beautiful. She was too quiet and cold—she hadn' no color nor sparkle 'bout her. I t'ought she was tired of al. de 'gratulations and hand-shaking, and so on; but she was too artful to show it, and smiled pleasantly at everybody. I stood in de hall, holdin' Judy's hands, wid my flowers all ready to pursent w'en she come in. I was de last to speak to her. She took my bouquet very gracious, and den she stooped and patted Judy on de head—she wanted to seem good-natured, to get de good-will of de people.

"'W'at a lovely child!' said she; 'is she yours, girl?'

"I don' know w'at demon made me answer:

"'Yes, mine and Massa Dudley's.'

"Nobody heard me but she, I spoke so low; she cast a glance at her husband, and then back to me—I knew I was as handsome as she was, any day, and I didn' care—I felt so wicked jus' den.

"She made no answer, of course; she was surprised at my impudence, and I ought to have been punished for it, I know; but her eyes spoke as plain as words, before she swep' by me:

"'I'll have you whipped and sold before long, girl.'

"I was sorry de next minit—not on my own account, but Massa Dudley's, and my own dear missus. I'd made an enemy, widout gaining anyt'ing by it—not dat I s'posed she'd t'ink of it long, or car' for it—such t'ings too common; but I was too han'some, and had been too impertinent 'bout it, to be 'scused as a common case.

"I was sorry I'd said it, 'cause I felt I'd done Massa Dudley an injury; I loved him too well to want to harm him; I'd a laid down my life for him, any day, dough he cared no more for me dan if I was cattle; it was only w'en de w'ite blood in me took fire and blazed up, dat I did sich hateful t'ings. White blood proud and 'vengeful—brack blood warm and kind. I 'dored him wid de wild heart of brack woman, and sometimes I hated him wid proud heart of white woman

—for, ye see, de blood is mixed in our veins, chil'ren—its all mixed up and fermenting, and it makes trouble. Dem blue eyes of Miss Dudley Gregory was cold and sharp as steel—dey went tru' me wid a pang, and dey made me feel wicked for a spell. But I was a member of de church, and tried to be a Christian; I prayed de Lord forgive me, 'fore I went in de dining-room, and I got de ugly feelin' down. I was sorry; I would have begged de young missus' pardon, if I'd had a chance. All I could do was to be submissive and humble—to put de *pert* all out my manners; so I waited on de company jus' as well as I knew how, and paid 'tention to nothing but my work.

"Dar was dancing and music dat ebening; de parlors were lighted all up like de sun; my breast was sad, I didn' know why, but I kep' 'way from de house, setting under de oak down by de river, listening to the murmur of de water, wid little Judy fas' asleep in my arms. De sound of de water kind o' got in my head, and whirled and sung so sorrowful—hark, chil'ren! do you hear de lake out dar talking?—it's saying de same t'ings now.

"Bym-bye, de house settled back in de ole ways; 'cepting dar was no more company coming and going; young missus was fond of showing off in such times, and Massa Dudley was proud of her looks, and dressed her splendid. She wanted me for dressin'-maid, I had such taste; but I begged Missus Gregory to let me off, which she was kind enough to do, and 'lowed me to gib up waitin', and take to cookin'. I didn' fancy cookin'-work, but it kep' me from de house, and give me peace of mind; it was hard, and sp'iled my hands, but I wasn't proud any more, and I prayed every night for de welfar' of de whole family. I *couldn'* like young missus, but I could pray for her. I never knew whedder Missus Gregory like her new daughter, or not; I t'ink she know she was vain and selfish; but she was so kind and charitable she would try to have good influence widout saying much 'bout it.

"Woll, time run along, winter and summer, winter and summer, t'ree, four years. Judy growed into a bright little girl, trottin' round, taking care of herself. If I say it, who was her mudder, de sun never shone on anodder such a chile—she was beautiful as an angel—*everybody* said so. Her eyes were as dark as blue eyes could be, wid long, drooped lashes; and her hair was just one soft fleecy cloud of shining rings, blowing 'bout her face; her mouth was red as a strawberry, and her skin was handsomer dan any white chile's could be—a sort of brown, not dark, rich and smooth and velvety, wid de red in her cheeks like peaches—and her motions! seemed she didn' move nor walk like common chile. She loved de grass, and trees, and talking water, well as her maumy use to; she use to frolic 'bout on de lawn like a bird, her little red dress darting 'bout in de light and shade. Missus Gregory give me purty bits of bright calico and muslin for her frocks, and I use to set up nights to make 'em han'some. Warm weather, she wouldn' have no shoes—'twan't allowed, and her little round feet were so purty and dimpled, I was prouder of 'em dan as if dar were open-work stockings and kid slippers on 'em.

"All dis time, dar didn' come no heir to de Gregory plantation; Massa Dudley give up hopes of dar ever being one, and it worried him more dan he was willing to let on. Missus Dudley didn't car', 'cause she'd rather keep 'bout in gay company, and be admired, dan be shut up in her chamber having children; only, when she see her husband was disappointed, dat made her jealous if she see him looking at oder people's babies. She was jus' as jealous as she was selfish.

"If little Judy come 'bout de house, she'd drive her away,

and when missus would reprove her, said she couldn't abide de nigger chil'ren round her—dey'r place wasn't in de house—dey made her nervous, de little brats did. Dar was nothing 'bout Judy to make any fine lady nervous—'less de angels demselves make 'em so. I bathed her every night, and brushed her curls, and kept her neat and tidy as a rose. She was a good chile; she loved everybody; her lip would quiver when de han'some pale lady spoke so cross to her. But Missus Gregory got so she like to have little Judy come to see *her;* she taught her to read, and let her run 'bout her chamber much as she mind to. You see, missus was in a decline; she didn' 'spect to live long, and she'd got over the aversion she once felt for poor little Judy; she couldn't go out of her room much, and she liked de chile's company; it 'mused her, and passed away de time.

"I's always b'lieved 'twas missus' soft manners and heavenly face made my chile so gentle and obedient; she sort o' caught some of the dying grace of that dear missus.

"'Spect Missus Dudley never got quite over being jealous of me and spiteful at Judy. I knew well 'nuff 'twas her first put it in Massa Gregory's head dat I ought to be married.

"''Twas a shame,' she said, 'for me to be wasting my bes' days, widout a husband! W'at good would I be to de estate, living single?'

"So Massa Gregory, Massa Dudley, and young missus, dey all said I must pick out a husband from some de hands on de plantation. I jus' told 'em I *wouldn'*—I didn' want no husband—I'd work hard for 'em as long as I lived; but I begged dem not to 'sist on my marrying. Somehow, I couldn't bring my mind to it; I'd smothered my passion for my master; I'd scourged it and whipped it down; and now I was living quietly, wid my chile and my Bible for company.

and I didn't want to rile up all my peace, taking up wid a man I didn' car' for.

"I went to missus 'bout it; and she put her foot down for once, dough everybody else commonly had der own way, dat it shouldn' be—dey should let me alone—if I didn't meet anybody I wanted, I needn't get married.

"So dey let me alone for awhile, till dar come a great trouble and grief to me—my dear missus died. It broke my heart to see her go; but she went so patient and willin'. She didn' forget poor slave-girl in dat solemn time. She made her husband and son promise never to sell me nor my chile, whatever happened. She left me her Bible, and several little trinkets she knew I'd prize; and she put round little Judy's neck a string of old-fashioned gold-beads she'd worn herself. Here dey are, now, chil'ren—look at 'em—I allers keep 'em in my bosom, day and night.

"'Bout a year after missus died, ole massa said I mus' marry—couldn' have no more foolin'; I was de healthiest, bes'-looking girl he owned, and I mus' have a husband. I cried 'bout it, but I couldn't help myself. White masters owns brack folks' feelin's as well as der bodies. So I was married to Jackson, massa's teamster, who had wanted me long before, but I'd given him de mitten out-and-out. He was right black—no w'ite blood in him, good-looking and kind-tempered, and he loved me and little Judy faithfully.

"We had a little cabin of our own fixed up more comfor'-able dan de most, 'cause I had a way of keeping t'ings nice, and Jackson like to see 'em so. I did de cookin' for de house—de most of it—wid a girl to cl'ar up and do de drudgery; den I had a good-sized room of my own, 'sides de kitchen, wid a table and set o' chairs, and walences 'round de bed, and a stand for de Bible, and a bit o' carpet. Little Judy was six years ole when I married Jackson.

"Woll, we had chil'ren—four in all. I took good car' of dem; but dey never seem to me *my own*, like Judy. Dey was nice pickaninnies, some mos' as brack as der fadder, some more like der maumy—but dey was no more like Judy dan dark is like light. I couldn' help being kind to my husband, he was so good and 'tentive to me—had allers liked me ever sence he was little, and I was so good to his chil'ren—but my heart clung to my own chile more and more, wilder and wilder—oh, Lord of mercy, how I did love my Judy!

"Jackson liked her, too; he wasn't jealous 'cause I favored her; he sort of worshipped her—he told me, of'en and of'en, she was an angel, and he was 'fraid suthin would happen to her. Ah! dat was an echo of my own heart. I didn' dar' to breaf when I t'ought of it. She was too purty, too good, too 'telligent for a slave. She could read any book she laid hands on. She knew all the hymns and psalms in the hymn-book missus give me for her. She was so innocent and pious. Sometimes she played wid de worst little niggers on de plantation; but she never seemed to take harm from 'em—dust wouldn't stick to her.

"When she growed old enough to be useful, I couldn't keep her all to myself. Missus Dudley wanted her in de house. She made her wait on company, and take care of her room, and do light chamber-work. I saw Massa Dudley look at her strange sometimes. He had no chil'ren, and I b'lieve his heart yearned after her. He needn' bin ashamed to call her his daughter—she was fair enough for a king's daughter. She wasn't to blame for her brack blood. And if she'd been sent up North, 'way from her maumy, no person could have told dar was a drop of it in her veins.

"All dese days I was a-working. I sewed nights for rest de serbants; I raised chickens and wegetables of my own.

dat I ever tasted—I sol' 'em in de market, and laid de money way—not even Jackson knew 'bout dat money. He s'pected I had some, but he didn' know how much, nor where I kep' it. When missus died, she gave me twenty dollars in gold, out of her own purse-money. Dat was de beginning. You see, I had it in my mind to buy my girl's freedom. Judy shouldn't be a slave. Long as she was a little girl, I didn't mind it; but I'd allers been resolved she shouldn' grow up to be a woman, and a slave—ever since de first hour her lips touched my bosom, I'd had it in my mind. Many colored persons don't feel so; but I'd had opportunities for reading and t'inking—and, oh! I'd had plenty opportunities for *feeling.* She *wasn't* a nigger, and she *shouldn't* be a slave! De Lord hadn' set de brand of bondage on her, and man shouldn' do it.

"If I'd had my choice, I'd rudder see her married to a man as black as Jackson, than be any white massa's missus: but I'd hopes of better things dan either for her. If I could buy her freedom, could take her up North, and put her in some school, or get some white family to 'dopt her, I was bound to do it. I was resolved not to let my own feelings stan' in de way—I'd give her up—she should be free white woman, marry good white man, and her chil'ren, and her chil'ren's chil'ren, should be free. On dis my heart was sot. For dis I worked w'en I might have been idle. I took no rest. I 'couraged her to get books from massa's liberary, and read and study, so she'd have a start if she ever got in a school. She did read and study many books—it was de only deceit dat dear chile ever practise—she was so fond of books, she'd borrow 'em widout leave, 'cause massa wouldn' have allowed it. Sometimes she'd read aloud to me, when I was sewing, fine stories 'bout happy white lovers, and I t'ink to myself she should some day be as fine and as happy as dey.

"I had an ole chany tea-pot dat had been t'rown away at de house, whar I use to keep my money—gold and silver, mostly gold. Many times each year I'd count it over and over, to see how much dat golden grain had growed. Fifteen year I was a-laying up dat money—fifteen year, and I had twenty dollars to begin wid. Dar was a heap of it. It got so much, I couldn't count it; and I darsn't get nobody to do it for me. So I bought an ole 'rithmetic at a book-stall in de village, for Judy to study, and I worried over dem figgers myself, till I could get 'long and count my money. De day Judy was fifteen year ole, I counted it, and I had a t'ousand dollars. I knew massa would hold her worth more'n dat; but I 'spected he'd remember his promise to his dead wife, not to sell her, and mebbe he'd feel kindly, and willin' to let me have my own chile for dat. I could hardly keep from going right to him and asking him; but de nearer I come to parting wid Judy, de harder it was; and I t'ought, as nothing happened, and she didn' seem in danger, I'd work another year, and try and get her a little something to send her 'way up North wid. I'd give my promise to massa to come back, if he'd let me go 'long; and if I couldn't find de right folks to 'dopt her and send her to school, I'd 'prentice her to some dress-maker, so she could get her own living, and be a respectable free white woman.

"Judy was so pious and so modest, she didn' think of her looks; she didn' guess how han'some she was, and how every one turned to look after her when she passed by. I didn' want her to stir out, hardly, I was so 'fraid somebody'd want to buy her, or some de colored boys would be stepping up to her and askin' de privilege of her company. Yer needn't feel hard, 'Perion, 'cause I didn' want her to mate wid a colored man; dar was none on massa's plantation dat I felt towards as I do towards *you*—dey was coarse kind of young men, and had no learnin', and dey wasn't worthy of my Judy. Heigho! do you hear dat water in de lake keep a-moaning, Rose? I wish dis knife was out in de middle dat lake—it's horrible de way dat knife keeps a-lookin' at me!

"Did you ever hear a clap of thunder burst in a cloudless sky?—w'en de sun is shining, and dar ain't no signs of storm? One day, 'bout t'ree months after Judy was fifteen I heard dat clap of thunder break. De blue sky dat was over me and my chile showed a little cloud no bigger dan a man's hand, and dat was de beginning of de storm. Don't look at me so, chil'ren! I'm a withered and branchless old tree, knotted and scarred—for ye see, de lightning struck me, and I couldn' never bear green leaves again."

Maum Guinea rocked herself to and fro in terrible silence, while her listeners dared not interrupt her mood, by expressions of the interest which they felt. Rose wanted to press the clenched hand to her pitying bosom, but she could not break upon the tide of recollections which were rising in the story-teller's soul.

"Hark!" whispered Hyperion, suddenly.

The three started, every faculty strained and held in suspense. There was some person, or persons at the ingress to the cave—the vines were carefully lifted aside, some one bent down and forced his way in, and, just as Hyperion sprung to his feet, revolver in hand, a well-known voice exclaimed:

"Don't shoot—it's me—Johnson."

He stepped forward and shook hands with the party.

"I've come to pay you a friendly visit," he said, smiling, as Hyperion returned the threatening weapon to his pocket. "Couldn' rest, 'less I know how you was gettin' along. See here, Rose, w'at I brought you!" He tossed a great apple into her lap, and another into Maum Guinea's; then he drew from beneath his jacket a loaf of bread, some slices of cold meat, and a small flask of brandy. "If you should get sick in dis damp hole, de liquor'll be useful," he said.

"W'at's our massas doing 'bout us, now?" was the first question.

"Dat's w'at I come to let you know You see, 'twasn't easy for me to get off, 'specially in de daytime, jes' now, w'en everybody's eyes is sharpened; but I was 'fraid you'd be gone by night, and I'd miss you. I jes' want to tell you to stay where you are for a spell yet. You're safer here dan anywhar else at presen'. I'll try and keep you from starvin', and let you know when I t'ink it's least bit safe for you to try to get off."

"De Lord bless you, Johnson!" said Rose, earnestly "How's Miss Virginny?"

"She's better dan any de rest; but she ain't to be trusted, 'course, 'cause 'tain't for her interest. But she told me, confidentially, she didn't care much if you wasn' found—she hoped you would get off—"

"Dat's my own dear missus, all over," interrupted poor Rose.

"But de rest of dem, dey're awful mad. De Judge, he's mad 'cause his plans all upsot, and Massa Talfierro down on him wid a vengeance; and de Colonel he raving—he's quick-tempered, you know, anyways. He says you're an ungrateful dog, 'Perion—ha! ha!"—and there was something bitter in Johnson's laugh, as if the thought of ingratitude did not appeal to his better principles.

"Ungrateful son, he means, 'stead of dog," muttered the *valet*.

"Massa Philip he takes it easy; whistles w'en his fadder scolds, and says you ain't to blame for running away with a girl so purty as Rose; only he's deuced if he knows who's going to tie his cravat for him, and twist his mustache jes' de right twirl."

"Poor Massa Philip! I *did* hate to leave him widout nobody to take right kind o' car' of him," said the soft-hearted "boy" with an accent of self-reproach.

"As for Massa Talfierro, he's bound to find Rose. He's hired men to hunt, and he'll help pay de expenses of finding de runaways. He's a kind of man dat never gives up. He's mad as blazes 'cause he hain't had his own way—he's use to it, dat's plain—and he don't mean to be fooled by a lot o' niggers. He's swore he'll have dat devilish girl yet—so you see w'at's before you, Rose,"—the girl shuddered, and clung to her lover's arm instinctively. "I shouldn' wonder if he did w'at he said. I'm boun' to do all *I* can to save you, Rose, and dat's why I'm here. Don't you stir 'way from here jes' yit. Dey's got watches at all de river landings up and down for a good ways; dey's adwertised and got everybody lookin'. Jes' you stay here and keep quiet. I'll try and t'row 'em off de track. By time dese yere perwisions gone, I'll try and make another trip out here. I must hurry back, or I'll be s'pected. I don't want to be s'pected, 'cause I can't help you so well. Be quiet, and stop till you hear from me."

He shook hands with them, and was gone. The party felt despondent enough; the dangers of their undertaking overwhelmed them; they brooded over them in silence and misery till the twilight deepened again into desolate night; but in all three hearts was the courage to meet death rather than surrender the hope they had cherished.

"Go on with your story, Maumy, please. I shall die if I ne here thinking and dreading about myself all de time."

CHAPTER XI.

MAUM GUINEA'S STORY CONTINUED—JUDY.

The shrouded graces of her form;
The half-seen arm, so round and warm;
The little hand, whose tender veins
Branched through the henna's orange stains
The head, in act of offering bent;
And through the parted veil, which lent
A charm for what it hid, the eye,
Gazelle-like, large and dark and shy,
That with a soft, sweet tremble shone
Beneath the fervor of my own.—BAYARD TAYLOR.

A weight seemed lifted from my heart,
A pitying friend was nigh;
I felt it in his hard, rough hand,
And saw it in his eye.—WHITTIER.

Uncertainty!
Fell demon of our fears! The human soul,
That can support despair, supports not thee.—MALLET.

"I'VE told you before, dat Miss Dudley Gregory was a gay woman, fond of company and dress. 'Peared like, as time went on, and she had no chil'ren to take up her mind, she grew more extravagant dan ever. Nobody dressed so fine as missus. She mus' take trips every summer up North, and have lots o' spending money, and trunks full new clo'es; and winter-time she must give parties and keep house full of visitors all de time.

"Woll, de Gregory plantation was sort o' wearin out. Dar had been too many crops of 'baccy raised on de land; it was a-growing barren; and de income of de estate wasn' nigh what it used to be, and de expenses was more, 'cause missus would live in high style. Every little while, of late years, dey'd had to send niggers to market, 'stead of 'baccy. De proud ole Virginny planters could raise good crop of niggers, if de land *was* barren. Massa Gregory couldn' afford to feed all de pickaninnies on de place. Every little while he sold a nice, growin' chile, and sometimes a field-hand he didn' need. Dat's de way me and Jackson lost our oldest chile—a fine boy. He was sold de year before w'at I'm telling you of took place. It was mighty hard to let him go; it made us sad a long time; but we had de consolation of knowing he was tol'ably well off—he was only sold to de nex' village, to wait on a lawyer who wanted an errand-boy; and we saw him sometimes, and knew he was well took care of.

"One fine April day I was busy making pound-cake and other fixin's for dinner and tea; dar was company at de house, and dar must be extra nice dinner. Judy was settin' in de door of our own room, working a collar for missus. De door was open 'tween de two rooms, and as I flew round, busy 'bout my work, I could see her, where she sot, and I kep' thinking I never saw her look so purty. Her head was bent over her sewing; her hair fell in curls all down her cheeks and neck; her cheeks were bright; her little w'ite apron was tied neatly over her dress, so as not to soil her work, and she was singing to herself very soft and low.

"'Dar, didn' I tell you?' I suddenly heard missus say, right in front of de cabin.

"I looked out and saw her standing wid a strange gentleum looking at Judy, who was so busy she hadn' noticed 'em at all.

"'Didn' I tell you she'd beat anything you ever saw?'

"'She's confoundedly purty, that's certain,' answered de gentleum wid her.

"'De handsomest colored-girl I ever saw,' kep' on missus. I wouldn' think of letting her go; but I *must* have money, and Dudley says he can't afford to let me have any more.'

"'But will he part wid her?'

"'Oh, I'll worry him into it. She's no use to us, in

pertikeler. I'd rather have the money; and she's just de girl for your wife, George—*you* can afford to keep her.'

"'Yes, she's jus' de girl,'—he laughed w'en he said it, and looked at my chile wid dose hateful eyes—I wanted to tear 'em out dat minit.

"'Judy,' called missus, 'I shall need you to help wait on the dinner—don't forget.'

"'Yes, ma'm,' said Judy, raising her eyes, so innocent and smiling.

"'W'at eyes!' muttered de strange gentleum—and de two walked away, leaving me as weak and cold as water, and Judy singing away as merry as ever. Not dat I rea'ly feared missus would make out what she wanted, for I knew massa had promised his dead wife; and I t'ought anyhow, I could buy my own chile myself, if de worst come. But reason as I would, I couldn' help feeling cold and trembly; I didn' know w'edder I'd got de pudding and sauce right or wrong; and all de time she was singing to herself, happy as a lark.

"W'en dinner was sent in, I hurried on a clean dress, and tol' Judy to stay whar she was—*I'd* wait on table dat time. I wanted to keep her out of sight, and I wanted to find out who de stranger was, and as much as I could from what might be said at dinner.

"'Why didn' Judy come,' asks missus, w'en she see 'twas me.

"'She's got a bad headache, ma'm,' says I, 'and I'll jes' take her place.'

"She give me a prying look, but I 'peared not to notice it; so I waited 'round, and listened to every word dat was spoke.

"Massa Dudley, he complained of hard times, and made some remark 'bout his wife's extravagance dat made her very angry; dey sometimes let der bad feelings show out towards each other, w'en dey was provoked; dar was half dozen guests at de table; but de man I had marked set nex' to massa, and appeared kind of confidential. I found out he was cousin of missus's, very rich, and he had a wife, but she wasn't wid him. He was de baddest-lookin' man I ever see; a middle-aged man, wid han'some features, only such a bad mouth, and such ugly eyes. He drunk a good deal of wine, and was coarse and loud in his talk, dough he was so very rich—he wasn' a gentleum, and I didn' believe he b'long to any true branch of de ole Virginny stock. Howsumever, massa was mighty polite to him, and paid him extra 'tention; 'cause he wanted to borrow money, I guessed, and I wasn' far from right.

"Dat night I didn' sleep, t'inking over matters. Nex' day Judy was sent for to come up to de house. I jes' went wid her, pretendin' I wanted my orders for dinner. W'en we come on de portico, dar sat Massa Dudley and Massa Raleigh, de stranger, and missus, waitin' for us. Missus she give me look dat paid back de one I give her de day she first set foot on dat spot—she'd never forgotten it, and she was going to pay it back wid interest.

"Massa Dudley didn' dare to look me in de face, nor my chile; he kep' his eyes fixed on de rose-vine front of him, and says, pleasantly:

"'Well, Judy, how'd you like a new home, and a new missus?'

"She didn' know what to make of de question; she looked at him and me and all 'round; but when she met Miss Dudley's eyes, she seemed to get afraid of something, and she caught hold of my frock, and said:

"'I shouldn' like to leave my maumy at all, master.'

"'Oh, you're a big girl, Judy—too big to talk about your maumy. Everybody leaves der maumy some time,' said he, making light of it.

"'W'at does dis mean, massa?' I asked, boldly, looking him full in de face.

"'It's not for servants to be putting questions,' said missus, tartly. 'I presume we understand our business.'

"'It means dat wife, here, and her cousin Raleigh have been striking up a bargain. He wants Judy, and she has consented to give her up. His wife is a nice, kind lady, and she'll have a splendid home.'

"'Didn' you promise your mudder, on her death-bed, you'd never sell us?'

"His eyes sunk; he had to clear his t'roat 'fore he could answer:

"'Well, *I* haven't sold her; I got fadder to make her a present to my wife, and *she's* sold her—she never promised. But you needn't fret, Ginny. You'll see her every year, when dey come here on a visit; and she'll have nothing in de worl' to do, but wait on a lady. She couldn' be better off.'

"'She couldn' be better off. Miss Raleigh will be very fond of her," said the stranger, with a kind of laugh dat made me feel as if I wanted to t'ar his heart out wid my teeth—all dis time he was a looking at my poor, modest, purty chile, as if he couldn' keep his eyes off her.

"She was frightened and pale; she kept close to me, and didn' speak, only once to missus, so pitiful:

"'Oh, please, missus, don't sell me 'way from maumy.'

"'I'd sell her, too, if my cousin wanted her; but he's got a good cook, and don't want to be bothered wid anodder. I wish he did.'

"'Couldn' you take Ginny, too?' asked massa, suddenly. I saw he pitied me, and was acting agin his conscience; but he hadn't strength of mind to stand out agin his imperious, selfish wife; he'd allers let her have her own way too much, till she'd got so she usually mastered him—'sides, I believe ne did need money dreadfully. Anyways, 'twas all *her* work —I won't blame Massa Dudley more'n I can help--I'd loved him once, as nobody else ever did love him.

"'No! no! she'd be in de way,' was the short answer.

"I knew why he didn' want de poor girl's maumy 'round.

"'How much will he give you for Judy?' I asked missus.

"'Eighteen hundred dollars, cash down,' she said, coldly.

"'*I'll* buy her,' I cried out. 'I can't pay you all, now; but I will—so sure as God lets me live, I will—and I'll give you a t'ousand dollars to-day, all in silber and gold.'

"'You!' said dey all, surprised.

"'Yes, me! a t'ousand dollars—and I'll sure get de rest.'

"'A t'ousand dollars won't do,' said missus, as hard as a rock. 'It will just pay my debts and leave me nothing to go to de Springs wid.'

"'Oh, missus!' said I, falling on my knees, 'don' refuse to let a mudder buy her own chile. Fifteen years I've worked day and night, and sot up late, and saved and contrived to get togedder enough to buy my own daughter. Don' go for to let anodder have her, after all I've done. You can take a t'ousand dollars and wait for de rest.'

"'A t'ousand dollars won't do,' said she again; ''sides, I want to get rid of her. I've no reason to like to see her 'round,'—here she gave her husband a hateful glance, and he blushed.

"I'll give two t'ousand—come, let's bid!' said dat brute man to me, dat 'fernal stranger, laughing at de joke of bidding 'gainst a nigger.

"'I's got no more to bid,' says I, 'but you oughter be 'shamed of yerself, t'aring a child 'way from her own mudder Come, Massa Dudley, ain't you going to put a stop to dis? Won't you take my money, and give your wife what more she needs, and let me keep my Judy?'

"'I'll give twenty-five hundred, now my blood's up, bidding agin a nigger,' jeered Massa Raleigh. 'I shall be angry wid you, cousin Dudley, if you disappoint me in dis matter. I've quite sot my heart on making my wife dis purty present.'

"'I can't afford to throw away fifteen hundred dollars at dis crisis,' says massa, not looking at me, 'and all for a whim of Ginny's. Her daughter ought to be glad to get so good a place; and she may have to go, sometime, under less favorable circumstances—for, by George, if affairs go on as they have lately, the Gregory estate will be in de hands of creditors before long. Yes, madam, dough you don't seem to know w'at your doing,'—and he gave his wife a fierce look.

"'Den don' make a fool of yourself, t'rowing 'way my cousin's offer,' she says, as calm and cool as could be.

"'I can't help you any, Ginny,' said master, after a moment's waitin'; 'I'm sorry, but I'm 'fraid Judy'll have to go.'

"I got up off my knees, and I 'spect I looked mighty fierce.

"'Dey say dis is a Christian land, massa; dat it is a good place to bring poor headen niggers to give 'em de light of de Gospel. I's had dat light, and I don' see yet w'at kind of Christians dem be dat spekilates in der own flesh and blood. I s'pose it's Christian to sell your own daughter, Massa Dudley. Look at her! She's de only one you ever had, to my knowledge, and you's done gone right well to sell her for money.'

"'Cl'ar, out, girl!' cries he, springing up off his chair in a rage—and de stranger laugh, and missus she laugh very soft and dreadful—oh, how I hated her, w'en I heard dat laugh.

"I took Judy by de hand, and we went home. 'Fore dinner, word came she mus' be ready to go in de mornin' de papers was signed and dar was no use making a fuss. De chile was done broken-hearted; she jes' sot and cried all day—she didn' want to go off wid strangers, 'way from her maumy. But she didn' guess de worst, as I did. She was so pure and modest, she didn' dream w'at she was took 'way fur. Her heart wasn't wrung by de anguish dat filled mine Ye see, I'd brought her up so pious, I knew she'd be shocked and grieved to def. My brain was a burnin' up t'inking o it; but I tried to keep calm, for I'd made a plan.

"Jackson didn' come home to dinner; he took his grub wid de hands in de field, and I couldn' see him till mos' night. 'Fore he come back, I wanted to fix my plans, so's to tell him and get his help. I knew he'd help me, if it cost him his life. He 'dored Judy, and it would jes' kill him to see her carried off by dat bad man.

"Woll, I let de chile set and cry: I didn' say much to her, for I was too busy in my mind. W'en Jackson come home, I hurried up his supper, and den I tol' him de whole story. He 'proved my plan, and was eager to help me. He wasn't selfish, my husband wasn't; he showed he had a good heart when my troubles come.

"Dar was a sloop a-loading with tobacky, not more'n a mile down de river, below us. I knew about it before; dat it 'spected to sail next mornin' early—it was bound for New York. I was goin' to take Judy and go aboard dat vessel. I didn' much fear but I should be able to bribe de capt'in to tak' us. I'd jes' seen w'at money could do wid an ole-family gentleman like Massa Dudley; and I t'ought if it could make him sell his own daughter, it wouldn' fail to make a poor capt'in take a good price for stowing 'way a couple of colored women 'mong his tobacky. If we got safe to New York, dar was plenty of things I could do. I could hide Judy 'way in somebody's school, who'd never know who she was nor whar she come from, and I could get my own livin', easy. Jackson was to try and git 'way wid de chil'ren, and find me, soon as he dar.'

"I took down de ole tea-pot full o' money. I made a belt and sewed in five hundred dollars in gold, and fastened it round my waist. I put a hundred and fifty dollars in my pocket to buy our passage—I wasn' going to let the capt'in know I had any more. I put a belt round Judy wid a hundred dollars, so if anything did happen dat we got separated, she'd have a little to help herself. De rest I left in Jackson's car', for my oder chil'ren—to keep it sacredly till he saw a chance to run away, and den to use it to help dem pickaninnies get der freedom.

"W'en he and I had talked it all over, we felt better. He said he'd rudder give me up, dan see Judy carried off by Massa Raleigh.

"W'en we'd settled it, den I took Judy and told her w'at I was going to do. She was so glad, she laughed and cried togedder. She was wise and careful, too; I wasn't afraid to trust her. I made her go to bed early in de evening to get rest; den I got out her clo'es, and went to overhaulin' 'em, mending 'em and folding 'em up; so if any body was spying 'round de window, dey wouldn' suspeck my purpose. I knew well 'nuff, missus would come spyin' round; and sure 'nuff, 'bout nine o'clock she burst in sudden, to see w'at I was about.

"'W'ar's Judy?' says she, by way of 'scuse, 'I want to give her some little things to fit her out for her journey.'

"'Much obliged to you, missus,' says I, curt enough, 'de poor chile's cried herself to sleep. I made her go to bed, against her journey to-morrow, and I'm mendin' up her things. You may keep yer presents—she wouldn' take 'em from you.'

"'Oh, very well,' says she, in return. 'You've got a t'ousand dollars have you, cook? Rea'ly, you're richer dan I am. W'ar do you keep it?'

"'Out at interest, of course,' says I; 'de lawyer dat's got my boy, is taking car' of it for me.'

"'Oh!' says she, and out she went.

"I didn' pray to de Lord to forgive me for dat lie. I didn' hardly believe dar was a God any more—I felt so bitter. Why did He make brack people, jus' to see such troubles? Why did He 'low me to bring up my girl pious and modest, jes' to let white man take her and defile her when he'd a mind to? W'at de use of trying to be good?

"I tell you, I had a great many thoughts dem hours. Bym-bye, I put my candle out, and I take my youngest pickaninny on my lap. It was a little girl, only two year ole—a nice chile, dat I couldn' b'ar to leave. But I had to. I had to jus' leave her in de hand of Providence; and how could I trust de hand of Providence, w'en I saw w'at it had done for me and mine? I sot a-holding my sleeping baby 'till two o' clock. Den I woke up Judy, and we was ready in a few minutes. We put on our bes' clo'es, so's to look decent w'en we got to de city. We kissed de chil'ren, fas' asleep, and shook hands wid Jackson. Dar was no time to cry and take on.

"He opened de door very soft; it was a dark night; it had begun to rain a little; we was glad of dat; for de sound of de rain and de wind blowing, kep' everybody from hearing us. I put an ole shawl over Judy's head and shoulders, and we slipped out on de lawn, and down to de river's edge Jackson darsn't go 'long; t'ought our chance was better alone I knew de way right well; I'd gone over it since I was a girl, and I kep' hold Judy's hand, and we run. De river it rushed on, sobbing like, for de wind was blowing—it was an old friend, dat river was, and I hated to part wid it. 'Pears to me, all de time to-night, dat lake out dar, is de James river.

"It was pitch dark still, w'en we come to whar de vessel was; but dey was stirring aboard of her, 'cause dey wanted to take advantage of de wind, and get down de river quick as possible. Judy begun to tremble so, I could hear her teeth chatter w'en we come onto de little dock, whar de light of de ship's lantern fell on us--I trembled too in every j'int, but I wouldn't let her see it—for I knew right well if the capt'in *should* refuse to take us, my chile was lost—I'd have to go back wid her and give her up. Woll, dey seen us standin' dar, and dey hollered out rough, 'W'at did we want?' and I tol' 'em I'd a special message for de capt'in and I mus' speak to him. So de capt'in swore at us a little, and hollered to me to speak out; but I tol' him it was private; and finally he let de han's help us on, and den I took him aside and whispered to him w'at it was. I tol' him me and my daughter wanted to go to New York; and if he'd give us passage in his vessel, and not let on we was dar, if anybody come to ask I'd give him a hundred and fifty dollars in gold. His eyes twinkled w'en I showed him de money. He asked if I had any more. I told him not anodder dollar; but I was willin to give all dat to get safe to New York wid my daughter Woll, I believe he was a Yankee capt'in; he didn't love slavery, and he did love money—so we made de bargain easy.

"He swore all de officers in Virginny shouldn' tech me; and he took us down in his own little cabin, and told us to be easy in our minds.

"Oh! how safe we felt w'en we got down in dat little close place—it was paradise to us; but we wasn't sorry w'en we felt de vessel in motion, and knew dat we was actually sailing for de ocean. I t'ought of my poor, forsaken pickaninnies, but I couldn' grieve den, I was so glad my chile was safe.

"W'en it come broad daylight, de capt'in had breakfast sot in his cabin; he give us two poor scared women a cur'ous look, w'en he come in; but w'en he saw Judy, he jus' seem astonished.

"'Jerusalem!' says he; and den he whistled to hisself, and says he:

"'You don't say dat young lady's a slave, do you?'

"'Yes, massa, I's sorry to say she got 'bout two drops black blood in her.'

"'Woll, she's good enough to eat to *my* table,' says he. 'Here, boy, put on two more plates, and give us something decent for breakfast.'

"He made us set down and eat wid him; he was jus' as 'spectful to my Judy, as if she'd been a lady, and dat made me take to him mightily. He wasn' fine gentleum; his hands was hard, and he talked purty rough; but he was a manly looking person, quite a young man to be a cap'tin, wid a honest, han'some face—somehow, we bof felt safe wid him, and Judy, she picked up her spirits, child-fashion, and smiled w'en he put mos' a whole br'iled chicken on her plate.

"He was out on deck mos' all day; but we had to stay in de cabin, for we darsn't show ourselves till we got out in de ocean; den Judy begun to be sick wid de rollin' of de vessel. You ought to see how dat great, strong man nussed her up, and brought her hot tea, and took car' of her as if she was a baby.

"She wasn't sick long; when she'd got over it, we rea'ly gan to enjoy ourselves.

"If it hadn't been for my chil'ren in de ole cabin at home, I should have been very happy; I was beginning to realize de hopes of fifteen years of toil and trouble.

"De capt'in was a very interesting man; he was a great talker, and he was so kind as to tell us all kind of stories to amuse us; den Judy she sung for him, to please him. She sung sweeter dan al. de birds in de world—she'd allers been called a wonderful singer; and de capt'in he never take his eyes from her face w'en she was singing.

"His name was Ephraim Slocum; 'fore we got to de end of our voyage he'd told us a good deal 'bout hisself; dat he had no parents living; dat his friends and relations live in State of Maine; dat he'd got his own education and made his own way, and he 'spected by end of anodder year to buy de vessel he was sailin', and be an undependent man. I liked his pride and sperit. It was different from ole Virginny pride; he wasn't 'shamed of work, and he liked to tell he'd made his own fortune. He use to study of evenings. He had maps and charts and 'rithmetics and hard books on his little table; but he didn't stick to 'em very close on dis voyage, 'cause he was too much taken up wid Judy.

"He gave up his own bed to us, and slep', like as not, on deck, hisself. Judy allers read her Bible and sung a hymn before she went to bed, and he use to stay to hear her. De chile was as gay as a lark; she liked de capt'in, and she showed it out so innocent, it pleased him dreffully. I could see he was wrapped up in her—dat he'd never seen anything in the world before, dat he t'ought so bright and so purty.

"He got me to tell him my story. I told it all to him: who Judy's father was, and why we came away, and how car'ful I'd brought her up, and w'at my hopes was about getting her settled 'mongst w'ite folks.

"'Yis, yis!' says he, 'she ought to be taken car' of, dat's sartain.'

"I 'fessed to him dat I had more money; for I had so much confidence in him, I wasn' afraid to let him know; I asked him to befriend me, w'en we got to de great city; to find us a safe, quiet place, whar we could stop, till I found a school for her.

"He promised; and he kept his word. He made us stay on his vessel 'till he'd found us rooms in a nice, plain house; dar was enough furniture in 'em for us to begin living, and we was to board ourselves—so we could be as retired as we wished. He kep' a sharp look-out, for fear massa had sent on officers to take us; and he took us off in de night, and brought us to our new home.

"Judy cried and sobbed w'en he shook hands wid us, and said good-bye; my own t'roat choked up so's I could hardly t'ank him for all his kindness.

"'Don't cry, little one,' says he, broad and hearty, 'I'm not going off forever. I shall be in New York several weeks, and shall come to see you most every day. If Miss Ginny t'inks she'll be in order to see company so soon, mebbe I'll drop in and take tea wid you to-morrow evening.'

"I had a mighty nice supper ready when he come. You know nobody can beat Ginny at cooking, and I did my best for him. He was in good spirits, and we had a nice time. I wasn' disturbed at all by his comin' to see us, and being so polite to my daughter; for he was so respectful, he seemed mos' 'fraid of her; and he never said rude things, nor jested before her. Fact is, Judy was so pure and purty, no decent-minded man could help being good to her.

"Woll, he kept coming, a'most every evening, long as he staid on shore.

"I saw how t'ings was going. I noticed Judy, w'at a change had come over her. She used to sit and never stir, day-times, thinking of something; and when I'd speak to her, she'd blush. And every time she heard *his* step come a flying up de stairs, I'd see her start, and her heart begin to beat, and her cheeks to get red, and she wouldn' hardly dare look up when he first come in. I see all de signs of de young girl's heart, when it first finds out w'at it's made for. t'ought he seen it too; for my chile was so artless, she couldn' put on no airs. I was a little oneasy; for I couldn' forget she had brack blood in her, and dat he knew it, dough nobody wouldn' have guessed it if dey hadn' been told.

"I felt anxious for him to speak out w'at he meant, or else to get Judy 'way, whar she'd have a chance to forget him.

"Woll, one day he come in, w'en Judy was out of an errand, and we got to talking 'bout w'at it was best to do wid her. He liked my idea of sending her to some boardin'-school; I had plenty of money to buy her clo'es and keep her dar a year; and as for myself, I could make my own livin', any time.

"He said he knew of a nice school up in Connecticut, whar a cousin of his had once gone; and whar de principal knew all 'bout him; he'd take her to dat school hisself, and tell 'em she was Southern girl, an orphan, who'd been sent up in his care from de South—and den he was silent little while, and I waited, feeling as if he'd more to say.

"'Mrs. Ginny,' he begun at last, 'you must have seen dat I love Judy. I do love her, wid all my heart and soul. I think she's too good for any man living. I mus' marry her —dat is, if she loves me, and will marry me. I can't help it. I'm a New-Englander; and I've my prejudices against black blood. I tell you candidly. I don't think it's right to mix it wid w'ite. But I'm so infatuated wid dat angel, I forget everything only dat I love her. I've made up my mind to ask her to be my wife. But, Mrs. Ginny, though I've overcome my prejudices, I never could dose of my relatives; I'd never like to tell 'em dat my wife had African blood in her —I'd never like 'em to know dat you was her mudder I tell you now, 'fore I speak to Judy, so you can decide for yourselves. If you're willing to keep it secret dat you're her mudder, and only see her w'en we come to visit you, it'll be all right. You shall be took good care of, and we'll both love you and respect you, as we do now. Only I'm so nfernal proud, I don't want my relatives to know 'bout you. You must speak as you feel. Dat chile needs a protector—even you, her mudder, can't protect her as I could. She's so beautiful, dar will be evil persons after her. I will make her a good husband—she shall be as happy and as honored as any daughter of de North. Speak, Mrs. Ginny; how shall it be?'

"'It shall be jus' as you want it, for *her* sake, Mr. Slocum,' says I, chokin' down de lump in my t'roat. 'I've allers wanted her to have a w'ite man—she's worthy of de best—and I believe you're among de best. I don' blame you for not wanting a slave mudder. I've always 'spected to give my chile up—I've been schooling myself to it for years, and I'm only too glad and happy to see her in such honest hands,'—here I broke down, crying, part with joy, and part wid sorrow, for it *was* hard to disown my own sweet chile, to give her up, as it were—but it was for Judy's good, and w'at else did I ive for but for *dat?*

"'You musn' feel bad,' he says, his own voice tremblin' a little. 'I know it's a hard thing I ask, but I can't help it. We're a proud family, Mrs. Ginny, if we have hewed out our own way—and I'm one of de grittiest of de stock. But dat chile of yours would melt a rock. Don' feel bad—I shall let her love her mudder as much as she pleases. And if I can fix it so's to settle in New York, we can see you a great deal; you shan't be parted entirely.'

"'Dat'll be enough for me,' says I, wiping my eyes.

"'Woll, now, let's finish up our plans; for I've got to sail again next week. You want Judy to go to school, and so do I. She's too young to be married yet, and I'm not quite ready. A year will fix us out all right. Let Judy go to school a year. She must learn music, sartain; she'll take to it like a bee to honey; and dat voice of her's must be trained. At de end of a year, I'll buy my vessel, and be an independent man; I can keep a wife in clover; she shall come back here, and we'll be married. Hurrah, it's glorious, isn't it? only so little Judy herself consents!'—and he laughed, and walked around de room, looking as bright as a dollar.

"Just den Judy come in, all sparkling and fresh from her walk; she took off de veil which I allers made her wear in de street, and she looked so lovely, de young man couldn' contain hisself—he went up, and took her hands, and kissed her on de cheeks, and says:

"'Your mudder says I may have you, Judy. Say, little one, w'at you say to dat?'—she looked at him and at me, and begun to color up. 'Will you love me, Judy, and be my wife w'en you get a little older?'

"She look frightened for a minit, and den she blushed, and said, softly:

"'I do love you, now, Mr. Slocum,'—and run to me and hid her face.

"Woll, we had a happy day, talking over matters and arranging 'em. Judy dreaded to go 'way into a strange school—she was timid, and had never left her maumy—but she knew her lover wanted her to be educated, and she was so proud, and so anxious to please him, dat it made her willing to try. He could only spare us two days to get her ready; he took her 'way to school, and left her dar. Heigho! I felt lonesome 'nuff, all alone in dat big city; but I had de comfort of feeling dat all was going right, and I set myself to work, to cure myself of pining for my chil'ren.

"Capt'in Slocum got me place to cook in a restaurant; had good wages, and got 'long nicely. All I was 'fraid of was dat somebody might spy me out, dat had known me in ole Virginny; but I didn' have to show myself out de kitchen; and if dey did get *me*, dey couldn' find Judy, and I knew de capt'in would take car' of her, if anything happened to me.

"I was so busy day-times, I hadn' much time to think; but nights I'd lie awake and please myself dreaming 'bout my chile. I laid up all my wages to buy her weddin'-clo'es. I's bound dey should be splendid, and dat she should have 'em from *me*, so's not to have to take 'em from her husband. Five, six times, during de year, Capt'in Slocum was in New York; he took his meals to dat restaurant, and I'd chances to talk wid him, and hear all 'bout how Judy was getting along. He'd read me her letters—dey was beautiful—I know dat. I got nice letters from her, too. I could read writing, handy enough, dough I couldn' write much myself, for want of practice. I'd send her messages in de capt'in's letters—he had special permission to write to her from de principal of de 'cademy.

"Woll, de year went by; it went as quick as any in my life. Sometimes it seemed long; but w'en 'twas rea'ly over, I was surprised, it was so short.

"I got a month's absence from my situation; for I wanted to go back to our ole rooms and help Judy make her wedding-clo'es, and 'joy her society while I could. After she was married, I 'spected to go back and keep my place—I had good wages, and I liked it well enough. Hush, chil'ren! w'at in de world was dat?"

"I hear nothing," said Hyperion.

"Only your heart beating, Maumy," said Rose.

"I thought I heard blood gurgling," resumed the story-teller, in a strange voice, which made Rose shiver and creep closer to her lover—"but it mus' have been de water in dat lake out dar—it never will keep still!

"Capt'in Slocum come ashore in time to go after Judy and bring her home. Things had prospered wid him; he had bought his vessel, and was in high heart. W'en I had Judy in my sight and in my arms I was mos' wild wid delight. I t'ought she was *perfeck* before; but I saw how much she had improved. She'd caught the best of everything she saw; de capt'in said she'd been de pride and favorite of de school—and I could see how proud of her he was hisself.

"'I'll give you t'ree weeks, Mrs. Ginny, to get her ready,' said he, when we'd settled down, after the first excitement. 'I've got to take a little trip that'll keep me over a fortnight, to arrange my affairs to suit; but I can't have any waiting after I return. Be sure and be ready, little one; I've waited a year, now. And take good care of my birdie, Mrs. Ginny. Don't let her fly abroad—the hawks may pounce on her. Do all the going out yourself. Keep shady, little one, till you get a husband, and den we'll snap our fingers at the hul' world.'

"He made light of his own words; but somehow he felt uneasy; I could see it; and when he'd kissed Judy over and over, and shook hands wid me, and said 'Good-bye' de last time, and de door shut on him, I felt oppressed, and wished de t'ree weeks was over instead of jus' begun.

"One day, he'd been gone about a week, we went out to do some shopping. We bof of us wore thick veils, and didn' raise 'em at all in de street.

"'You shall have a white silk wedding-dress, my chile,' says I. 'I've set my heart on dat, and we'll go to Stewart's and get a good one.'

"I 'lowed Judy to pick out de pattern suited her best. I was so happy seeing her so animated and happy—I paid for de silk as proud as a queen, and we took home a bundle of beautiful things.

"Dat evening we was setting sewing in our room. Don' you speak to me, chil'ren—jus' let me talk as fast as I can, and get tru' wid dis—we was settin' sewing. We had a bright light to sew by; de table was covered wid lace and han'some things; Judy was running up de bread's of de white silk; it glistened like pearls all over her lap and de floor; I was making de boddice. I'd fitted it very nice—I was a good dress-maker. She didn' put her frock on, w'en I'd basted de new one, for I wanted to try it on again; she sot dar in her petticoat and corset, and I kep' noticing de dimples in her shoulders, jus' as soft and fair as dey was w'en she was little baby. She had taken off de gold beads missus gave her, which she allers wore, and laid 'em down on de table, till I was tru' a-fitting her dress. She was singing to herself, and stopping to 'mire de glittering of de silk every little while.

"We sot dar sewing, never thinking of nothing, only de wedding, w'en de door suddenly opened, widout nobody knocking; and w'en I looked up I saw Massa Raleigh standing dar, and two officers behind him. De needle jus' dropped out my hand, and I turned stone cold, but I couldn' move. Judy she knew him, right 'way, and she gave one scream went right tru' my heart.

"'So,' says he, 'my little bird,' (dat's just what Ephraim called her w'en he went away,) 'you flew off from me, didn't you? I've found your nest at last—just when I wasn't looking for it. If you hadn't put up your veil when you got interested in dat bit of dress-goods to-day, I shouldn't have tracked you. Are you ready to go home with your master, now?'

"We just stared at him—we could neider of us speak.

"'You live right snug here—lots of purty things! Hope

you haven't sold yourself to anybody else, my girl,' and he looked about suspiciously.

"'No, she hasn't,' I spoke up, for I understood him. 'For God's sake, let us alone, Massa Raleigh. Judy's 'gaged to be married—dese are her wedding-clo'es. Her husband's well off, and he'll give you twice what you gave for my chile, if you'll only let us alone till he comes back.'

"'I ought to have some interest, after lying out de use of my money a year,' he says, wid a wicked laugh. 'So, she's 'gaged to be married, is she? Woll, I pity de man dat's got took in. He ought to thank me for coming and claiming my own, before de knot was tied. Who is it?'

"'It's a capt'in of a vessel—a nice young man,' says I, 'fore I thought.

"'Aha! de same sloop dat helped you get 'way, I'll be bound. No, curse him! if it's that d—d capt'in, he shan't have her, if he offers twenty t'ousand dollars. I'll punish him for dat trick.'

"''Twasn't dat one,' says I, but he was too sharp to believe me.

"'Come, Judy,' says he, 'put your frock on, and come 'long. I'm in a hurry.'

"'Oh, Massa Raleigh, let me stay till Ephraim comes back,' cries my chile. 'I'll give you my word and honor I won't try to run away. Only let me stay till I see him; and if he can't buy me 'way from you, I'll go home wid you den.'

"'Got to leave town to-morrow, and mus' take you 'long. No, no, Miss Judy, "a bird in de hand is worth two in de bush,"—you've played me one trick.'

"She threw herself down and clasped her hands about his knees.

"'Please, please, Master Raleigh, let me stay wid my mudder till he comes!'

"I saw his wicked eyes gloating over her lovely head and shoulders; he stooped down and patted her on de neck:

"'Not a single night,' says he; 'I've been kep' out my property long enough. Come, girl, get what duds you want, and come 'long.'

"'May I go, too?' I asked.

"'No! you cussed, impertinent nigger—you made all de trouble in de first place. Massa Gregory may cotch you when he can—I shan't help him. Come, girl, get your bonnet. What you standing dar for?'

"Her big eyes opened like a frightened deer's; she looked at him, but didn' stir. I prayed hard and fas' to de Lord, but he didn' 'pear to hear me. Oh! how I prayed dat Cap'n Slocum would come in and knock down all dose cruel men, and save my chile—but he was hundred miles 'way—dar was no help.

"'Here, fellows, help her dress if she can't help herself,' says Massa Raleigh, and he picks up a bonnet and goes towards her.

"'I'll be d—d if I do!" I heard one de men say—de oder one stepped forward; Judy ran to me and clung 'bout me wid her hull strength; dey tried to force her 'way, but we bof held out. Dey tore de clo'es half off my poor chile.

"'For de Lord's sake, and sake your own chil'ren, don't give up my poor girl to dat bad man,' I pleaded wid de officers.

"'Dey darsn't refuse to do der duty. She's mine; I paid roundly for her, and I'm going to have her; you jus' behave yourself, ole girl, or you'll get hurt.'

"Wid one strong wrench he pulled her 'way from me, and dragged her to de door.

"'Save me, mudder!'

"'I will, chile. Dat man shall never take you alive, Judy

"'Shan't hey?' said he, wid a chuckle dat drove me raving mad.

"I sprung at him and tore her 'way ag'in; I was strong as a tiger; I got her 'way, and held bof his arms so he couldn' stir, dough he cussed and swore, and tried hard to get his pistol out his pocket.

"'You jes' run, Judy,' says I, 'and don't you stop for me. Run 'way, and hide, no matter whar—only don't you come back here.'

"'Take hold of her, fellows,' says Massa Raleigh, twisting and turning, but I held him like a constrictor.

"'Blast me if I do,' said de same man spoke before. 'If I'd known *dat* was de kind of slave you'd set me to cotch, you wouldn' have got me here,' and he looked at my poor, beautiful white chile. 'She's whiter dan I am, and a darn sight purtier. Come Jem, let's leave here.'

"'I'll have you fined and 'prisoned, you rascals,' shouted Massa Raleigh.

"'Cap'n Slocum pay all de fines, and reward you besides, says I. 'Judy, why don't you run?'

"'I don't like to leave *you*, mudder.'

"'Never mind me, chile. I can take car' myself. Like as not dey'll keep me, in hopes of catching you; but don't you show yourself roun' here. Mind!'

"She took up an ole shawl, and run like a cat out in de hall, and away. De men dey bof laughed.

"'Bully for her!' says one.

"'I'd as soon help cotch my own sister,' says de oder.

"'Hold on to him, ole girl. You're a tough one,' laughs t'odder.

"'Don' bite him.

"'Why don' you kiss her?'

"'She's a trump!'

"Woll, you better b'lieve Massa Raleigh get mad. Dar I was a-holding him, and dem officers laughing at him—down South, dey wouldn' dar' to laugh at an ole Virginny gentleman; but dese fellers was independent—dey t'ought it very good joke. Judy hadn' much more'n time to fly down de stairs, 'fore I felt my strength giving out; and de nex' thing I know I didn' know nothin'—he'd flung me down on de floor so hard dat I was stunned entirely.

"When I come to myself I was in de hospital—my arm was broke a-falling on it; and I hadn' been dar but t'ree, four days, 'fore Massa Dudley come after me, and made me go back wid him. I don' believe he cared much dat Judy had got away from his cousin; he let me go back to my rooms and see to things. De officers had locked it up, and took car' of things. I found Judy's gold beads on de table, and I took 'em to remember her by. I never 'spected to see her again. All I was 'fraid of was, dat Massa Raleigh would cotch her. I saw de officer dat was friendly to me dat night. I thanked him for letting my chile off; and I begged him to keep watch, and if she come round to enquire for me, to tell her what had happened to me, and to warn her 'gainst Massa Raleigh—dat he was still in de city, watching 'round. And I told him 'bout Cap'n Slocum, and to tell de cap'n, for me, to take good car' my chile—I never 'spected to see her ag'in, and he mus' be good to her. 'Cap'n Slocum,' says I, 'will pay you for all your trouble, whatever you're mind to ask. You won't lose by being kind to my Judy till he comes back,' —and he promised to hunt up de capt'in, and let him know what had happened.

"So I just prayed de Lord to keep my white lamb from de wolf, till her husband dat was to be, should get back to take car' of her; and I come away wid my Massa Dudley back to ole Virginny.

"My heart was sick and sore to leave New York widout knowing what was Judy's fate. If I could have seen her settled for life, wid a good man, I shouldn' have felt bad to come back a slave—for I wanted to see Jackson and my chil'ren. But I couldn' help fearin' w'at might befall her 'fore Cap'n Slocum got back; or thinking, p'raps, *he'd* get shipwrecked or lost, and de poor chile never have any friends in dat great city. It was brooding ober all dese things, that made my heart as heavy as lead.

"Woll, I never knew, till I got clean back to de plantation, dat I had no husband and chil'ren for to see. Dey was sold down South—every chick I had, and Jackson too. Massa was so mad when me and Judy run away, dat he jus' sold Jackson right off, for helpin' us escape—sold him 'way down to de Florida Keys. Den Massa Gregory died; and de young folks was eatin' up de plantation as if it would last forever—dey'd sold all my pickaninnies, every one.

"'Tain't an easy thing to go childless—'specially when your chil'ren ain't dead, but scattered all over, you don' know whar, nor what has happened to 'em. My poor heart has done nothing but ache—it done gone aching now, and is jus' dumb and cold—it don't car'. I never heard 'bout Judy. I don't know dis blessed day whedder she's safe and happy, or what become of her dar. I take out her gold beads, and look at dem, and pray for her—but what's de use?

"Sometimes I think I'd like to see my youngest pickaninny—she was a little girl, too—but what's de use? I don't even know what State she's sold to.

"When I wake up in de night, I hear my chil'ren hollerin and cryin'—I hear de whip on der backs, or 'see em tired and hungry—oh, I has awful dreams.

"Woll, I went round so stupid-like, thinking of my Judy, and de rest of 'em, dat I wasn't much use. Missus got dreadfully out of patience wid me; and finally, she got massa to sell me down to New Orleans. I was such a splendid cook, he got a good price for me. I was in New Orleans but a little while, when Massa Fairfax bought me. I use to keep a-looking out all de time on de street, to see if I could see any my chil'ren, in New Orleans, and dat master said I was lazy. Masters don' like der niggers to get de dumps.

"So I's dragged out life jus' any way I could. I thought dar wasn' no more sap in de ole tree, sence it was struck; but when I see you two chil'ren living my troubles over again, dar put forth one little green branch. I couldn' help taking to you and trying to help you.

"If I could only know what had happened to Judy! It gnaws at my vitals all de time, de fear dat something has gone wrong wid her.

"If we only get away from here, and make our way up North, mebbe I shall find out about Judy—mebbe I shall see her. Oh, Rose! what if I should see my chile again!"

"Cheer up, Maumy! maybe you will. Who knows? I hope you will, Maumy."

"I'd walk dar all de way, on coals of fire, o hear from Judy."

CHAPTER XII.

THE YANKEE CAPTAIN.

Why must we look so oft abaft?
  What is the charm we feel
When handsome Harry guides the craft,
  His hand upon the wheel?

His hand upon the wheel, his eye
  The swelling sail doth measure:
Were I the vessel he commands,
  I should obey with pleasure.

He would seem taller, were he not
  In such proportion made;
He wears as frank and free a brow
  As golden curls can shade.

Fresh youth, and joyance, and kind heart,
  Gleam in his azure eye;
And though I scarcely know his voice,
  I think he cannot lie.—MRS. HOWE.

COLONEL FAIRFAX was walking up and down the portico in front of his mansion, with that hasty step which sounded as if he were endeavoring to walk off some mental irritability. The crisp January air was having its desired effect; the knitted brows gradually relaxed, the step grew more slow and regular, and the planter's countenance toned down to its usual placid tints. He had been excessively fretted by the escape of two of his most valuable slaves, and by the result of all the attempts which had been made to track them; he thought he, of all men, ought to be spared such trials of his patience, when he had always been considered one of the kindest and most indulgent of masters. He sympathized with his neighbor, Judge Bell, in the unpleasant predicament in which he was placed, by the sudden disarrangement of the business affair he was about to conclude with such satisfaction to himself and his creditor.

"There's neither gratitude nor common sense in any of the race," soliloquized the Colonel. "What did they want to cut up such a freak for?—leave comfortable homes, protection and plenty, for cold, hardships and poverty—like as not, to starve in the swamps—or, what is worse, to go up North, and perish of cold and hard work. I did think that boy was a little above the average—but it seems what wit he's got has been used to his own ruin! A pretty piece of sentimentality between a couple of darkies—ha! ha! A runaway match —took Maumy along to tie the knot, I suspect! Ridiculous ridiculous!"

"I presume Hyperion caught his sentimentality from constant association with *me*, father," laughed Philip, coming out in time to hear the above. "You see, he apes my dress and my manners, and now he's going to imitate me in my love affairs."

"Why, you never eloped with any silly young lady, did you?" queried the Colonel, growing good-natured under the smile of his only son.

"No—I *haven't* done such a thing, so far. But I rather think I should be hurried into such a course, if I found somebody else about to step in and carry off my lady-love, against her consent and mine."

"Nonsense, Philip! The mistake you make is in applying the same rules to your servants as to yourself—as if the delicacy of their feelings was to be consulted in all our arrangements. Ignorant, thoughtless, brainless, indolent, troublesome children—I wonder how they'd fare, if we didn't look after their interests better than they know how themselves?"

"I'd trust Hyperion to take care of himself, anyhow—the rascal! I wish he'd come back and attend to my room—I haven't had anything decent since he went away."

"Well, I've lost two, and the Judge only one—but I guess

he feels his loss the more keenly--it's upset his arrangements finely!"

"Good enough for him!—he'd no business to go and dispose of that girl to such a person as Mr. Talfierro. I'll say so, if he is Virginia's father. I don't believe *she* feels very badly about Rose's running off."

"Oh, of course not! You young people can afford to be very pretty in your sentiments, and very careless of your property, as long as you have us to take charge of you. But I think, by the time you've had charge of a plantation for twenty years, you'll look at these things in a business point of view. Talfierro is getting out of patience. The Judge was over this morning, to see if he could borrow money from me, towards making up the amount he owes him. I expect I shall have to let him have a part of what he wants. If we don't hear from the fugitives by to-morrow, I've promised to try and accommodate him. Blast 'em! don't I wish they all had a sound whipping for their tricks?"

Philip did not reply, his attention having been arrested by the sight of a horseman trotting leisurely along the level road; it was so seldom travellers passed by, they always excited more or less remark. This one, as he reached the avenue diverging from the road into the planter's private grounds, turned his horse's head towards the mansion, much to the excitement and arousal of a dozen negro children in "the quarters," and half as many men and women lounging about the yards and offices.

By the time he had reached the place of dismounting, he was surrounded by a small throng of curious spectators, who hardly among them all could manage to take the bridle of the animal for him, but who seemed to consider their chief duty to consist in the display of an astonishing quantity of glowing eyes and "ivories."

"Does Colonel Fairfax reside here?"

"Oh, yis, massa! Dis is Colonel Fairfax's, suah."

"That's a Northerner, or I miss my guess," said Philip, aside to his father, as the stranger walked up to the porch.

With the courtesy native to him, the planter stepped forward to greet the new-comer, inviting him in before inquiring name or business. He was sufficiently well-spoken and well-dressed to warrant the invitation to the library extended to him, and which he accepted, with an apology for intruding upon the time of the host. Nevertheless, although he apologized for intruding, he did not immediately state what business brought him; but showed himself an interested stranger to the country, inquiring with intelligent curiosity into the peculiarities of sugar-planting, climate, etc., of that part of Louisiana. The three were in the midst of an animated conversation, when they were summoned to dinner.

An invitation to partake of that meal was accepted as frankly as it was offered. There was something about the stranger that amused and entertained his hosts, while it compelled their respect. It was certain that Captain Slocum, from Maine, as he introduced himself, was not a gentleman after their own model; he had no high-bred manners, no courtly polish—yet he committed no breaches of etiquette, was neither uncouth nor unrefined, but had an air of his own, frank, earnest, and—acquisitive. Yes, it was acquisitive, no doubt, and faithful to his New England parentage—not the acquisitiveness of the miser, but of the ardent mental strength and growth, reaching out all the time, and absorbing the elements about it. His looks were in great contrast to those of the two Southern gentlemen, with their sallow complexions, and that air of languor, or at least, repose, peculiar to their climate. His face was fresh and florid; his eyes blue, bright and keen; his features clear-cut and handsome. He talked incessantly, and his language was not always chosen for its elegance; though nothing coarse fell from his lips, since Mrs. Fairfax was at the table. No gentleman could have been more deferential, than seemed natural to him, when he addressed himself to her. It was difficult for the Colonel, accustomed to the exclusive *castes* of southern society, to judge where to place his guest, who certainly was not "poor white trash," and just as certainly was not a "first-family" born gentleman, laying his claims to their respect upon the ground that he had inherited wealth and indolence from the blood and toil of others. Captain Slocum had an air of courage and self-reliance not born of bowie-knives and revolvers, but of innate strength of will, that was exhilarating to come in contact with—one could forgive him for a little roughness, as they could a winter wind for the vigor and healthful energy which it provoked. He came across others like a salt breeze of that ocean with which he was familiar.

Philip, who had not so much talking to do as his father, and consequently more leisure for observation, noticed that the stranger scanned with a searching eagerness the faces of the women who came in to wait on the table; and that his eyes glanced at every new-comer, and out of the windows and doors, as if looking for some one.

"Hope he has no designs on our property," thought the young man. "Can't afford to lose any more at present. But, pshaw! he isn't an abolitionist, I'll be bound! He talks too much common sense."

While the dessert was being brought in, Captain Slocum broached the subject which had evidently been on his mind, underneath all others.

"The business which brought me here to-day, Colonel Fairfax, was to inquire after a colored woman whom I have heard belongs to you—have you a slave, an elderly woman, called Maum Guinea?"

"I wish I could tell you something about her, sir. I've as much curiosity to hear from her as you have, I presume," was the answer, with a good deal of irritation in the tone.

"Then you no longer own her?"

There was so much disappointment in the tone of the question, that the family looked at him in surprise.

"Why do you wish to know?"

"Don't look at me so suspiciously," half-laughed the stranger. "I have no intention of stealing her, nor of inciting her to run away. But I should like to buy her, very much indeed. In fact, that was the principal object of my long journey to Louisiana; and I should be willing to give you all she is worth possibly to you—she's getting rather old, you know, and can hardly be called a first-class servant any longer,"—a touch of Yankee business carefulness suddenly dashing the eagerness of his manner. Now, the Captain would have given one of his little fingers for the property in question, if he could not have obtained it otherwise; but he did not choose to betray this willingness until necessary.

"Maum Guinea is good for her work many years yet—there's no better cook this side of New Orleans."

"She's a capital cook," responded the Captain; and his mind went back to certain exquisite suppers served up in a little room in a secluded corner of a great northern city, years ago — wonderful suppers, whose daintily-concocted dishes derived an inimitable flavor from the piquant sauces of sentiment and secrecy which no scientific Soyer ever combined—a face of marvellous beauty beamed upon him from the other side of the table, and Maum Guinea, dignified and stately as some antique Egyptian empress, in her richly-colored silken turban, dispensed elegant hospitality at his right hand. As this vision rose before him, like an enchanting mirage in the desert of memory, he forgot the present for a moment, and was aroused from a deep reverie by the planter remarking:

"If it's a first-rate cook you are after, I think I know a neighbor who would part with a woman I could recommend."

"I want Maum Guinea herself. Did I understand you that she was not with you now? Could you give me any clue to her?"

"I wish I could, Captain Slocum! I wish I had some clue to her myself. The fact is, the wench, favored and petted by all of us though she was, up and run away about five days ago, and the devil of a trace can we get of her."

"I'm sorry, extremely sorry,"—and the stranger looked all he said.

"Not so sorry as I am, sir. I regarded her as a very valuable servant. More mind and judgment than most of 'em—a great comfort to Mrs. Fairfax. Another of my best boys went with her. Fact is, our servants give us more trouble than they're worth. What with sickness and deaths, and accidents, and runaways, and improvidence, they keep us constantly in hot water. I wish they were all back in Guinea!"

"Have you given up all hopes of recovering the fugitives?"

"Why, no, not all hopes. We have officers on the watch at the different steamboat landings for twenty miles up and down the river; if they should manage to reach the water, I doubt if they could get off. Where they are, I cannot guess. We've searched the woods and swamps thoroughly, and still keep a sharp look-out. They might possibly be concealed in some jungle yet, in the woods back of the plantation, if they could get enough to keep them from starvation, and could endure the cold. 'Twas a pretty brisk night, last night, for them to lodge out of doors. They're easily chilled, sir. There were three of them One of my neighbor's girls ran away with a boy of mine, and Maumy went along to see 'hat 'twas all right, I suppose."

"Aha! just so!" and again the Captain's mind recalled certain circumstances of the past, which rendered it quite probable to him that Maum Guinea might sympathize with a pair of distressed lovers, and aid them in efforts to accomplish their hopes. "Well, Colonel Fairfax, I do not see as I can take any farther steps in this business at present. I hope that you will succeed in finding your servants; and in that hope I shall remain in the village as long as there is the slightest prospect. If you should find Maum Guinea, I stand ready to purchase her at any reasonable price, and therefore desire that she shall not be punished in any way."

"Oh, I never punish my people to hurt or disable them, sir. If I do get her back, probably I shall be willing to dispose of her; for if she's discontented and uneasy, we shall not have so much confidence in her. Where are you stopping in the village, Captain?"

"At the St. Charles Hotel, where I should be happy to hear from you, if you have any news to communicate. I will no longer trespass upon your hospitality, but with many thanks for your kindness, will bid you good-day."

They had left the dining-room, in the course of their conversation, and the stranger now resumed his hat and gloves and stepped on to the portico. The planter felt curious to know the reason of his especial interest in Maum Guinea, but there was nothing in the demeanor of his visitor which encouraged him to inquire; and he allowed him to ride away, with his curiosity ungratified.

That evening Philip paid his tri-weekly visit to his betrothed. The light and laughter, the music and jesting of the family-circle gathered in the parlor, were very pleasant for a while; but it is surprising what a fondness the most common-place lovers acquire for moonlight and solitude, whispering breezes, starlit walks, and all the sympathetic influences of out-door nature. So it was not long before the young man was wrapping a shawl about Virginia, and the two, arm-in-arm, slowly promenaded the pleasant verandah, in the sweet whisperings and sweeter silences of "love's young dream." A slender crescent of silver shone in the dark-blue sky; a heavy dew, which was gradually congealing into frost, sparkled over the lawn.

"You are not in earnest, Virginia, about making me wait a year?"

"Mother thinks I'm very young to be engaged, Philip."

"Well, you're not too young to be married, if you are to be engaged," laughed the lover. "You half-promised me you know, the last time we talked about it. As long as there's nothing in the world to prevent or interfere, what's the use of losing a whole year out of one little life of happiness?"

The young girl wondered, too, "What was the use?" but it was not in her feminine nature to yield immediately to such pleasant argument.

"Since Rose ran away, papa has felt troubled about his affairs. I'm afraid my *trousseau* will not equal my wishes, if I do not wait until he gets his business straightened out a little."

"*Trousseau!* nonsense! you just want to provoke me, little one! I shouldn't know or care, if you had but one dress to your name."

"Well, *I* should—and so would you! It's very pretty of you to say so—but we must do as other people do, for all that."

"I suppose your father has not heard from the fugitives?"

"Of course not. And for my part, I'm glad of it—I really am, Philip. I'd rather put the wedding off a year, than to see Mr. Talfierro carrying my poor Rose off. Poor girl! I hope she isn't cold or hungry."

Philip admired the bright tears which rushed into the young girl's eyes as she thought of the hardships which might imperil her pretty favorite.

"I think she really loved Hyperion; and any one could see his heart was bound up in her. He could not take his eyes off from her, when she was around. If papa had known just how the case stood, I do not believe he would have sold her. Wouldn't it have been nice, Philip, to have had them married when—when—we were, you know,"—very timidly—"they would have been such useful servants, and so happy together."

"It would have been charming," responded he, pressing the little soft hand. "If I could only find them, I would buy Talfierro's claim out, myself, and make you a wedding-present of your waiting-maid."

"Oh, *would* you? What a generous, kind-hearted man you are, dear Philip."

"Dear" Philip! She had never ventured to call him that before, and the lover was in ecstasies.

"If I had to dispose of my favorite riding-horse, and half my trinkets, to raise the money, I would do it gladly," he pursued, animated by her grateful admiration. "But the deuce of it is, Virginia, we can get not the least clue to them. That Maum Guinea is a terribly sharp woman! It's her doings, I feel sure, their getting off so cunningly. By the way, there was a person at our house to-day, who wished to buy her—came on purpose. A Northener, too, and opposed to slavery, as he did not hesitate to tell us. I liked his honesty. I'd trust him with my people, without fear; a man who had the courage to speak his mind as moderately and as frankly as he did. I am curious to know what in the world he wants to purchase Maumy for."

While he was speaking, a dark figure flitted out of the

negro-quarters, and took up a position at a corner of the verandah which was buried in shadow, remaining there, listening and motionless, while the young people continued their conversation.

"I wish we could get track of them, Philip."

"I wish we could. The stranger was evidently so anxious to secure Ginny, that he would have paid a good round price for her."

"It's strange what a Northerner could want of a slave."

"Yes; and what he should have come down here for, to look her up. He told us he had traced her from her old home in Virginia, to her master in New Orleans, and from there, here. He seemed much troubled to be disappointed at last."

"What did he seem to be?"

"He gave his name as Captain Slocum; he's been captain of a vessel some time, but not recently. He's got some personal interest in her, I'm sure."

"I've always thought Maumy had some secret history. She's a strange woman."

"It's a pity she took it into her head to run away just now."

"Poor Rose! I can't help thinking of her, this chilly night. I am afraid she is cold,"—and Virginia shivered inside the warm folds of her shawl. "Every time I waken in the night, I think of her. She's always taken care of me, since we were children together, and I feel lonely without her."

Philip wrapped the shawl closer about his betrothed, and they resumed their walk, forgetful soon of the unhappy fugitives, in their own consciousness of love and safety. The dark figure which had skulked at the corner stole away, and as it emerged into the moonlight of the open lane, it proved to be that of Johnson. He had been driven to this resort in his anxiety to learn the plans of his master with regard to farther pursuit of the runaways.

"I mus' see 'em to-night," he muttered, "ef I can anyways possibly get off. Dat overseer, he's 'spicious of me; he keeps mighty sharp watch over me now-a-days. I mus' see 'em to-night—'kase I'm sure Rose is hungry, and mos' worn out a-waitin' for news. 'Sides, I mus' tell Maum Ginny what I heerd 'bout *her*—'spect she'll know whedder it's good news or bad."

But Johnson had no chance to get off that night. The overseer came down the lane, and ordered him in pretty sharply—it was past the hour at which slaves were allowed to be out, and as he had some reason to suspect Johnson of being in communication with the runaways, or proposing to follow their example, he was keeping a stricter watch than ordinary over his actions. Johnson knew that he must be suspected, as he usually enjoyed privileges denied to the common slaves.

The next day he contrived to get sent to the village on an errand. He did not hurry himself, once there, but lingered about the hotel, to catch a glimpse of the person who was interested in Maum Guinea. Not having heard her story, he had no clue to the link existing between her and this northern sea-captain. He did not even know whether his purpose was dangerous or friendly; but he resolved to find out, and to allow this knowledge to control his actions. If this were a friend of Maumy's, and a northern man, perhaps he might aid the whole party of fugitives in making their escape. He had a kind of confused idea that the whole northern race was engaged in the benevolent pursuit of freeing colored people from bondage.

After disposing of his master's errand, he proceeded to the St. Charles with a basket of eggs, which he disposed of to the steward for his own benefit, the eggs being a part of the "lawful spoils" which occasionally fell to his portion, and kept him in pocket-money. When he came up from the kitchen, he lounged against a post in front of the house, taking a survey of the various persons coming in and going out, lingering in the bar-room or smoking cigars about the doors. He was not long in determining that the light-complexioned man, sitting on a chair in the verandah, tilted back against the wall, reading a paper and casting occasional sharp glances about him, was the person he was in search of. Johnson hung around for some time, not knowing how to approach him; and finally went into the bar-room and purchased two or three papers of tobacco, and a bunch of cigars, which he placed in his empty basket, and sauntered out along the verandah.

"Buy a fus'-rate segah, massa?"

"I don't smoke."

"*Don't* you? Mos' gentleum does. Buy some 'baccy?

"Don't use it, boy."

Seeing the fellow did not move on, the stranger looked up, slightly annoyed; something in the manner of the mulatto caused him to forbear ordering him off, and to glance at him again.

"Massa from 'way up North?"

"Why, yes. I reckon I'm not one your yellow Southerns!" The Captain began to think this was some discontented slave, who, perceiving him to be a Northerner, was trying to work upon his sympathies. He had no idea of making trouble, or mixing himself up with the business of others, and he surveyed the intruder rather coldly.

"Massa wanted to buy a fus'-rate cook?"

"Not unless I find just the right one."

"I hearn somebody say you was 'quiring 'bout Maum Ginny."

"Well, what of that?"

"Oh, nuffin'!"

Captain Slocum saw there was something behind the assumed indifference of the man, who now picked up his basket as if to walk away.

"Do you know anything about Maum Guinea, boy?"

"I *use* to know 'bout her 'fore she run away."

"Do you know anything about her *now?*" eagerly, but lowering his voice.

"I's a berry pertikler friend of Ginny's, massa. I don' want to see no harm happen to her. I's glad she's cl'ar'd out."

"So am *I* a very particular friend of hers—the best she ever had, or ever will have. I'm *sorry* she's cleared out. Because I came here, hoping to do something good for her. She would be glad to hear from me."

"Do you rea'ly t'ink she would, massa?"

"I know she would. If I knew anybody that could give me a clue to her whereabouts, they'd never regret it. Don't look frightened, boy—I don't want to steal her—I mean to pay for her handsomely."

"'Twasn' *dat*, massa," answered Johnson, in evident trepidation. "I mus' go now," and he glanced nervously at the parlor window, close beside of which Captain Slocum was leaning, and behind whose curtains he saw, as he followed the startled glance of the mulatto, the handsome but disagreeable face of an elegantly-dressed man. "I don' know nuffin' 'bout Ginny, sence she run away, but I *use* to be great frien's wid her Sorry she's gone off, jus' dis time," and as he stooped to pick up his basket, he continued in a whisper: "Somebody a-listenin', massa; but I's comin' round ag'in to-morrow," and he was hurrying off across the square before the Captain had time to realize what he had said. Johnson had been home but a short time, before Mr. Talfierro rode up to Judge Bell's in no very good humor; though he bowed with his usual suavity to Miss Virginia as he passed her in the hall, on his way to her father's library.

"I've just overheard your boy Johnson in confidential communication with that confounded Yankee who's hanging about here, Judge," began the gentleman, as soon as the compliments of the day had been passed. "If you don't keep your eyes open, you'll lose more of your property. It's my belief, that he's nothing more nor less than a northern abolitionist. And further, I believe that Johnson knows, this minute, all about the runaways, and where they are. I'm tired of this fooling. I shall start for New Orleans to-morrow afternoon, if nothing is heard of the girl in the mean time. Either the girl or the money, to-morrow, Judge. You know I've been vexed about this, and kept waiting for a week of very valuable time."

The Judge had no doubt, in his secret soul, that the time of Mr. Talfierro was of immense value; he acknowledged that he had reason to feel irritated and out of patience; said he should take Johnson to task, in the hopes of getting some satisfactory information, and that if none were obtained, the gentleman's claim should be settled to enable him to get away the following evening.

Talfierro then related the suspicious nature of the interview he had witnessed, and the two separated, mutually inflamed against the innocent Northener for his kidnapping propensities.

CHAPTER XIII.

A DANGEROUS KIDNAPPER.

"Sometimes a place of right,
Sometimes a place of wrong,
Sometimes a place of rogues and thieves,
With honest men among."

He deserves small trust,
Who is not privy councillor to himself.—FORD.

THE holiday life of the negroes on Colonel Fairfax's plantation, was exchanged for the toil which was to occupy them until Christmas came again.

The banjo and fiddle were hung upon the cabin wall, the smell of roast pork and 'possum came to the ebon laborer only in dreams.

It was upon a sparkling January morning that the field-hands turned out to prepare the ground for the cane-planting

Captain Slocum, who had met Philip in the village, the previous day, had been invited by him to ride out and acquaint himself with the first steps in the process of making sugar; he had accepted the invitation with pleasure, and it was still early in the forenoon when the two rode forth and joined the overseer, who was getting his gangs of men into working order. The two chatted pleasantly together.

The sturdy Northerner took an especial fancy to the gay and generous young man, whose character was written on his expressive face. But while that congeniality of feeling was springing up between them which comes of mutually generous impulses, a storm was brooding at the house, of which they perceived no symptoms.

Judge Bell, his usually agreeable mood ruffled by the fact of his having a five-thousand-dollar note to pay in the afternoon, had come over to communicate to his neighbor his well-grounded suspicions that the plausibly-speaking stranger was playing the base part of a kidnapper.

"Talfierro overheard the whole conversation between him and my boy, Johnson; and it proves his guilt conclusively. I believe that he has not only been the agent in getting the others away, but that Johnson and others of our most valuable people are in the plot, and awaiting the first opportunity for getting off," said the excited Judge.

Such news was of the most inflammatory character. Worried and disappointed by their previous loss, neither of them were in the mood to hear of farther depredations, nor to be put to farther inconvenience, now, when a busy season was about to begin; their anger rose against the despicable meddler who was even at that moment beguiling Philip into betraying information to him which he was to use against them.

Having obtained the solicited loan from his friend, Judge Bell rode back in all haste, to the village, in the first place to settle his account with his New Orleans creditor, and in the second place to get out a warrant for the arrest of Captain Ephraim Slocum as a kidnapper, and procure the services of the sheriff in carrying it into effect.

This latter step had been taken, and the two, going to the hotel, expecting, perhaps, to find the person returned to his dinner, did indeed meet him there under circumstances calculated to deepen their suspicions. Notwithstanding he had been strictly forbidden to leave the plantation that day, they saw, as they crossed the square, Johnson again in conversation with the stranger; so absorbed was he in what he had to say, that he did not perceive his master until his hand was laid heavily upon his shoulder. His evident alarm and agitation proved still further the consciousness of some guilty secret.

Instead of eating the comfortable dinner which he had ordered at the hotel, Captain Slocum fasted that day, upon bread and water, in a little apartment of the square log house which served as the parish jail. There was not much satisfaction in kicking the wall, or tramping about the narrow oom, or using strong language, deep not loud—but such as it was, the Captain took the full benefit of it.

"I'd rather pay a hundred dollars an hour than be kept here, at this crisis," he muttered. "She may be starving, or they may get away! Confound the luck! I wish I could, at least, have finished my talk with that mulatto. He might have done something, in my place, while I was shut up in this hole. I suppose, though, that he is a prisoner too, and perhaps being punished. Jerusalem! what an institution!"—and he dashed his boot against the wall, making a wreck of the plaster in that part.

"I'll thrash 'em!" he continued, after his irritation had again risen, momentarily subdued by the satisfaction of shattering the plaster—"I'll thrash those two old fogies within an inch of their lives, when I get out of here. They may bring on their bowie-knives and revolvers—I won't condescend to use anything but a raw-hide on *them!*"

He was in no very courteous mood, when, just before twilight, the jailor unlocked the door, ushering a visitor into his apartment. It was Philip Fairfax.

"I come to tell you how mortified and grieved I am at the hasty step which my father has taken," said the young man. "I know that he is mistaken in his suspicions—I could swear to it, Captain Slocum—and I feel that no apology can atone for these unpleasant proceedings. Rest assured I shall use all my influence to get you out of this as quickly as possible."

"Thank you," was the dry response.

"I am indignant myself," continued Philip, "when I see how touchy and suspicious my own people are. They make themselves ridiculous by their fears and their extreme sensitiveness. If our institutions stand on a firm basis, they need not be so eager to defend them, nor so afraid of harm to them. I hope that I, for one, am free from such weakness. I despise a meddling abolitionist as heartily as any one; but I have no reason to suspect you of being one, and until I have, I give you my confidence and friendship freely. Do not visit your first displeasure at my father upon my head also; but allow me to ask if there is any way in which I can serve you. I am anxious to do so."

Captain Slocum was too ardent in his own feelings to resist the earnest manner in which Philip spoke; he shook hands with his visitor, and invited him to occupy the only chair of his apartment, while he seated himself on the little table where his bread and water still stood, vainly inviting him to partake of their luxurious refreshment.

"Is that the dinner that rascally jailor gave you?" suddenly inquired Philip, as his eye fell upon it.

"It's good enough for a kidnapper, isn't it?" queried the prisoner, smiling,

The young gentleman sprang hastily to his feet and knocked on the door with rather more than his usual indolent softness.

"Go to the St. Charles restaurant and order everything decent there is to be had. I'm going to take supper with this gentleman."

The peremptory tone of the order did not admit of argument; the jailor became suddenly very obliging; a clean cloth soon covered the table, and shortly thereafter the two sat down to it, carrying on their conversation during the pauses of an excellent repast.

"What have they done with the slave whose communication with me has furnished such evidence of a conspiracy?" asked the Captain.

"Judge Bell has confined him in the guard-house on his plantation for the present."

"He would allow *you* to see him, of course?"

"Oh, of course. No one suspects *me* of wanting to get rid of my own property, or my father-in-law's," laughed Philip

This was the beginning of a long interview, at the close of which the two separated, feeling still more confidence in each other.

CHAPTER XIV.

HOW THE FLIGHT ENDED.

My heart grows sick with weary waiting.
BAYARD TAYLOR

Oh! they listened, looked and waited,
Till their hope became despair;
And the sobs of low bewailing
Filled the pauses of their prayer.—WHITTIER.

Sweet, as the desert fountain's wave,
To lips just cooled in time to save.—BYRON.

"OH, Maumy, I's so tired, and so hungry, and so cold!"

"Poor chile! you'll perish, sure enough, if we don't get out of dis, mighty quick. 'Perion! what you settin' dar for, wid yer face in yer hands? Can't you cheer up dis poor baby? Jes' rub her hands—dey'r cold as ice! See here, honey here's a few drops more of brandy. It'll warm you up."

"You need it yerself, Maumy. You give me de last piece o' bread—you've eat nothin' for two days, I know. Drink it yerself, Maumy."

"I shan't do nothin' of de kind. I's strong, and got

courage. You's a chile, Rose—poor girl, you haven't much sperit—no wonder! 'Perion! it's for *you* to be brave, and help her bar' her troubles. It don' look well to see a man settin' wid his face on his knees—givin' up, while thar's any thing to be done."

"What *is* to be done, Ginny?" asked Hyperion, looking up showing a face worn and gaunt. "If dar was anything to be *done*, I'd do it. Its jus' setting here, waiting, dat uses me up. I can't bar' to see *her* a-sufferin'—dat's what takes de sperit out of me. I could starve to death myself, and willing rudder dan go back—but I can't stand to see *her* so hungry and mis'able."

"Dar's no use waitin' any longer to hear from Johnson. If we hadn't waited on his advice we might have been far 'way while our stren'th lasted. Now we've got to start off wid empty stomachs. You must try and kill a coon, or cotch a fish, or somethin' 'fore we start to-night, or I fear Rose'll give out de very first night's tramp. She's weak as a chicken, now."

"Poor Rose!"—the half-despairing, altogether devoted look the lover gave the girl showed that all his anxiety was for her He made no complaint of his own sufferings. Although he had not touched food for forty-eight hours, he cared not for himself, if only *she* were comfortable; they had cheated her into partaking of the last morsel, the day previous, and had themselves gone fasting.

"Yis, we must get off to-night," continued Maum Guinea. "If you don't get anything to eat in de woods, I mus' travel back to de plantation, and trust to luck to get something dar."

"Oh, how dare you, Maumy?"

"I'll jes' keep a sharp eye out, and I'll get in some cabin, or de corn-bin, or I'll cotch a chicken—see if I don't, without getting caught, too. So, you jus' cheer up, chil'ren."

"It 'll take all one night to do dat."

"Dat's so. I'll have to get 'nuff to las' more'n one day cause we shan't make out to start till next evening."

"Maybe I'll cotch a fish," said Hyperion. "I's got a big pin dat I's made a good hook out of, and I's got a bit of string."

"It's bin such a long, long day," moaned Rose, "and it ain't getting dark yet. 'Pears to me de sun'll never set."

"'Pears to me de Sun of Righteousness will never rise," muttered Maum Guinea.

"Dar's no light for colored folks dis side of Jordan."

"Let's all go out and drown ourselves in de lake," whispered Hyperion.

"Don' talk about it, 'Perion," answered Maum Guinea, with startling energy, "don' talk about it! Do you know, dat's what dat water been a-sayin' to me ever sence we come here! Night and day—night and day, it jus' calls me and calls me to come rest from my troubles."

"Oh, don't say so, eider of you," shuddered Rose. "I ain't ready to die, yet,"—and she turned and pressed her lover's hand to her lips with a passionate gesture, full of the hope and warmth of youth and life.

And he—how could he feel ready to die, with that loving face before him, and those clinging arms reaching out towards him? He did not. It was only the passing impulse of a momentary despair. His resolve to do and dare, and only to perish in defence of what was dearer to him than life, rose up higher than ever in the midst of surrounding difficulties. His eye kindled, his lip compressed, the fire of a desperate will flashed out from his thin, haggard face.

"You shan't die, honey; you shall live and be free and happy," he said.

She tried to believe him; she crept closer to him.

and laid her head on his breast, trying to forget that she was famished and weary--that her bones ached and her flesh was sore and her heart faint.

So they sat a little while in silence and thought, that dark group, in the dim and dew-dripping cavern, waiting for night.

While they sat thus, they heard a long hoped-for sound. Johnson parted the screen, and stood before them once more.

"Have you brought us food?"

"Laws! I forgot all 'bout you must be starved!" he exclaimed, glancing almost in terror at their haggard faces. "But never you mind dat, now. Jus' come out dis ugly place, now and forevermore. Come!"

"'Tisn't dark yet. S'posin' somebody sees us," hesitated the *valet*.

"Never you mind dat! Don't s'pose Johnson would get you into danger, do you? Dar's nobody 'round dat'll hurt you. Come out!"

They did not stop to guess what he was so anxious to get them outside for; obeying him by impulse, they emerged from the low passage, and stood on the bank of the lake. As they turned to look toward the setting sun, they discovered a party of whites surrounding them—Colonel Fairfax, his son, Judge Bell, and several others.

"Betrayed!" cried Hyperion, with a fierce glance at Johnson.

Rose gave a dreadful scream, and threw herself against his breast.

One arm he placed about her; with the disengaged hand he drew out the revolver from his pocket. Maum Guinea pulled from her belt the keen knife which glittered there. Motionless, desperate, threatening—resolve and despair pictured upon the sickly yellow of their faces, their black eyes flashing, the miserable fugitives awaited the attack.

"Hyperion, my boy, put up that weapon," called out

agony for fear you'd starve to death, or get off, during our brief imprisonment. But it's all right, now, Mrs. Guinea, all right! Won't Judy be a happy woman when she hears from us? We're living in New York city now—in a brown stone house of her own. I've got her picture here—hers, and all the babies'. What do you say to that, Mrs. Guinea?"

He drew an ambrotype case from his pocket. The woman took it in her hand, and by the last beams of the red winter twilight, she pored over the lovely group—the beautiful young mother and her dimpled children. Then her full heart gave way, and with sobs and tears, she fell upon her knees and thanked the Lord for all his mercies.

The next summer, a certain extremely happy new-married couple, on their way from the South to spend the season at Newport, stopped at the brown-stone mansion of Captain Ephraim Slocum, to see him, and the pretty wife of whom he was so proud. Very welcome were Mr. and Mrs. Philip Fairfax; they were received with a perfect extravagance of joyful hospitality, for the Captain was a man who loved his friends as he hated his enemies—with all his soul. His gentle wife was the marvel of beauty her mother's fondness had painted her; and no prettier children ever laughed around the lap of a grandmother than those who frolicked in the light of Maum Guinea's wordless affection.

Mr. and Mrs. Farifax brought their *valet* and waiting-maid with them to the North; they felt secure in the strong ties of gratitude which bound the couple to their service—the laughing, brilliant, animated couple married the same night as themselves—Rose as happy in her pink tissue, as her mistress in her pearly satin—who had no farther thought of deserting those who had made life to them now seem like a long CHRISTMAS HOLIDAY.